THe
gIFt

Jul 17

Other Titles from Emily Books

Problems
by Jade Sharma

I'll Tell You in Person
by Chloe Caldwell

THE gIFt

(Or, Techniques of the Body)

BARBARA BROWNING

COFFEE HOUSE PRESS
AN EMILY BOOKS ORIGINAL
Minneapolis and Brooklyn
2017

Coffee House Press books are available to the trade through our primary distributor, Consortium Book Sales & Distribution, cbsd.com or (800) 283-3572. For personal orders, catalogs, or other information, write to info@coffeehousepress.org.

Coffee House Press is a nonprofit literary publishing house. Support from private foundations, corporate giving programs, government programs, and generous individuals helps make the publication of our books possible. We gratefully acknowledge their support in detail in the back of this book.

Library of Congress Cataloging-in-Publication Data

Names: Browning, Barbara, 1961– author.
Title: The gift / Barbara Browning.
Description: Minneapolis : Coffee House Press, 2017. | "An Emily Books original."
Identifiers: LCCN 2016039379 | ISBN 9781566894685 (softcover)
Classification: LCC PS3552.R777 G54 2017 | DDC 813/.54—dc23
LC record available at https://lccn.loc.gov/2016039379

Printed in the United States of America
24 23 22 21 20 19 18 17   1 2 3 4 5 6 7 8

Some will say that all we have are the pleasures of this moment, but we must never settle for that minimal transport; we must dream and enact new and better pleasures, other ways of being in the world, and ultimately new worlds.

—JOSÉ ESTEBAN MUÑOZ, *CRUISING UTOPIA*

NOTE

The nine dances referenced in the text (signaled by still images and semi-fictitiously credited to the narrator) can be found at https://vimeo.com /album/4104760. Password: poussin.

THe
gIFt

Part I

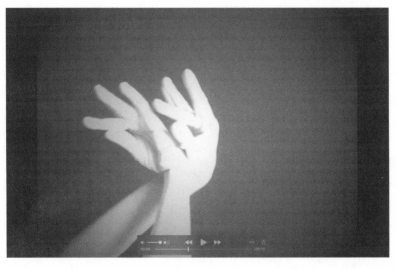

ON JANUARY 31, 2011, I RECEIVED WHAT APPEARED TO BE A BIT of spam in my e-mail.

The message began, "Hi barbara," and went on to explain that the sender was "Dr. Mel," a board-certified psychiatrist in Winnetka, Illinois, specializing in the treatment of obesity: "I use Phentermine for patients who have had success with that medication in the past. I also use Liquid Diets and can also use the HCG program. I have been practicing thirty years in Winnetka. The first ten new patients get 90 free Fiber Capsules with their first office visit. Check me out at winnetkaweightloss.com. Love Mel."

This e-mail came from noreply@totalautopilot.com, but I noted that Mel had included his personal e-mail at the bottom, so I decided to respond. I wrote: "Hello, Mel, and thank you for your message offering me your information and the possibility of receiving free Fiber Capsules for obesity treatment. I am a congenitally skinny person, and I live on the East Coast. Still, I appreciate your concern. I was actually more interested in the fact that you signed your message with the word 'Love.' That was so nice. I was just wondering why you love me. Feel free to answer if you have the time. Love, Barbara."

A few minutes later, Mel wrote me back: "wow i guess because I believe in the love cure. A great lady in California writes about the love cure, and love is a good thing to spread around. I sort of feel that way when I send an e-mail whether or not it is well received. Lately McDonald's and other food sellers are into luv and 'lovin' it' and that is OK too. It is OK to be Lovin' it when it comes to McDonald's. Most of my e-mails go to patients and self love is the intention of their weight loss efforts. Pride, Self Love, Gratitude are the feelings that come from being well formed. The purpose of the program is self love, not weight loss. So I guess I hope you love yourself today. I wish you love. Mel."

That was interesting. Naturally, I paused to think about how effective Mel's weight loss plan was if he was telling his patients that it was "OK to be Lovin' it when it comes to McDonald's." But then I considered that perhaps Mel's therapeutic stance was moderation in all things, including moderation.

I myself am an extremely moderate person. But as you can see, even that phrase, *extremely moderate,* is a contradiction in terms. And in truth, sometimes I am excessive, though I try to express my excess in ways that are easy to ignore—for example, recording ukulele cover tunes for people. I had started doing this a few months before this e-mail exchange, prompted by the hospitalization of a friend of mine. I made a few covers for her, thinking they might cheer her up. Then I noticed that a Facebook friend was having a birthday. I seemed to remember that he liked Iggy Pop when we were in college, so I recorded "The Passenger" for him. Suddenly it seemed like Facebook friends were having birthdays every day. Since I'd recorded a song for that guy, I felt I should do the same for the others. Then I started taking requests. It got a little out of control. I decided it was a conceptual art piece.

Actually, I decided it was a conceptual art piece a few months into the process, while reading Lewis Hyde's *The Gift,* which is a meditation on the relationship between Marcel Mauss's famous anthropological treatise of the same name—an account of gift economies in a global and transhistorical context—and the notion of artistic "giftedness." I was reading Hyde for a graduate seminar I was teaching on theories of the fetish. Mauss's essay had long preoccupied me. Hyde's extension of its propositions into the realm of creativity may seem to turn on an arbitrary quirk of language, these two seemingly disparate meanings of a single word, but it's kind of intriguing. I don't mean to imply, by invoking Hyde here, that I'm gifted on the uke. On the contrary, my musical gifts, both as a singer and an instrumentalist, are, in keeping with my temperament, extremely moderate. I have similarly mediocre talent as a dancer. In these domains, I'm really better at appreciating art than making it. But it occurred to me that maybe if I began (or, to be

BARBARA BROWNING

honest, continued) super-producing both asked-for and unasked-for recordings of my uke covers as gifts, I could possibly help jumpstart a creative gift economy that would spill over into the larger world of exchange. The recent implosion of the global financial system made it evident that we needed to try something else. My idea may not have been particularly revolutionary, but I thought it might be a start. The super-production of my very modest gifts seemed to me, precisely, to realize that paradoxical "moderation in all things, including moderation." Whether or not this was the therapeutic stance of Dr. Mel, I guess you could say it's mine.

The next step in the correspondence was clear. The affectionate closing of Mel's most recent message provided an obvious choice of song, and it happened to be a tune I adore. I have some powerful associations with the melody of "I Wish You Love." François Truffaut used it in *Stolen Kisses,* a film that takes its title from the original French lyric by Charles Trenet. The most famous renditions in English are probably Nat King Cole's and Frank Sinatra's. Blossom Dearie put a perky spin on it. But my favorite version by far is João Gilberto's gorgeous bossa nova interpretation in his tender, Brazilian-inflected French.

I found the chords for the song on the internet. It wasn't in my ideal range, but I didn't bother to transpose it (transposition is quite a challenge for me). I tried recording it in my lower, smoky Julie London register, but it sounded pretty forced, so I went up an octave instead, producing a high, tremulous warble with, if I do say so myself, an affecting air of mild desperation. I sang the song in English and then again in French for good measure. I popped it off to Mel.

It took a little longer this time for him to write me back. I imagine he was trying to decide if I was a lunatic. But when he answered, he answered warmly: "thank you. Beautiful." He went on to say that years ago he'd been a professional musician, playing in clubs on the South Side of Chicago, but he'd had to give up the boozy piano-playing life to make it through med school and open his weight loss clinic in the suburbs. He said that now on rare occasions he noodled around on a Korg. His message ended indicating that I had intuited something perhaps profound: "I wish you love is a favorite so you got it." But this time he didn't close with "love"—just "Mel."

It didn't surprise me that Mel had been a musician. All my life, nearly all of my amorous relationships have been with musicians—or at least lyrical types. Which is not to say that I was having amorous feelings toward Mel. Still, while I tend to play dumb about these things, I was aware he might find it a little flirtatious of me to send him a warbling home recording of such a romantic song. I didn't intend for my gift to be flirtatious, but I did intend for it to be inappropriately intimate. I could claim I was provoked by Mel's own oddity, indiscriminately larding his business spam with "love." But let's face it, I was raising the stakes, and it wouldn't be unreasonable for Mel or somebody else to suspect some kind of erotic investment in this exchange.

In fact, that seemed to be the interpretation of my lover, Olivia. In my excitement over the unexpected intimacies taking place between Mel and me, I blind copied her on my message to Mel containing my cover of "I Wish You Love." She is, unlike me, an artist with a pretty high level of self-exigency, but I thought she might find some charm, if not in my plunking and warbling, then at least in Mel's and my utopian efforts to be "lovin' it." Unfortunately, she failed to note that the original addressee of the message was Dr. Mel, and when she read my minimal text, "i made this for u," she assumed I'd recorded the cover for her. When she realized it was intended for Mel, she didn't take it that well.

Really, I didn't have any erotic aspirations in regard to Mel, but the question does bring me back to Lewis Hyde. "In the world of gift," Hyde writes, "you not only can have your cake and eat it too, you can't have your cake *unless* you eat it. Gift exchange and erotic life are connected in this regard. . . . Scarcity and abundance have as much to do with the form of exchange as with how much material wealth is at hand." For Hyde, that's the link between the redistribution of wealth and eros. To him, and to me, the beauty of the gift is that, like sex, it confounds our sense of what it means to give pleasure and to receive it. The more you give, the more you have.

Take, for example, the uke covers. If I solicit a request from someone, they may think I'm asking what I can give to them. But every request sends me down a path of pleasure. "Genius of Love" by the Tom Tom Club. "We Almost Lost Detroit" by Gil Scott-Heron. "This Guy's in Love with You" by Burt Bacharach. "Kiss Me on My Neck" by Erykah Badu. You really don't think about how weird or delightful or righteous the lyrics are, or how quirky or gorgeous the original arrangements were, until you do your own dumbed-down version. And then you find yourself checking out other people's covers on YouTube. How many weirdos are out there for you to fall in love with as they croon into their laptops? When I make a cover for someone, that person may or may not enjoy it musically. But in the best of all possible worlds, the recipient feels compelled to *do* something with the gift—mine (although my musical gifts, in both senses of the term, are pretty negligible) or the true musical gift at the origin of the song. Hello, Burt Bacharach is a fucking genius.

Who knows if my antics prodded Mel to sit down and noodle around on his Korg—or even to record his own cover tune and embed it in the next batch of weight loss spam he sent out into the ether. If he did that, the nudge was the best gift I gave him. But I didn't get any more messages from him. I think he might have taken me off his mailing list.

If he did unsubscribe me, I don't think it was out of fear or offense—I think he just realized I wasn't likely to become a patient at his weight loss clinic, especially given our geographic distance.

There's a probable explanation for his having sent me weight loss spam from Winnetka in the first place. I occasionally get other spam from that area—like updates from the botanical garden in Glencoe and a Highland Park Toyota dealership. There seems to be another Barbara Andersen living near there. She apparently created an e-mail address very similar to mine, on the same domain, except since I had nabbed "barbaraandersen" first, she added "64," presumably the year of her birth. Either she or these businesses she frequents make a little typo when they enter her contact information into the system—they forget the 64. I also occasionally get family photos or personal messages that have gone astray. I politely reply to the senders, saying, "oops, sorry, but I think you sent this to the wrong barbara! i live in new york!" Sometimes they apologize, but mostly these exchanges just fizzle out.

On June 1, 2013, I went to see a performance by my friend Tye. That was just last night. I'm still processing it.

Tye hadn't mentioned it to me, and it wasn't widely advertised. It just happened that a mutual friend sent me an e-mail about the event, and she said it was sponsored by the Whitney Museum. So I looked at the Whitney website, and it said that the performance would be at The Kitchen, which is an experimental theater on Nineteenth Street on the far West Side, near the river. The website said the show was free, but you had to reserve a space, so I sent an e-mail asking if there was room for me. At the last minute, I got a message back saying I'd been bumped up from the waiting list, which I didn't know I was on, but I had to confirm right away that I could be there or someone else would get my space. So I confirmed, walked over, and got there about fifteen minutes early.

The performance was to begin at eight. The building was locked, and no one else was there. After about five minutes, someone else showed up—a short, bald white guy with glasses. He was friendly. We both wondered why it was closed and why we were the only ones there. At about 7:55, Tye walked up, and we embraced. I introduced him to the guy I'd just met. His name was John. Tye said there would be two other audience members—and indeed just then another appeared—a tall, delicate guy with black nail polish. His name was Joe, and Tye seemed to know him. Tye said to John, "You, I didn't know, but I Googled you and saw your picture. In fact, it was somebody else with the same name, not you. I chose you because of the picture of that other guy with your name, because he looked like someone I often collaborate with." He must have been referring to Tom, a distinguished older gentleman with white hair who's appeared in many of Tye's pieces.

Anyway, Tye didn't seem to mind that this John didn't look like Tom. I guess it was sufficient that *conceptually* there was a Tom look-alike there.

Then a very beautiful young woman walked up and tried to ring the bell. She explained that she was writing an article about Tye for the magazine *Art in America* and wanted to see as much of his work as she could, although she hadn't received confirmation that she had a seat. Tye politely told her there was no room for her, though he'd be doing this piece once more a few weeks later, and she could try her luck again if she wanted. As she walked away, I told Tye that if he wanted to give this journalist my place he could, and John said the same thing, but Tye said no, he'd chosen us for a reason. The last audience member was a guy named Matthew, who is the head curator at The Kitchen. He was already inside, in his office.

Tye unlocked the door and led us in. He took us up two floors in the freight elevator, and then we went into a stairwell leading down to the administrative offices. Tye hollered down to Matthew, and he walked up the stairs to join us. While we were in the freight elevator, before Matthew joined us, Tye explained that he'd been given $1,500 by the Jerome Foundation as a commission for two performances of this piece in the Dance and Process series. He'd also been given $100 for his artistic fee and $400 for materials by the Whitney for two additional performances of the same piece, but for the first time ever he hadn't overspent his materials budget. Usually he ends up losing money when he makes a piece because he likes to build fairly elaborate structures, and that's expensive. But in this case he hadn't spent anything, so all the Whitney money had gone toward the conceptualizing, discussion, and performance of the piece.

I'm pretty sure we were doing the math in our heads. If you think art has calculable monetary value, and if you divided those total fees by four audiences of four people each, then each of our free tickets was worth $125.

That ticket value accounts for the funding only, though I suppose the hope is that art's value will exceed the initial investment made to create it. I suppose this is the hope with any investment. I actually forgot for a moment about the other performances, so I was thinking my seat was valued at about $500. That would be pretty steep, though to my mind, worth it. But it might have been hard for the four of us to swing that kind of ticket price—particularly Joe, as he was a graduate student. Anyway it's a moot point, as nobody asked us for anything.

After Matthew joined us, Tye led us through the top floor, past some ragtag sofas, and into a storage room. It was twilight, and the only illumination was the natural light coming through two sky-lights. It got darker as the performance progressed. Tye told us we could sit wherever we wanted, except in his chair. He took a seat on a padded office chair. Matthew and I took the other two chairs in the room. Joe and John sat on the floor. There were some card-board boxes, an old desk phone, and some wooden planks leaning against the wall. Someone had attached a handwritten sign to the wood saying: "BE CAREFUL."

Tye turned on an old electric metronome that he held in his lap, faceup. It was loud, and it had an orange light that flashed. He appeared to be manipulating the beats per minute, but only very slightly, diminishing the tempo bit by bit, and the sound also changed a little with the way he held it in his hands. It was dim, and there was a muffled, rattling noise coming from the air shaft running through the ceiling. Tye looked as if he was occasionally consulting his wristwatch.

It was kind of a minimalist musical performance but also a light show. And for the hour that it lasted, the light was changing in the room. It felt very intimate, and Tye was staring into the flashing orange light, and I thought at one point it might make him have a seizure, just staring into that flashing light for so long, with the irritating, loud electric beat.

Later when I got home, I texted him to say how much I liked the piece. He texted back that he'd practiced piano to that metronome as a child, and he only recently learned it had belonged to his father when he was young as well. Tye said, "He didn't play well—plowed through pieces, rushed, poor articulation, heavy touch." Tye has had some conflict with his father over the years. But then he said, "This narrative was not supposed to be foregrounded." I figured that.

While we were watching, we were all very careful, like the sign said. Then he walked us out of the building, and we exchanged thank-yous. Tye stayed to speak with Matthew, and John and Joe and I began walking downtown. John looked a little stunned. He said, "That was amazing." Unfortunately, he had something else to do, or maybe he was overwhelmed or exhausted or didn't know what to say, so he peeled off, but Joe and I decided to get a beer and talk about what we'd just seen. Joe also loved it. We talked about some of Tye's other work we had seen. We were both at a performance in a gallery that was conceived in collaboration with another artist. In that piece, Tye dragged a young woman back and forth across the floor for a long time. This woman looked to me like she was probably a dancer (Tye often works with dancers), and that under other circumstances she would have been able to move herself, but in the performance, she was entirely limp from the waist down. Tye was careful with her. He kept quietly asking if his grip was OK. But he wasn't gentle—you could see red marks where he held her, and he was sweating from the work of moving her around. I kept thinking that if indeed this woman had the use of her legs, it must have been very difficult to cede her weight so entirely—maybe especially if she were a dancer.

The woman with whom Tye had conceived this piece was observing all this from a wheelchair. At one point someone took her into the small bathroom at the back of the gallery. I was sitting nearby, and I could hear their muffled voices in there, apparently negotiating the way he would help her use the toilet.

I'm skipping some details. It was awkward for the audience to enter at the beginning. The top layer of flooring had been pulled up and a corner of it rested for a time on the lap of the woman as she sat in her wheelchair. That meant the flooring was pressing into her legs as the audience walked across the wood. Tom was there.

After the extended episode of dragging that young woman back and forth across the floor, Tye climbed a ladder, stood precariously at the top of it, and put his mouth on a pair of long, irregularly shaped pieces of metal protruding from the ceiling. Later I learned that the metal pieces were the spine of a friend of his who had died. This friend had a degenerative disease, resulting in the surgical implantation of this two-piece metal spine. Tye only recently told me that the young woman he was dragging across the floor was in fact the sister of his collaborator in the wheelchair. The reason she was in a wheelchair is that she has a degenerative condition similar to that of the friend that had died. It turns out that her sister does too. The friend that died was also trans. Tye is trans.

After holding his mouth against his dead friend's spine for a while, Tye came down from the ladder and left. Everybody looked around, wondering if it was over. Eventually we decided it was, and we all left. Many of his pieces end sort of like that. You also often don't know when they begin.

Joe loved that piece too, but had no idea about the friend that had died or his spine. His mouth dropped open when I told him. Then we talked about what Tye reveals and what he conceals, and why. Tye generally tells me if there's something he wants to remain a secret or if he's giving me information that's OK for me to share. He's very intentional about everything. Later I'll show him this manuscript and ask him if it's OK to say these things.

When we were texting back and forth last night after the metronome piece, he wrote, "I thought Sami might be interested in tonight's work." I said, "Oh yes, I'm going to write Sami about it." I did.

Sami doesn't know Tye, and Tye doesn't know Sami, but they know of each other, through me. Sami is my collaborator, and he lives in Germany, in Cologne. We've never actually met in person. This is another case of inappropriate intimacy. We came to know each other in the spring of 2012, through my ukulele habit. It was around then that I decided to start putting my sound files up for free download on the internet. I usually send them directly to my victims, like I did with Dr. Mel, but once I've given them, I feel it's good to make them available for regifting to anyone who might want one. I was partly looking around to see how others were handling this proposition of promiscuously distributing their own sound files, and I was partly scoping out other uke enthusiasts. I Googled "ukulele covers."

If you go down this rabbit hole and if you listen to some of the millions of uke covers floating around out there, you will find yourself repeatedly glazing over, thinking to yourself, "This person is a genius. Oh no, wait, this person is an idiot. No—genius—or—no, wait . . ." I don't mean to sound dismissive—you could very well think this listening to my covers as well. Sometimes I think it myself, listening to myself. There are some famous virtuosos on the instrument, like the late Bruddah Iz and the YouTube sensation Jake Shimabukuro. But your typical uke cover artist is somebody who seems to feel comfortable with his or her technical limitations. My own website proffered this word to the wise: "Limited instrument. Limited voice. Limited production values. Use your imagination." That's how I listen to my own covers, and I've learned to do it with others'. Somehow, the vaguely incompetent version still manages to communicate what the cover artist heard and loved in the original. It's a little like listening to someone singing softly and unselfconsciously along with their iPod on the subway. You know they're hearing something proficient, maybe even magnificent, and probably super-produced, and all of that is somewhere behind their anemic tracings of the melodies. I like listening for the things you can't hear.

So if you Google "ukulele covers" and if you spend enough time slogging through the blogs and vlogs of weirdos on four strings, eventually you might stumble upon Sami's site, a relatively streamlined page with a brief bio, a photo (which he changes sporadically, depending on his mood), and some thumbnail images that, when clicked, open up the various categories of sound files he's posted for anyone to download. One category is tagged "ukulele covers," though the "album" image you click on says, *Dreams of Bora Bora*. This is written in childlike script under a similarly childlike drawing of a stick figure playing the ukulele under a palm tree. When I found the page, I clicked on *Dreams of Bora Bora,* and a list of tunes popped up, the first being, improbably, "Paganini Caprice in A Minor: Tema con Variazioni (Quasi Presto) (Excerpt)." I clicked on the little arrow and the song began to play. I stopped breathing.

I had never heard the ukulele played like that. I'm not sure if anyone has. The piece displayed extraordinary clarity, speed, and precision, and yet also exquisite sensitivity in the moments of pause and suspension. This caprice is famous for its technical demands:

left-hand pizzicato, parallel octaves, rapid-fire arpeggios. Sami had somehow discovered a manner of subtly bending the notes on a fretted instrument that evoked the expressivity and nuance of a violin. In the slower sections, his harmonics were ethereal, otherworldly. But when the capricious theme reemerged, it was with an unbounded vigor. The only word for it was astonishing. I wondered who else had heard this.

I listened to some of the other tracks on *Dreams of Bora Bora*. Some were more standard ukulele fare, beautifully played, though none displaying the level of difficulty of the Paganini. On several tracks Sami sang, and his voice was honeyed and bluesy, deep in register, and very sexual. But the track that had blown my mind was the caprice. I thought, "I want to make a dance to this."

I also make dances sometimes. I make them in my house and film them either directly through the Photo Booth app on my MacBook or through a little low-def Flip video camera that I have. Sometimes I post them publicly, and sometimes I show them to people on my iPod. I like small screens. My dances are generally pretty minimalist, like my music, and they seem to look best in a small format. Occasionally I'll give one as a gift, as I do with the uke covers. I usually save them in the smallest file size possible, as I don't want to overwhelm anybody's inbox with a large file. I wondered if Sami might like to receive a dance. I also wondered what it might mean for me to try to rise to the occasion of that Paganini caprice.

I read Sami's brief bio: "Hi I'm Sami, living in Köln and also Berlin. Classical training on santoor, violin, and piano from childhood, guitar age 11, playing all styles, also singing. Thanks for lend me your ears and I'm appreciating your feedbacks on my music. :)" The photo next to this text showed a handsome young man with a somewhat unruly mane of black hair and a dark brow, his eyes downcast, with a violin tucked under his chin.

I scanned the other albums posted to the site: *Jazzman* (this included mostly standards on piano but also some vocal performances with acoustic guitar), *3 Bs* (Bach, Beethoven, and Brahms on both piano and violin), *Family Traditions* (Indian classical and improvised music on the santoor), *Aufgaben* (the most technically demanding pieces for piano, violin, and classical guitar—including Paganini, and also a number of Sarasate compositions), *Balkanization* (Gypsy jazz), *Metalman* (electric guitar shredding), and *wtf?* (apparently tossed-off and disarmingly charming acoustic covers of pop songs). WTF? Good question.

He appeared to have no taste. I don't mean this in the negative sense, I just mean that everything seemed to appeal to him. There were a couple of Whitney Houston covers up there. At the bottom of the page there was a contact link, and I clicked it. A little form popped up asking for my name, e-mail, and message. I wrote, "sami, i'm also a ukulele enthusiast and a dancer. i think your paganini caprice is extraordinary. i'd like to make a dance to it; would you mind? love, barbara." A few hours later, I got an e-mail reply: "Hi Barbara, sure thanks, it would be great for you making a dance to my uke :). I love to watch people dancing, maybe because I'm not good in it myself. OK have fun, cheers! Sami." I wrote back, "sami, my great pleasure in life is that i do all kinds of things i'm not really good at. like playing ukulele, for example. OK, let's see if I can rise to the occasion of your paganini!" He wrote back, "I can't wait for see what you do :). Also I would like to hear your uke ;)." I obligingly sent him an MP3: Peter Frampton's "Baby, I Love Your Way." He wrote back, ridiculously generously, "It's sublime!" I said, "hm, that would be a pretty ample definition of 'sublime' . . . also, shouldn't you be in bed? it's even late in new york!" I was calculating the time difference, and it seemed a little weird that he should be up yacking away with some oddball incompetent ukuleleist and internet stalker in New York at roughly six in the morning Cologne time. He said, "Its six hours later hear then my wonderful NY, I already had my nap! OK, sweet dreams ;)."

Over the next couple of days, we exchanged a few more messages in short spurts like that. Sami's were littered with goofy emoticons and vague references to his ineptitude at dancing. I told him I liked choreographing for "nondancers," which was a classification I didn't really believe in, and he said something about how in his case it might need to involve crutches or a morris chair, which I had to look up. On the third day, I peeked at his website again and noticed that he'd posted a new picture of himself. He appeared to be seated, nervous, looking slightly off to the side. The small image was from the waist up, but if you clicked on it, it expanded, and you could see his whole body. His left pant leg was rolled up, exposing a bladelike titanium prosthesis.

I offered to choreograph a dance for him in a chair. He responded that he'd just read an interesting poem about sitting in a chair, and he quoted from it, a sad line about solitude and just sitting there and a tear falling from a plexiglass eyeball. I'd just read an interesting poem as well, and I typed it out for him. It was by Matthew Dickman, and it was called "On Earth." Sami wrote back, "that's fuckin beautiful." It was.

It was Olivia who'd shown me that poem. She knew Matthew from when he'd been living in Hudson, New York. She teaches poetry writing at Bard in the summers, and she'd met him at a dinner party of writers up there. Maggie Nelson was also at that dinner. Olivia said Matthew Dickman was smart and charming and shy and awkward—but the shy and awkward part may have had something to do with meeting Olivia. She can be a little intimidating.

Maybe you want to know why. The obvious answer would be her literary reputation. Aside from her own work, she's considered the definitive translator of Brecht's poetry. Then there's her steely beauty. At sixty-two, she seems to be growing more luminous by the moment. She's very muscular. But I think the thing that sometimes takes people aback when they meet her is that her feelings are very close to the surface. She can be funny. But her intensity is a little frightening. She has some lines from Brecht tattooed around the muscles of her right thigh. It's that sonnet that begins, "Als du das Vögeln lerntest, lehrt ich dich." When you learned to fuck, I was the one who taught you. Sometimes, when we're fucking, I think, "It's true."

But I was telling you about Sami's website. In addition to the new photograph, Sami had also posted some new sound files. He'd written a brief commentary accompanying a violin gavotte that noted that you could hear his breath and his fingers in the recording. It wasn't clear to me if he was saying this apologetically or if he wanted listeners to pay attention to subtleties in the recording. I wrote him that most of the music I liked was very quiet and that my church was the Church of João Gilberto the Divine. I described his singing of "Estate" on his *Live in Montreux* album—the way you can hear the spit on his lips and you can hear the hairs in his nose when he breathes. It's like he's singing softly right into your ear—so intimate. But I said I also loved Maria Callas, and Hendrix, and I loved Sami's astonishing, virtuosic playing, as well as some of the goofball, idiot savant ukulele doodlers so rampant on the internet (and I noted that I would immodestly put myself in their camp). He told me I wasn't a doodler, though he loved to hear anyone play, regardless of their capacities, if they played out of love of music. He said he particularly liked all those composers who wrote music to exercise their own virtuosic skills. He understood that desire to be absorbed in a challenge.

Sami said, "Music is my only way to communicate my emotions as I have hard times with nonverbal communications . . . I'm a common freak ;)." I said, "I think it's safe to say that most of the people I know and practically all of the people I love would put themselves in the 'common freak' category, except for the ones who would prefer to be called exceptional freaks."

Tye sometimes uses the term *freak* in reference to himself. I don't think he's used the term *exceptional freak*, though he is entirely exceptional.

Sami and I spurted some more messages at each other, often at odd hours. I told him I sometimes wrote poems as well, and he asked to see one. I sent him this:

When we lived in a storefront on Elizabeth Street

198A
Elizabeth is between
Spring and Prince. It was

1992.
There were Dominicans and
Chinese on our block.

There was a Puerto
Rican super named Johnny.
He claimed the Chinese

liked to dry fish on
the radiators. I'm sure
that this was not true.

Our landlord was an
Italian guy named Oscar.
I just Googled him.

A current tenant
called him "so uptight he can
crack walnuts between

his a** cheeks." I guess
some things don't change, though I bet
the rent's quadrupled.

Back then I lived with
my Brazilian boyfriend. He
played drums. We had to

pretend to be a
drum repair store. We put a
sign in the window.

In three years, no one
ever brought a broken drum
to our house, though one

junky tried to sell
us an accordion he'd
probably stolen.

I got pregnant. My
son was born at the New York
Downtown Hospital.

I walked there when I
went into labor. All the
babies were Chinese

except for Leon.
When I brought him home, I dressed
him up and put him

on display in the
window of our store. I'd made
him lots of outfits

out of velvet, with
ruffles. I was going for
a kind of Jimi

Hendrix look. I have
some photos of those outfits.
One day Leon's dad

said he was going
to Brazil to play drums in
the carnival. He

never came back, so
I had to move to Princeton,
New Jersey, where I

was teaching in the
English Department. It was
very quiet in

Princeton. I lived there
for one year, and it was the
saddest year ever.

Not because I had
to leave New York, but because
that was the year the

love of my life died
of AIDS. Not my baby's dad,
but the boyfriend I

was with for eight years
before I met my baby's
dad. He was also

Brazilian. Sometimes
I go back to the storefront
on Elizabeth

with my son. He's a
man now. I tell him that the
whole block used to smell

like bread because there
was a bakery on the
corner that made good

Italian bread. He
says he can remember the
smell very clearly.

That poem was entirely true. I wrote it because somebody had asked me to participate in a reading of short pieces about the Lower East Side. They told me I would have five minutes to read. I thought about the period when I lived there—so much had happened. I thought, "How can I say that in five minutes?" I thought, "I know, I'll try to write it in a haiku." After the first seventeen syllables, I wasn't done saying what I had to say, so I kept going until I got to the end. I guess this is another example of immoderate moderation. Saying too much and too little. I was embarrassed to show it to Olivia, because she always seems to know when to cut things off. And also when to really let them blast.

Why did I want Sami to know all that? I don't really know.

Sami wrote back a day and a half later. He said he liked the poem. He remembered going once to a gallery on Elizabeth Street when he was in New York. He said he also had a son, he was ten, and his name was Franz, but he went by the nickname Kakay, which had been Sami's nickname too, when he was a boy. Sami said he wished he saw Kakay more often. He also said that he'd looked up my books and had ordered one of my novels, because I made him curious. He told me which book he'd ordered. I said, "if you read that novel, you will see that i say i have a twenty-three-year-old vietnamese lover named duong van binh who lives in berlin. i don't really have a young vietnamese lover in berlin—although one day i may, because often things i imagine end up coming true. so if i go to visit my lover, maybe you and i can meet for tea. :)"

Sami didn't write back for a couple of days. This was OK, I didn't think much of it, but on the third day I decided to visit his website just to see if he'd posted any new music. That was June 12, 2012. When I checked the website, he'd changed his profile photo and removed all but one track—a painful, heartfelt cover of Pink Floyd's "Goodbye Blue Sky." The only commentary under the track was: "Bye—Sami." The photo he'd left was a black-and-white, contorted shot of his naked back, arms writhing over his head.

I stared at the picture for a minute and that minimal text. I wondered what to do.

I sent him a message saying, "you seem to have evaporated! :(i hope you don't mind if i still make your dance. it was so much fun being surprised by you every day. xo" Sami wrote me back about twelve hours later apologizing and saying that he'd had a panic attack. He said he really needed to be very careful about how he "dosed" his human contact, or he flipped out like this. He said he found emotions confusing, he could really only express his own through music, and in conversation he was often over-whelmed by irrationality. Social interaction was difficult for him because it wasn't logical but emotional, and social cues for irony or hostility or affection often eluded him. He said he himself never smiled, and he had a very difficult time reading other people's facial expressions. It wasn't my message that had put him over the edge but rather some other listener, who had sent him something like thirty messages in one day, enthusing over several of the tracks he'd posted. He hadn't meant to frighten me or anyone else with that picture or with that song, it was just what he'd been feeling, but he'd love it if I'd still make the dance. He said he'd enjoyed our conversation, and he just had to be careful not to pretend to be someone different from the way he really was, which was autistic.

I told him that a friend of mine had a daughter who'd been diagnosed with Asperger's and I wondered if that was what he meant. I said I found it very relaxing to be with my friend's daughter because she didn't mind just hanging out together without talking. I said she had some difficulty hugging, she liked to type on a typewriter, she counted things obsessively, she liked the video game *Zelda,* and she played the saxophone. I said I appreciated people who didn't have very high affective expectations and that I sometimes frustrated my lover because I was very rational—I didn't get jealous, I didn't get angry, I didn't understand why people couldn't have more than one lover the way parents can have more than one child or we all have more than one friend and it doesn't mean we love them less. I said I'd enjoyed our correspondence as well, but he should never feel obligated to respond to my messages, as I was pretty good at entertaining myself. I wondered if my emoticons were disconcerting to him because they emulated facial expressions, and said I'd just been following his cue as he seemed to use them a lot. I said he should eat well and try to get some sleep. I said it was raining in New York, and I'd just recorded a uke cover he might like of a beautiful song by the French singer Barbara. The song was called "Pierre," and it was about the rain.

Sami wrote back again very quickly saying, "i have an asperger." He said it was an aspect of what we call in English "savant syndrome," though he preferred the German term, *Inselbegabung*, which means "insular talent." I wondered for a second if I should feel bad about having used the term *idiot savant* to describe the uke doodlers. I'd meant it as a joke, but that's what they used to call people like Sami. From early childhood he'd been able to remember complex melodies after hearing them only once, but he couldn't remember faces of people he'd known for years. He loved emoticons. He said that as a child he had an "emotion clock" with a hand that pointed at different emoticon-like faces so that he could indicate his own affective state. He mostly couldn't bear being hugged—as a child it made him scream, which got him in trouble—and he also liked counting and collecting things, and he liked to mimic accents. He found eye contact extremely uncomfortable because it conveyed too much information. He thought what I said about love was interesting.

He said that, to be honest, if he didn't receive a response to one of his own messages, he'd start to panic, wondering if he'd written something inappropriate, which he sometimes did. Sleep was a challenge for him, but he almost always ate well, and he loved to cook Indian food. He'd smoked a little weed and was starting to feel a bit calmer, and he was going to go back and practice some Bach partitas because that always helped him to come down from a panic attack. He ended his message saying that New York was very special, and he would always love it. He didn't say when or why he'd been here.

I wondered if Sami might find it helpful if I could suggest a way for us to maintain our interaction at a level that wouldn't overwhelm him. I proposed that we limit our correspondence to one message a day each. I said he should never feel obliged to write, but if it would be helpful for me to write to him reliably, even briefly, once every day, I could do that. He seemed to like this idea. Writing was sometimes a little difficult for him, but he liked to send his friends long voice messages, and perhaps he would send me one.

I said I'd like that.

When we first met, Olivia and I also talked about how often we should write each other. Actually, she was the one to bring it up. I'd explained to her my thing about moderation. When it became clear we were going to keep seeing each other, I made what seemed to me to be a reasonable suggestion—that I spend one night a week at her place in Inwood and she come downtown to stay with me another night. We were both fairly compulsive about our own work and agreed that we didn't want to constrain each other from seeing other people, erotically or otherwise. But she seemed incredulous that I'd want to parcel things out like that, so rationally. It wasn't that she wanted more, necessarily. Maybe she'd have a month where she couldn't see me at all. Maybe she'd want to drown in me for a week. It was the same with writing—after a drought of several days, there'd be a flood of emphatic e-mails. Actually, in a calmer moment, she wrote me an e-mail about that—in pentameter. This was her being funny, but not really. Her message said, in part:

BARBARA BROWNING

26

> Sometimes writing seems to say too much—
> the exclamation points, so hyperbolic,
> ellipses, EVERYTHING IN CAPS!—but then
> I realized, the problem really isn't
> excess, but its opposite. Love's lingua
> franca's a frank tongue that slides the groove
> where we connect, that licks the slit sex
> of friendship. Every other kind of language
> fails somehow. I think the only poem

that satisfied us both was when I held
your nipple in my mouth and with my fingers
traced tiny circles on the bud
of your sex, while it reached up to meet me.
THAT was poetry, the way our bodies
stretched towards each other, like a plant
stretches towards the light . . .

There was more. She said she could try to moderate her e-mails, but
not our sex. It was hard to argue with that.

Aside from *The Gift,* Marcel Mauss's other most influential piece of
writing is an essay called "Techniques of the Body." In it, he considers various techniques for doing things that we sometimes assume
are natural, not cultural—like squatting, or walking. Mauss says,
"I made, and went on making for several years, the fundamental
mistake of thinking that there is technique only when there is an
instrument. I had to go back to ancient notions, to the platonic
position on technique, for Plato spoke of a technique of music and in
particular of a technique of dance, and I had to extend these notions."
Mauss calls the body "man's first and most natural instrument"—or
better yet, his "first and most natural technical object."
    The essay considers various bodily techniques—beginning with
childbirth positions, moving through breastfeeding, crawling, sitting, walking, running, dancing, jumping, climbing, falling, swimming, lifting, throwing, washing, eating, drinking, copulating. Of
this last, Mauss makes this radical and assured assertion: "Nothing
is more technical than sexual positions." Since his entire discussion of technique is founded on Plato's understanding of technê
in relation to dance, the implication is that there's nothing more
choreographic than the sex act. I find that very interesting. But
he also dwells on the technique of sitting, which I mention because
of Sami's leg, and the dance I offered to choreograph for him in a

chair. And walking, which pertains to Tye, and his relationship to postmodern choreography.

Around the corner from my apartment, on the south side of Washington Square Park, there's a Baptist house of worship called Judson Memorial Church. In the late 1950s, the church began welcoming and encouraging the work of avant-garde artists living in the neighborhood, and in 1962, a group of experimental choreographers began to create and perform work there. The Judson Dance Theater was a collective of choreographers who would come to be seen as the innovators of a style broadly termed "postmodern." Maybe the simplest way to characterize their work would be to say that they, like Mauss, wanted to reconsider the distinctions between dancer/nondancer, and between the technical and the natural.

Steve Paxton was one of these dance artists. He would go on to create a choreography in 1967 called "Satisfyin' Lover" which is basically a score for untrained dancers to walk across the floor. It's really beautiful, if you like that kind of thing. Another of the Judson choreographers was David Gordon. He made a famous dance, "Chair," in which he and his wife, Valda Setterfield, explored various possibilities with two folding metal seats. Yvonne Rainer was also active in the group. She wanted to strip dance down to its essential language. In 1965 she wrote her "No Manifesto," which outlined what she didn't want in a dance:

> No to spectacle.
> No to virtuosity.
> No to transformations and magic and make-believe.
> No to the glamour and transcendency of the star image.
> No to the heroic.
> No to the anti-heroic.
> No to trash imagery.
> No to involvement of performer or spectator.
> No to style.

No to camp.

No to seduction of spectator by the wiles of the performer.

No to eccentricity.

No to moving or being moved.

Probably her most famous choreography from this period is "Trio A." It was originally performed as three simultaneous solos (herself, Paxton, and Gordon). It's a long movement phrase, perfunctory although sort of demanding. It requires concentration and some agility, if not grace. It seems adamantly bent on avoiding those things she said no to in her manifesto, but it's not unbeautiful. It's pragmatic and neutral.

The first time I saw Tye perform was March 9, 2011, at a launch party for a feminist art journal I work on, *Women & Performance.* We were publishing an issue on trans performance, and the issue editor had commissioned Tye to make a piece. He arrived at the party looking a little flustered. He had some power tools, and was wearing a green cap, dark pants, a long-sleeved shirt, and work boots. He asked somebody from the audience to read his text out loud for him, and he proceeded to get to work assembling a life-size replica of the rose window in Judson Church. He asked for help with that as well, and both the reader of his text and his building assistant were given green caps identical to Tye's. In the course of the performance, Tye asked the building assistant to keep supplying him with screws, and also with fake blood capsules, which Tye was biting down on. Red gore began to stream from his mouth. He continued working as though nothing unusual were happening. When he was done with the construction, he stripped off his shirt, pants, and boots. Under all that, he was wearing a white T-shirt, athletic shorts, and white ballet slippers. He got a little blood on his white slippers. I remember being concerned about the slippers being stained.

The text that Tye had his surrogate read out loud began, "Hi, everyone. My name is Tye, with a *Y*." Surrogate Tye said he was excited to be there, though he groused a little about the name of our journal. He asked if we'd considered renaming it *Women & Transpeople & Performance.* Then he admitted that his critique of the name of the journal, which was sponsoring the event, was something like going to a dinner party and complaining about the meatloaf because you're a vegetarian. He said, "But I'd love to have a moment of transparency." Then he went over the economic terms of the performance, which were, in his words, "very generous" by dance-world standards: $300. Then he went through his budget for the evening, which included renting a U-Haul and hiring a friend at a rate of $15 an hour to help schlep. After subtracting the costs of the materials, which he enumerated in detail, he was in the hole by $766.56. But this wasn't "totally fair," because he'd built the apparatus he was reassembling for a Judson Church performance, "Dog House," which had left him $386.12 in the red. In figuring out the budget for this evening, he paid himself (or would have if he weren't in the red) $15 an hour for the carpentry work he'd already done, but he said he was donating his actual performance time as a kind of "community service." He described the conception of that earlier piece, "Dog House," and the various glitches that came up in its realization. There were references to the fetishization of Judson as the birthplace of postmodern dance, the recent weird enthusiasm on the part of the art world for dance, the myth of Sisyphus and the story of Giselle, to which he always seemed to be returning. He said he never knew how to end his pieces. He was into endurance, which should guarantee an ending when the artist can't take it anymore, except that he had an unusual tolerance—and appetite—for pain. He mentioned a piece he'd made at Dance Theater Workshop that had sixteen endings and an interruption.

Then he quoted several bloggers who had written about the performance. They described Tye's body and his gender in a variety of ways. The only consistent thing among the descriptions was that they referred to him as "short." He said, "Am I really that short?" I'm guessing Tye's about 5'5". He then said something about his realization that a big part of art-making for him was about wanting people in the audience to want to have sex with him. Then he asked a prominent scholar in the room if he'd be on Tye's MFA thesis committee. That was awkward. He said his program wouldn't offer this scholar an honorarium but he could give him a little scale model of the rose window. The guy said yes. Of course, what else could he say?

I didn't mention, toward the beginning of the piece Tye had said, "I almost have my MFA. I'm twenty-four thousand four hundred and twenty-four dollars and eighty-four cents away."

After the thesis committee invitation, he gave a kind of CliffsNotes reading of the meaning of the first performance in which he'd constructed the life-size replica of the Judson Church rose window. It went, in part: "Rolling out the window was the first in a series of alterations I made to the space. I hoped to suggest, if not create, a fascistic postmodern dance regime. Followed by an assassination. Which ostensibly opens up the possibility for regime change. But the change is never realized. Instead, my body is made subordinate to the regime I constructed. The window instantly becomes a relic. Which of course increases its value. So suddenly I'm subordinate to a very expensive architectural ruin . . . that's also a theme park. For sadists." This went on for some time. He explained that the long-windedness was also structurally necessary so the music, which was playing in the background, could hit its climax. The music was Elton John's "Funeral for a Friend."

Keep in mind, all this was being read by Surrogate Tye. Real Tye was drilling screws and bleeding from the mouth.

When the climax came, it was time for Tye to peel off the work clothes and get down to his ballet gear, which is when audience members were instructed that twenty-four of them were needed to volunteer to lie down on top of Tye, one at a time. This was a replication of part of the choreography of another Judson piece Tye had done, in which twenty-four male artists were called up, one by one, to lie on top of Tye. It seems there was something of a mirroring in the act, but also some kind of osmotic exchange.

Eventually, he got his twenty-four volunteers. I found that part profoundly moving.

Six months after Tye's "Performance for *Women & Performance*," about one thousand people Occupied Wall Street, which is to say, on September 17, 2011, protesters marched through the financial district and settled into Zuccotti Park. The encampment remained in place until shortly after midnight on November 15, when the NYPD gave notice that protesters would be removed due to ostensibly unsanitary conditions. A little while later, they cleared everybody out. About two hundred people were arrested.

I was very disheartened that night. I hadn't joined the encampment, but Olivia and I'd been going down to Zuccotti, hanging out a bit, and talking with people. We were particularly warmed by the library they'd set up, and we'd deposited some books there. It was called "The People's Library." She gave them her Brecht translations. I put one of my own novels in the alphabetically appropriate fiction bin, earmarking the page where my narrator recommends to her secret lover a book by the anarchist anthropologist David Graeber.

The Occupy movement, like Yvonne Rainer, said no to the glamour and transcendency of the star image and to the heroic. So you won't hear anybody calling Graeber anything like the "leader" or the "mastermind" of the movement, least of all him, but most anybody would have to acknowledge that he contributed a perspective to its early formation that was both strategically and intellectually important. (He'd also resist that "anarchist anthropologist" label, as he's given to saying that anarchism is not an identity but an activity.) He'd been active in the G8 protests, and had written about them as an anthropologist. He was famously denied tenure at Yale, which a lot of people seemed to think had more to do with his political activities than a rejection of his scholarship, because he was pretty manically productive on that count, and while his work elicited a range of responses, there were plenty of advanced scholars who were calling him one of the most provocative minds of his generation. He had an encyclopedic knowledge of the history of anarchist philosophy and its practice in diverse cultural contexts.

He'd thought a lot about Marcel Mauss. I've long been sympathetic to Graeber's take on him. There's a chapter on Mauss in Graeber's *Toward an Anthropological Theory of Value: The False Coin of Our Own Dreams*. It's tendentious. The prevailing reading of *The Gift* holds that it presents at best an ambivalent account of gift economies. That is, most people will tell you that Mauss demonstrates that receiving a gift obligates you to reciprocate, which is not always such a great thing, and in extreme cases it can lead to a potentially destructive cycle of ostentation, debt, and compelled payback. One doesn't have to turn to Native American potlatch to find this—it's easy enough to identify cases of pathological gift giving in our own culture, like the freakishly violent displays of acquisitiveness that take place each Black Friday, the official opening of the holiday shopping season. But one would like to think that other attitudes could prevail. Graeber's reading of Mauss would hold that there's another logic possible. I'd call it something closer to that of having your cake and eating it too.

Graeber says that in *The Gift*, Mauss was trying "to get at the heart of precisely what it was about the logic of the market that did such violence to ordinary people's sense of justice." We know better, that is, but it seems we need to be reminded. Mauss suggests that if we look at cultural practices that reject a market model of self-interest, we "shall find in this reasons for life and action that are still prevalent in certain societies and numerous social classes: the joy of public giving, the pleasure in generous expenditure on the arts, in hospitality." This is what tips Mauss's account away from obligation and into self-generated and self-generating pleasure (a socialist version of "let them eat cake"—and have it too).

But there's something even more interesting than the happy story of gift economies as sustainable and humane social models. It's the moments when Mauss talks about cultural contexts within which people think of gifts as animated objects—things with souls. He says that among the Maori, one's sense of obligation on receiving a gift doesn't come from a sense of debt to the giver, but rather from the fact that the object itself has a spirit. That's what compels you. He says that in the Trobriand Islands people speak of gifted bracelets and necklaces as dogs that are "playfully nuzzling one another"—which is why one would reciprocate, to let the dogs sniff at each other, because they want to. Mauss loves that metaphor. He says that in Fiji, people give gifts of their currency, which is sperm whale teeth, and the teeth are treated like dolls. People decorate them, and take them out of a basket to caress them and talk about how cute they are. Surely all of this is ethnologically suspect— much like that observation in "Techniques of the Body" about that "specifically Pacific" sexual position—but it's pretty charming. And I love the political implications Mauss draws from all this. In his version of the story, gift giving is neither about the giver's magnanimity, nor about his or her attempt to lord it over somebody. Property itself wants to circulate. My gifts want to sniff at your gifts, like curious dogs. Of course you only arrive at this conclusion if you take Mauss seriously when he talks about animated objects. That's how I like to read him.

I felt a little funny about leaving my novel in the fiction bin at The People's Library in Zuccotti Park, because even though I wanted to leave it as a gift to the ragtag little community camping out there, I knew it was a lot to ask, to think that one of them might take the time to read an obscure little postmodern novel like mine, when they could be reading Brecht or Noam Chomsky or Silvia Federici or Fred Moten or David Graeber himself—or, if they were into fiction, William Morris or John Steinbeck or Octavia Butler. But my novel was like a little dog that wanted to be sniffing around the other books in that bin, so I left it there.

Almost all the books from The People's Library got trashed when the police dismantled the encampment that November. Part of the "cleanup" involved a lot of water being sprayed on things.

After I showed Sami the recording I'd made of "Pierre," he asked me if I'd considered recording a cover of something by Léo Ferré, another great composer of French chansons. I hadn't, but the suggestion made me curious, so I began listening to a bunch of Ferré's songs. I also read a little bit about him. He was born in Monaco, and his repertoire was pretty evenly divided between melancholic love songs and rousing anarchist anthems. Sami wondered what I might do with "La Solitude." I ended up recording that one, as well as several others, but the first Ferré composition I took on was "Les Anarchistes." I thought I'd spam David Graeber with it. I'd met him once, in December of 2011, shortly after they'd shut down Zuccotti. He was giving a free seminar at Judson Church. I was surprised that the crowd wasn't bigger. It appeared to be a mix of graduate students and some older activists and autodidacts. Olivia went with me. She was chewing on the end of her long silver braid the whole time. She looked vaguely irritable. I'm not sure if this had anything to do with the fact that I'd recommended him to my lover in that novel. Graeber spoke a lot, very casually and yet masterfully, which is also how he writes (Olivia found it a bit mansplaining in tone, even though she was in agreement with his message). There were some questions from the audience, ranging from the very basic to the complex, all of which he answered with equal seriousness. When the talk was finished and we were folding up our chairs, I walked over to Graeber and handed him a copy of my book. I said, "Your work has meant a great deal to me. You appear very briefly in this novel." He looked just a little taken aback, but he nodded and stared at the back flap for a minute.

I had to go. Olivia was waiting for me out on the sidewalk.

On June 25, 2012, I sent Graeber the Léo Ferré ukulele cover. It wasn't that hard to find his e-mail online, as I knew he was teaching at the time at Goldsmiths. I wrote, "Hello, David Graeber. You may remember I went to hear you speak in New York several months ago and handed you a novel I'd written, saying you made a cameo appearance in it. Sorry if I appear to be cyberstalking you—I mean it nicely." I went on to tell him that I'd recently given a character in my novel Graeber's newly published theoretical treatise on debt, and my character was now reading it enthusiastically. That was true. Perhaps that sounds opaque or coy, but I thought he'd understand. Many of my fictional characters are closely or loosely based on real people, as I suppose are the vast majority of characters in the history of literature. I like to continue to have intellectual and sometimes intimate or erotic relationships with these people even after I've made them fictional. I feel the same way about my former lovers—and sometimes these categories overlap. I realize some people might find that strange—another form of possibly inappropriate intimacy—but it's pretty important to me. Maybe this will help you understand Olivia's disgruntlement that day at Judson. She's politically averse to erotic and affective constraints, but she says it's naïve to disavow feelings like jealousy and possessiveness. You should read that sonnet by Brecht. I also told David Graeber that I'd recorded a ukulele cover tune in his honor. I said I was sure he knew of Léo Ferré, and clearly Ferré's version was superior, but mine was from the heart, and it was for him.

Amazingly, David Graeber wrote me back almost immediately—just like Dr. Mel. The complete text of his message was, "Actually that's quite a nice rendition."

I thought it was interesting he didn't say thank you. Then I remembered that he has a whole little meditation on saying thank you in his book on debt. He says the problem with bourgeois politesse is that it automatically implies some kind of obligation, which goes against the logic of what he calls "baseline communism": from each according to their abilities, to each according to their needs. In fact, in some languages, the word for *thank you* is an acknowledgment of obligation—it's *obrigado* in Portuguese. Even in English, we sometimes say, "Much obliged." But maybe we shouldn't be.

Sami sent me the first voice message in July of 2012, after we'd been corresponding for a little over a month. As I said, he'd mentioned that he sometimes liked to do this with other friends, but the first time he sent me a recording of his spoken voice, it was prompted by a conversation we'd been having about accents and about some peculiarities in his written English. From the bits of it I've reproduced, you will have noticed that he didn't appear to be a native speaker of English, and yet almost all the text on his website was in English, as was most of the music he sang. He was living in Germany but never sang in German. He'd recorded a few songs in French and a couple in Spanish—all without any discernable accent as far as I could tell. I mentioned something about how much I loved "Águas de Março," and almost immediately he posted a gorgeous version on the *Jazzman* set list. I wasn't sure what was more mind-boggling—his spontaneous rendering of the complex chords and syncopations on the guitar, or his nearly perfect, relaxed pronunciation of the Portuguese. The song has one of the longest and most intricate lyrics in the history of popular song. I asked him how he did that. He said he liked trying to master accents and fake his way through languages he didn't really understand. And that was when I got the voice message.

It was about twenty minutes long. Most of his voice messages are about that long. It was riveting—not so much because of what he was saying but because of his voice, and his breath, and the sighs, and the hemming and hawing that came between the words. His speaking voice, like his singing voice, was deep and very—this is really the only word for it—musical. His accent was, roughly, British, and his spoken English made it seem more "his" language than you would have guessed from his writing. By then he'd told me a bit about his upbringing—he was born in Delhi to a Pashtun Indian father and a German mother. They were both classically trained musicians, and during his childhood they moved to London, where he lived until he was a teenager and his parents' marriage collapsed. The move to Europe was partly provoked by anti-Islamic sentiment in India after the assassination of Indira Gandhi. Sami's family wasn't directly threatened—most of the violence was directed against Sikhs—but it wasn't a good time. He said in London they lived in Brent with the other "curry munchers," and the South Asians called him "gora" (white), and the whites called him "paki." When Sami was fourteen, his father left them, and his mother took Sami to Cologne, where her family lived. He went to high school there, and that's where he met his best friend, Farrokh. They played in a rock band together. By his own admission, Sami was a handful in adolescence, a combination of innate sensitivity and hormones. When his mother kicked him out of her house in exasperation, he went to live for a time with Farrokh's family. He was also very close to Farrokh's sister, Minoo. She was now a photographer, and she was the one who took many of those portraits of Sami that appeared on his website. He said he was often uncomfortable being looked at, but with Minoo it was OK. Her photographs were very beautiful. Once in a while, he'd even look at the camera. In those shots, it was Sami's eyes that appeared to convey too much information. He was handsome, but his eyes were unsettling. When I told him that, he said everyone said that, and he joked about being a basilisk.

But back to that question of language—Sami said that after having lived in Germany now for twenty years, surely German was his "best" language, but he'd retained something of a British accent when speaking it. He liked it for speaking and thinking, but not for singing. He seemed a little embarrassed when I mentioned some of the syntactical quirks in his written English—mostly in his constructions of the future tense. In the voice recording, he said it made sense that he would make errors in the future tense, because the future was the most difficult thing for him to imagine. He hardly ever made plans more than a month or two out. This was particularly frustrating to his ex-wife, who often wanted to make arrangements for his meetings with his son. He said he found it difficult to imagine anything too far in the future, and in truth, he'd always imagined he wouldn't live very long. He didn't say this in a particularly dramatic way. He actually sounded kind of cheerful about it.

So in his early childhood, he'd been exposed to several languages, and it seemed none really felt to him like a mother tongue, but all of this is perhaps somewhat beside the point, since in fact words—any words at all—weren't Sami's first language. He didn't speak for the first four years of his life, until his parents put him in front of a piano, and he began to play. And everyone was astonished. And then he began to speak, a little.

Sami's diagnosis didn't come for some time. His early childhood was tumultuous, as you can imagine. His father's family was large, and in his words, there were always relatives around trying to hug and kiss him or else hit him in order to teach him to respect his father or uncle or aunt or cousin or uncle's cousin or the neighbor who was married to his cousin's cousin . . . For Sami the hugs and kisses were as terrifying as the hitting. He described the little girls at the school playground. They also wanted to hug him, and he'd scream and throw a fit. He sent me a photo in which he must have been about six or seven—shortly before his family left Delhi. A group of brown-faced little children stood in plaid uniforms, the girls in skirts with white blouses, the boys in shorts showing their scraped little knees. The other children's expressions ranged from radiant to quizzical. Just one beautiful, delicate boy averted his gaze entirely from the camera. Sami looked like somebody had rubbed chalk on his face. He looked terrified. I also had the impulse to hug him, even though I knew it would make him scream.

So in that first voice message, he spoke a little bit about what he liked and didn't like about German, what languages he liked to sing in and why—and he laughed a little, and sighed, and said "um" and "ah" and "hmm." That's what we call phatic language—words and sounds that don't really convey any information, but just serve to maintain a sense of contact in a conversation. I wrote him about phatic language after that, and it became a kind of running joke between us, because some of his voice messages seemed to be about 80 percent phatic. The interesting thing about this message was that the topic of it was the same as its substance: his speaking voice. When he'd finished, he signed off, almost as though he were signing a letter. He said, "All right, then, good-bye and have a nice day. Sami." There was a pause, and then he said, "PS: Well, the only thing I'm faking when I'm talking is, um, the modulation of my voice. I didn't always do this, but I learned it and somehow I, well, I mastered it, in order to sound, um, a little more human. Um. Because people just, um, modulate their voices when they're talking, and I learned that. So, yeah, well, that's the only thing I'm faking. Just in order to sound less . . . like an alien. OK, then, well, cheers, good-bye." There was a little break in the recording, and then he added a PPS: "Well, I just listened to this, and I'm sorry my breathing sounds like it was, um," and he laughed, "like Darth Wader or something," and he laughed again. "It's not always like that, I promise." Because he speaks German, Sami sometimes pronounces the letter *v* like a *w* and the letter *w* like a *v*. I thought that was funny. Darth Wader.

He didn't sound like Darth Vader, though it's true that his breathing was audible. It was like that recording of João Gilberto singing "Estate," where you could hear the spit on his lips and the hairs in his nose. I liked it.

I mentioned my correspondence with Sami to Olivia. I was a little nervous about it. I thought she might find his story interesting, but sometimes it's hard to tell how she'll respond to things. It was OK. I brought it up one day while she was taping her knee for a long bike ride. She narrowed her eyes a little but kept taping her knee as I spoke. She sort of focused on that term, *Inselbegabung*. She agreed with Sami that sometimes German was better for communicating certain things.

Exactly one year before I began corresponding with Sami, just shortly after "Performance for *Women & Performance*," Tye graduated from the MFA program in visual arts at Columbia. It's an interdisciplinary program that encourages or at least allows for performance and conceptual work, in addition to the more traditional forms of painting and sculpture. Tye's way of describing his work—and other people's ways of describing it—has morphed over time. The one thing that seems to drive him crazy is when you call him a *conceptual artist*. He prefers *artist*, period. One bio that I found from this period reads: "Tye Larkin Hayes is an interdisciplinary artist, whose performances and sculptures address shifting subjectivities and power relationships among human bodies and objects. Influenced by the Judson Theater and his training as a classical ballet dancer, Hayes's dance pieces explore ballet as a form of manual labor rather than an elite spectacle." Tye told me he didn't write that bio, and he doesn't like it. He also doesn't like to be referred to as *Hayes*. It's *Larkin Hayes*. There was a more compressed bio on the invitation to his *Women & Performance* performance. It just said: "Tye Larkin Hayes makes performances, objects, and the occasional video. All of it is dance." That was a good one.

I went to Tye's MFA thesis exhibit at SculptureCenter in Long Island City in May of 2011. He'd invited me because I told him how much I liked his "Performance for *Women & Performance*." In fact, he also asked me if I'd like to participate in the crit at the end. I felt honored. The piece was called "Duet . . " and there was a series of live performances involved. Tye had constructed an L-shaped wall in the middle of a large white gallery space and a long runway-like raised floor that cut sort of diagonally through the space designated by the wall structure. Actually, the construction of the raised floor and its subsequent deconstruction were a part of the performances. Leaning up against the back side of the wall he'd built were the remnants of a number of prior performances that had taken place elsewhere—a small maquette of the sanctuary of Judson Church, the life-size replica of the rose window, some leftover Gatorade bottles, some questionnaires he'd had people fill out (he asked some seemingly inappropriate questions about personal finances and debt), and so on. Affixed to the back of the adjoining piece of dry-wall, he'd mounted the wall text for the piece. It read:

Tye Larkin Hayes
Duet . .
Canvas, wood, cornstarch, paper, foam, foam core,
cotton, polyester, spandex, vinyl, plastic, acrylic,
aluminum, electricity, sweat, yellow 5, transsexual,
Thomas von Frisch
Live Performance Schedule:
Duet   Saturday, May 7 at 3 p.m.
Duet,   Saturday, May 14 at 3 p.m.

Commencement Tuesday, May 17 at 3 p.m.
Final Critique Sunday, May 22 at 3 p.m.

Please be prompt.

That "Please be prompt" is characteristic. Tye is polite but firm. When people arrived at the designated time for the performance, Tye was already sweeping the space and starting to get to work. He was dressed in baggy athletic shorts and sneakers and one of those green work caps. Actually, I'd arranged to meet a friend at the first performance, an artist who was unfamiliar with Tye's work. When I got there, I explained to her that it was Tye sweeping the area with a big push broom. She said that she'd seen this adolescent-looking guy at work and assumed it was a young student intern of the art center cleaning up in advance of the show—an undergrad or maybe even a high school student. Tye removed his shirt as he worked. He started using a power drill to assemble the raised floor. There was a boom box plugged into an extension cord, and it emitted a lot of irritating static. Tye was joined after a while in his labor by Tom, that distinguished older gentleman with white hair. Tye would tell him, quietly, what to do, and he would cooperate. Tye began covering the platform with marley, which is the sheet vinyl often used to cover dance flooring. When Tye constructs surfaces on which to dance, they're generally sprung, which means there are two wooden surfaces with a pocket of air in between to absorb the shock. This is how floors are made in dance studios, and when the surface wood cannot be perfectly sanded and varnished to protect the dancers' feet, marley is often laid on top.

At one point, when the platform had been fully assembled, Tom attended to Tye as he precariously performed a number of repetitive and difficult ballet maneuvers down the length of it. He'd prepared the surface, but it was still a dangerous situation, given the narrowness of the platform and the precision that it required for Tye not to go careening off while executing these difficult maneuvers.

In the corner of that drywall construction, there was a built-in seat—a tall, narrow rectangular projection that he eventually sat on. In one of the performances, Tye quietly instructed Tom to climb onto his lap. The surface of the projection was not actually large enough to support two people like that, and Tye had to use quite a bit of strength to hold on to Tom and keep him suspended. Tom was facing into the structure so we couldn't see his face, but it was clear that they were both very concentrated on the task of remaining there like that. You could see that Tye was sweating, and he kept having to adjust his grip and Tom's position. It looked very uncomfortable.

On May 14, Tye deconstructed that raised floor with Tom's help and rebuilt it at a new angle, along with a second, lower, unsprung platform, running alongside the first, six inches wide and covered with marley. They repeated the lap sitting.

On May 17, Tye performed port de bras movements with Tom walking slowly by his side. They repeated the lap sitting, but this time they were joined by the photographer who had been documenting the performances. Tye often choreographs any documentation of his work, so the documentation is part of the work, not the other way around. So Tom sat on Tye, and the photographer sat on Tom, and it was very precarious and difficult and a little sexual.

At the final performance, the day of the crit, Tye was almost done cleaning up when everyone arrived. He circulated through the audience and hugged a few of us in a very intentional way. As in the *Women & Performance* piece, some designated audience members were given green work caps identical to Tye's. I was wearing one of these. Afterwards I realized we were his committee members. When he approached me, I stood, and we embraced. He was shirtless and warm. I think I can say, immodestly, that I am pretty good at hugging. That is, I tend to be physically affectionate, and

I'm sensitive to other people's need for personal space, but I also usually pick up on a desire for contact and the degree of pressure and tenderness somebody wants or can tolerate. That's a sort of skill you consciously develop when you study tango or contact improvisation, but some people develop it just by hugging carefully. So whether it's due to an innate sensibility or some consciousness of hugging as a technique of the body, I think I'm good at it, but Tye is extraordinary.

I'm not the only one who's told him that. He once performed in a restaging of Yvonne Meier's famous experimental dance, "The Shining," in which audience members were led through a maze of cardboard boxes into a pitch-black space where they had different kinds of contact with the dancers. A famous choreographer was in the audience, and Tye ended up pressing his body against hers on the floor. She couldn't see him, but she knew it was him in the dark because of the specificity of his touch. She'd only seen him dancing once, but she could sense that, from the quality of his contact. I find it difficult to describe except to say that it's highly focused. It was months later that they met, when the choreographer told him this.

I experienced the hug with Tye that day as a pas de deux, concentrated and very specific. I felt very aware of my responsibility to correspond to his skill. Although he was naked from the waist up and a little sweaty, and although our embrace lasted for minutes and was so concentrated, I wouldn't characterize it as erotic, though I think there was some kind of love in it. It was definitely dance.

After all the hugging, Tye narrated for the audience what had happened during all the other performances. His narration was long, awkward, and meandering. He kept going over and amending a lot of seemingly meaningless details but would forget big chunks and then correct himself. The description went on and on. People began to wonder if it was ever going to end, but finally it did, and then the committee stayed on to tell Tye what we thought was interesting or significant. He took notes and nodded appreciatively.

I don't remember what I asked or said at the critique. I believe I had some kind of insight, but right now all I can remember is the hug.

If you Google Tye, you may find an old *New York Times* article referencing his technical abilities, but it's not about hugging. The *Times* once ran a profile of Tye's younger brother, Jesse. The article was titled "Portrait of the Dancer as a Young Man (in Pain)." That's interesting, as it would seem to be a possible title for much of Tye's artistic oeuvre. But it was, in fact, about the summer Jesse was on scholarship, studying at the American Ballet Theatre. He was fourteen. The article said that he got into ballet because of an older sister, Tye, a "phenom who could do 32 fouettés—the whipped turns that are one measure of a ballerina's skill—when she was 11." That article was written before Tye started identifying as trans, and I've never asked him if it irked him to have it floating around on the internet in perpetuity. Because it was in the *Times,* it pops up pretty quickly on a search. If it does irk him, I'm not sure if the more irksome part would be the pronoun or the suggestion that his virtuosity was a question of ballet technique. Maybe he likes that article. If you read it, you can tell he and his brother were very close. They still are.

While Sami finds it very difficult to hug or even shake hands, he's not averse to sexual touch. The topic came up fairly early in our correspondence. When I told him that I was a novelist, he said he'd ordered one of my books. I was flattered that he took an interest, and I thanked him. He said there was nothing to thank him for, that he looked forward to reading it—but I imagine all writers feel gratitude for their readers, just as Sami had extended thanks to his anonymous listeners "for lend me your ears." Sami wrote me the day it arrived in the mail, and the next day he'd finished it. He said he liked it, and he pointed out, in particular, a fairly graphic passage in which the narrator described a hypothetical—as in, proposed—blow job. Actually, she puts it much more gracefully than that. The passage, if I do say so myself, was pretty deft—that is, the language was graceful, but so were the specifics of the imagined act. Anyway, it ended with a question to the addressee: "Wouldn't that be nice?" Sami said something indicating that yes, it would.

That made me happy. I'm an imaginative person, and I don't require a lot of encouragement, so I imagined something small but somewhat intimate with Sami and included it in my next message. Not surprisingly, this freaked him out a little. That was embarrassing. I apologized. He wrote back that I hadn't done anything wrong, it was just a little confusing to him. But then he told me that, in fact, he loved sex, and maybe he loved it even more because it was the one kind of contact that wasn't painful to him. Well, he could also have nonsexual, affectionate contact with a few people sometimes—particularly his son. Later he would send me several photographs of the two of them together, some from Kakay's early childhood, some more recent. In these pictures, they were often touching, and indeed, they seemed very close. But as I was saying, most casual contact was uncomfortable for him, if not excruciating. But sex he liked, and it was the one other thing, besides music, that he was very good at. He didn't say this in a boasting way. There are many things Sami says he's bad at. I already mentioned dance. He also claims to have a terrible sense of humor, although in my experience that's something that comes and goes with him. His speaking voice, as I said, is charming, but according to him it could sometimes get quite awkward when he was nervous. At times, he said, he would stammer, and the worst was when he'd begin to flap his hands around uncontrollably. Sometimes he'd sit on them to stop it. There were particular parts of his body that were extra sensitive. He really couldn't bear to have his back touched, for instance—it sent him into a panic.

Sex, he said, felt like music. It was something he could understand. When he spoke of it, he used musical terminology. So when he spoke of music, sometimes it seemed almost embarrassingly sexual—even for me. I asked him something about the tone of a violin piece he'd posted—something by Fauré—and he described the technique of bowing sul tasto, and he also spoke of playing the "sweet spot." I thought it was one of the dirtiest messages anybody had ever written me. Not really, of course—strictly speaking, it was all about the placement of the bow over the violin strings. But you see what I mean.

Part of the reason we were talking about bowing technique was that Sami had just made a trip to Amsterdam to buy a very special new bow from the great maker of baroque replica bows, Basil de Visser. It was carved from snakewood. Sami sent me a photograph. The tip of the bow also looked entirely obscene. You are probably thinking I just have a dirty mind; I promise, it's not just me. Even Sami mentioned it.

Since Sami was waxing poetic about the beauty of the new bow, I wondered if he'd ever thought about getting a snakewood leg. He had more than one prosthesis. Apparently, the titanium blade was particularly suited to athleticism, which I would have guessed from seeing all those photographs of Oscar Pistorius. But he had another that more closely resembled his former leg. I sent him some pictures I found online of beautiful carved prostheses— one from the Victorian period and another made more recently by an artist. He seemed to like these. It was interesting to think of his prosthetic leg as though it were a musical instrument or a work of art. But it was even more interesting for me to think of his violin bow as a prosthesis.

Shortly after I met Tye, we had an e-mail exchange about sex, objects, and animation. Because I liked the text from the *Women & Performance* piece, he sent me another performance text, something he'd had a classmate read out loud for him at a crit at Columbia. The text began in a fairly chatty, cheerful way: "Hi, everyone. Thanks for coming to my crit." He said he didn't usually find the crit format particularly productive for his work, but that his new M.O. was to take full advantage of all the opportunities, since he and his fellow students were all paying through the nose for the program. He did the math on how much they were all spending per day, and then per hour, in order to get the degree. First he did it by dividing the day rate by twenty-four, but then he said he didn't think it was fair to pay while they were sleeping, so he refactored the hourly rate based on the hours that instruction was actually going on—between ten in the morning and ten in the evening. That put the hourly rate at $28.57. He said, "You're all paying almost thirty dollars to critique me right now."

He mentioned that he'd been kvetching all semester about the lack of queer mentors in the program and how difficult it had been for him to schedule this crit such that a queer faculty member could facilitate. As an undergrad, he said he'd had a lot of queer teachers, and he told some anecdotes about his teacher for Video I and II. Tye said he'd had a crush on her, which made for an excellent learning experience. This professor was friends with some famous "dyke art stars" like Catherine Opie, Catherine Lord, and Yvonne Rainer. He said these art stars always had Thanksgiving dinner together. Tye remembered going to his mom's house for Thanksgiving dinner and jacking off in his childhood bed while thinking about the dyke-art-star turkey dinner. He imagined the stuffing of the turkey. He said, "Of course, we all know Yvonne's hands well."

Yvonne Rainer's first experiment with film was a short called *Hand-Movie:* six silent minutes of her moving her fingers around in front of a white wall.

He told some other stories about his undergraduate education that involved a lack of funds and creative ways of finding places to sleep and to have sex. He gave a pretty graphic depiction of some of the sex he'd had in the classroom where they held crits. He explained how he'd gotten a couple of subpar grades on account of lack of access to equipment, and somehow this trailed into a story about how he'd prepared to commit suicide during his high school chemistry class, and his lab partner was weirdly concerned about Tye getting a zero for the day. This led to an account of his performance in a high school production of *No Exit*. He said he liked stages and lighting, but actors made him nervous because as they spoke they seemed to know exactly what their faces looked like, although for some reason dancers didn't bother him in quite the same way. And he told the story of a tall, beautiful practitioner of Alexander Technique that he slept with for a while, and how this woman kept telling Tye to stand up straight. This was before his top surgery, and he had a tendency to collapse his chest and round his shoulders. She told him he needed to think about Alexander Technique all the time. Tye said, "Even when we're fucking?" She said, "Yes." Apparently if you're really good at Alexander Technique, you can make three fingers feel like a fist.

That was interesting.

After I read this text, I wrote Tye, "You write so well. I'm now wondering if I should take Alexander Technique." He said Feldenkrais was better. I said, "But does Feldenkrais increase penis size?"

Tye balked at the word *penis*. We had a mutual friend who had just gotten a tattoo of one of Henry Darger's paintings—a butterfly girl with a little penis—but the tattoo artist had urged her to minimize the sex because "you don't want to go around with a dick on your arm." I had joked, "Who doesn't want a dick on their arm? Think of all the great maneuvers!" I said some people might not want dicks on their arms, but evidently many people would like a bigger penis, or we wouldn't be getting all that spam. Tye insisted that cocks and dicks were all well and good, but that the term *penis* was simply too biologically literalistic—he said it wasn't favored in the trans community. I said well, yes, I didn't think there was any community that thought the words *penis* and *vagina* were particularly hot, maybe precisely because they sounded too literal, which just went to show that maybe everybody secretly knew their Lacan even if they thought they didn't.

I told Tye, "I guess I never associate language about sex with a communal language (even though I keep talking about communism) because lovers have an obnoxious tendency to make up a private lexicon (like couples who have nicknames for each other's sex parts—Alice and Gertrude being probably the worst perpetrators)." I said that I'd once had a lover who sometimes affectionately wrote me about my penis the morning after we'd made love. (She was referring to my fingers.)

Tye apparently had a number of cocks, some anatomical, one prosthetic. It was made of silicone, and he insisted that when he fucked with it, he could feel everything. He said, "It's an extension of my body." I had no trouble buying that. I said, "My body is an extension of my body."

He liked that. I think he said, "That's fucking beautiful." It's funny, I just realized that's almost exactly what Sami said when I sent him that poem by Matthew Dickman.

Regarding the animated nature of objects, like the silicone prosthesis, I quoted to Tye early Marx on how man is a sensuous object, and so can only express his life in real, sensuous objects. The passage ends: "To be sensuous is to suffer . . . Man as an objective, sensuous being is therefore a suffering being, and because he feels his suffering, he is a passionate being." This is the erotic version of what Mauss said about animated objects.

At the end of our e-mail exchange about sex and prosthetics and a communal erotic language, Tye said something uncharacteristically prim, and I chided him, "Sex is good, clean fun!"

He said, "What kind of sex are you having?"

I said, "I only share that kind of information in totally public forums like academic books and novels." I was joking, but it was kind of true.

Sami also has a silicone prosthetic leg. He doesn't talk about feeling things with the prosthesis, but he suffers terribly from phantom limb pain. I imagine you're curious about how he lost his leg. You would think this would be something he talked or thought about a lot, but in fact, it happened very quickly, and while there have been repercussions, it's not by any means the trauma that haunts him most. It was a skateboarding accident, about three years ago. He was riding in the street when, as he put it, an enormous SUV came to "park" on his left knee. They tried to save the leg, but it was so badly damaged that osteonecrosis set in and his foot turned black. He said it was a relief when they finally took it off.

In the hospital, he obviously couldn't play piano, and even violin, guitar, and santoor weren't practical while he was stuck in bed, so they brought him a ukulele. At first he tuned it like a violin. That was the origin of that Paganini caprice. He practiced it in the hospital and recorded it when he got home. But he also banged out some cheery uke standards to distract himself from the pain, and he joked about the escapism and the "dreams of Bora Bora."

There was a period of rehabilitation, and physical therapy to learn to use the prosthesis. He said the hospital staff was, for the most part, very caring and gentle. There was one therapist who read about his autism on his chart and started speaking very slowly and emphatically, as though Sami were a child, but the others were sensitive, patient, and kind. He'd remained friends with one of the young doctors who attended to him, a woman named Chinonye, and he still called her if he was having particular difficulties with pain. The phantom limb pain was a problem, and because he was neurologically atypical, some of the standard therapies weren't effective. Antianxiety meds ironically made him very tense. Hypnosis backfired completely. Even the mirror therapy they recently developed was a flop. Acupuncture helped a little, but mostly they'd end up giving him morphine.

A month or so after we began corresponding, just after he went on that trip to Amsterdam to buy the new bow, his pain began to get worse. At first he thought he'd overdone it, wearing the prosthesis on the flight. It was his first airplane trip since the accident. But after he got back, it kept getting worse. Finally, Chinonye said it looked like a neuroma, meaning that the nerve near the amputation had grown back in a tangle. Sami said there was a possibility they'd do another surgery to try to untangle the nerve, but there was no guarantee it wouldn't grow back the same way. In fact, the odds were that it would. They prescribed an opioid, fentanyl, which came in the form of little lozenges. I read a bit about fentanyl on the internet. According to Wikipedia, it was one hundred times stronger than morphine. It was absorbed very efficiently because it was lipophilic. I joked to Sami that *lipophilic* meant it "loved fat," which sounded nice. The more worrisome part of the Wikipedia article was that a rock star, Jay Bennett, had overdosed on it, even though he was taking it under medical supervision. He was the guitarist for the band Wilco. Paul Gray, the bassist for Slipknot, apparently also overdosed on it, in combination with morphine, but it looks like he may not have been taking those drugs under doctor's orders. There was even a noirish suggestion that Mossad agents might have tried to kill the Hamas leader, Khalid Mishaal, with fentanyl in 1997. I wondered if the agents offered him the lozenges like they were hard candy.

When I told Sami what I'd read, he started calling his lozenges "killer candy." I was a little worried, but I hoped maybe it would be effective.

It was hard to think about him being in pain. He sent a couple of voice messages in which you could hear how labored his breathing was. Sometimes he wouldn't even say anything for a minute or so, he'd just breathe. I don't think he was trying to be melo-dramatic or anything; I think he'd just forgotten for a minute that he was recording, because of the pain, or maybe also because of the painkillers. But he'd send these messages anyway. If they weren't so sad, they would be kind of funny, with those long, unselfconscious silences.

One day I was recording a cover of a beautiful song by Susana Baca, "De los Amores," and it's about pain, the pain of love, and of caring. She sings, "Del dolor, fui el primero pescador. No soy bella. Como duele, el esmero, como duele." Of pain, I was the first fisherman. I'm not beautiful. How it hurts, to care so, how it hurts. I laid down the uke track, then the vocal, and then in a quiet part, I laid down one more track, very faintly: me, breathing, or trying to breathe, in the catching, labored way Sami had in a recent message. I sent it to him and told him I'd stolen the breathing from him, and I thought it was the best part of the recording. He said he loved it, and he said it sounded sexual. Of course it did.

Coincidentally, maybe, right around this time, Olivia wrote me an e-mail in the form of a cinquain:

> She liked
> to moan sometimes
> like an animal. You
> couldn't tell if it was pain or
> pleasure.

Oh, I didn't tell you about the ukulele cover I recorded for Tye. It was a request: Nicki Minaj's "Roman in Moscow." It was pretty atrocious. When I sent it to him, I said, "Well, you can't say I didn't try." I just listened to it again. Yow. In addition to my lack of skills as a rapper, there were some pretty obvious glitches where I had to fix an error, and you can hear the digital splice. Plus the fan on my laptop kicked in—I use the internal mic, and when the computer overheats you can hear it trying to cool itself. That was before I discovered I could put the laptop on top of a ziplock bag of ice cubes. I also figured out after a while how to camouflage the splices. Back then, if things got too crackly or hummy, I'd just add a track of fake scratchy vinyl and hope that nobody would notice.

I wasn't just embarrassed about my lousy performance. It also seemed pretty weird for me to sing that lyric—it was shocking, even for me. But I don't like to say no to a request. "Motherfuck you with a big dick, I'm a racist, I'm a bigot, bitch I'm thicker than a midget. Yeah I'm crazy, just a smidgen. Motherfuck me, get my waffle, and some candy from Monaco, unh! Hold on, fuck you! Brace yourself, buck tooth. Yeah I golf, putt too. Swallow balls, nuts tooooooo-oooooooooo-ooooooooooo."

Despite all the flaws, Tye seemed pleased with his cover.

There's another gift I failed to mention—one that Sami made for me. A few days after he'd read my novel, he composed an achingly lovely jazz piano piece titled after my book. I wrote him quickly, "Oh Sami, it's beautiful!" He said, "I'm so glad you like it. I'm making more—I'll show you soon." I don't think he slept that night. Eighteen hours later, on July 22, 2012, he delivered to me an entire jazz suite, each section titled after a small detail—an image from my narrator's dream, the name of a hotel where she'd stayed, something funny she'd said. One piece was titled "Wouldn't That Be Nice?"

I don't know if I can be objective about those compositions, but they took my breath away. And there was also the sheer audacity of composing and recording an entire suite of jazz piano pieces in a twenty-four-hour frenzy. That part was almost a little scary. If I were to try to find a shorthand way of describing Sami's musical sensibility in these pieces, I'd say they were reminiscent of Keith

Jarrett's *Köln Concert,* lyrical meditations on a simple figure, sometimes bluesy and sexual, sometimes deeply poignant. Maybe it's weird to even try to be objective about them—like judging the literary merits of a love letter. I just told Sami they made me cry.

Yvonne Rainer made *Hand-Movie* in 1966 while she was hospitalized after a surgery. It was about all the dancing she could do. Later on, for a time, she would completely give up choreography for experimental film. Tye had said, "Of course, we all know Yvonne's hands well," but actually, I only watched *Hand-Movie* recently. It kind of shocked me when I saw it because I'd been making hand dances myself. Mine don't really resemble Yvonne Rainer's. Hers has a tone similar to that of "Trio A." The affect is very flat. It's silent, and while the movement is challenging, there's nothing graceful about it. She has an impressive ability to move her fingers independently, but it's the kind of thing that makes you think she'd be good at thumb wrestling or card tricks, not dancing.

My hand dances are a little more intentionally beautiful. I made the first one just shortly after I sent Sami the song with the breath in it. I'd promised to make a dance to the Paganini, a real dance, with a real choreography, but I didn't feel I was quite ready to do it. For all that I could rationalize to myself an aesthetic of amateurism, I thought that particular musical performance called for a certain degree of preparation. I knew I was going to need to work on it. I wasn't sure exactly what that would entail.

But I wanted to make him something, so I made a hand dance. I just filmed it on my computer, in my bedroom, my two hands against the dark red wall. It was very short, and there was no music. My hands looked like birds, or like lovers. Often when I wake up, I do a little dance like that with my hands—I watch them in the full-length mirror on my door, which faces my bed.

After that embarrassing exchange in which I imagined something sexual, and he was mildly freaked out, Sami had come around and told me it had been a little confusing to him at first, because my book had made him start to imagine things, but he wasn't sure he wanted to. He'd had a lover for a little less than a year, a woman with two little daughters who told him she'd like to have another child, with him. Her name was Sabine. She lived in Berlin. Sami had been commuting there to work as a studio musician when he was well enough. He met her, they got involved, and soon they started talking about her moving to Cologne with the children. He liked the idea of it but was worried because he often needed to be alone, and he knew from experience it was difficult to live with him.

He'd met his ex-wife, Juliane, when they were both still studying. She fell in love with him watching him play music. She was very beautiful, and he couldn't believe she wanted him. They made love all the time, she got pregnant, and they quickly decided to marry. Her parents weren't particularly happy about it, though they adored Kakay. He told me he laughed inappropriately out of nervousness during the wedding ceremony. Things went downhill pretty fast. She was a dentist now, and she lived with somebody else, and Sami mostly exasperated her. Kakay would come regularly for visits and for piano lessons with Sami. Sabine visited Sami with her daughters sometimes, and Kakay liked her, and he liked playing big brother to the little girls. But Sami was pretty sure things wouldn't work out—and they didn't.

Anyway, when we started writing, it was around the time when Sabine was starting to get fed up. I think he told her about our correspondence. She also saw the jazz suite, and that didn't go over too well. But there were plenty of problems already, beyond even Sami's difficulties with contact and intimacy. She didn't like Cologne, and she wanted to be close to her family. Also, she was intimidated by Sami's talent. Even though she was far better equipped than him for everyday life, she wasn't an artist and felt intellectually inadequate around him. Sami tested very highly in school, and he's extremely well read. He's fluent in several languages, though he doesn't really sound like a native speaker in any of them. He knows a lot about art history, and he has an encyclopedic knowledge of various musical traditions.

He showed me Sabine's picture. She's very pretty. He called her "my Nordic princess." In the picture, she wore no makeup. She had just a slight frown, and she looked at the camera as though she were confronting a challenge. I asked Sami if he'd taken that picture, and he said yes. Her daughters were in the picture as well—little towheaded angels. The four-year-old looked down shyly, and the two-year-old smiled gleefully. Sami said that each of them was very much as she appeared in that photo—those were their personalities. He said, "I'm not sure if it's weird I'm showing you this. I thought it was important."

I can't imagine what Sabine was thinking when she came up with that idea to have another baby with him. I mean, I can see the appeal, but it didn't seem like a very pragmatic idea. Anyway, when it really fell apart, Sami wrote me about it, and he sent that picture. He was sad, but he also knew somehow this was for the best. She'd met somebody else, and she had a new plan, though she said she'd miss him.

A little while after that, he told me if I wanted to imagine something, it was all right. He'd imagined something.

That message was actually very beautiful. He sent it on August 29, 2012. In some ways, it was shy—maybe the word is circumspect—but in parts it was very lyrical. He divided the message into sections, and he gave them musical names: Scherzo amoroso (a sort of jokey apology for his shyness), Allegro più amoroso (here he confessed to imagining something), Interlude: Adagio con dolore ("You have to know that one of my earliest experiences was to be rejected, punished, and left alone for what I am"), and Vivace giocoso (right now, he felt happy). His message was somewhat discreet; I'm being even more discreet. But it probably won't surprise you that my response was very affable. I wrote some things. I sent him that hand dance, the short, lyrical one where my hands looked like lovebirds. And a little later, I sent him another hand dance that I really can't show you.

It was around this time that my mother had a terrible accident. Well, as it was happening it didn't seem so terrible, but it turned out that it was. She went out to lunch with a couple of ladies from the retirement community where she lives, and they were stepping off a curb to cross the street when one of them lost her footing and began to fall. She knocked into my mother, and my mom tipped over too. She broke her fall with her right arm and fractured her wrist. She also bruised her hip. They put a cast on her, but after a few days, her hip really started to bother her. They gave her some pain meds. She was hobbling around for quite a while. It turned out they'd missed another fracture in her right hip, and because of the way she was favoring that side, she ended up bearing the weight on the left side and eventually fractured her coccyx just by walking off-kilter. That's when the pain got unbearable. She's eighty-five.

This makes her sound fragile, and I guess physically she was, but temperamentally she's the kind of person she herself would characterize as a "tough old bat." She was really pissed off, for example, at the other old lady who fell on her (having broken her fall on my mom, she emerged from the episode without a scratch). My mother's cantankerous, a smoker, and a realist. She's also a lefty, a feminist, an atheist, and a right-to-die activist. Her refrigerator magnets say: "Intelligent Design: Helping Stupid People Feel Smart Since 1987," and "My Life. My Death. My Choice." That's why it threw us all for a loop when she got hurt—not the injury itself (after all, she was old, and these things happen), but the way she responded. She really couldn't handle the pain. I went to visit her at the hospital in Ohio. Her doctor had recommended she stay in the hospital for a while. She could get out of bed to use the bathroom and so on, but she had to use a walker and mostly remain lying down until the fractures healed. She was moaning quite a bit and dozing off, probably partly because of the pain meds. When she'd wake up, she'd sometimes make some acerbic remark about the incompetence of the nursing staff or of that lady that fell on her, but sometimes she'd be in so much pain she'd just get a glassy look in her eyes and say, "Help me. Help me."

My older sister, Carolyn, lives much closer than I do—about a two-hour drive away—and my mother had long ago given her medical power of attorney just in case something like this were to happen. She also gave my sister detailed instructions about her DNR paperwork. Carolyn had been driving down regularly and helping our mother through the crisis. She'd been great. I felt a little useless by comparison, but while I was there I tried to contribute what I had to offer, which mostly consisted of stroking our mother's arm or hip or forehead and saying, "There, there." I also read aloud to her, some stories from the *New Yorker,* but she'd fall asleep after the first paragraph or so. Her doctor seemed to think she was going to heal, but she looked really broken in her adjustable bed, lying there, just moaning like that. *Help me, help me.*

I wrote Sami about it after I got home, because he knew what that kind of pain was like. I told him, "I had a beautiful dream last night about my mother dying. In my dream, she'd had enough, she wanted to go, so she rented some kind of magical, quiet flying machines for herself and me and two other women. One must have been for my sister, but I didn't see her. Anyway, we were on these things that were sort of like children's swings, just flying silently over the ocean, with the night sky. The moon was full, and the stars were out, and just as we were over a placid, beautiful smooth part of the ocean, my mother felt it was time. She arched her back over her swing, and her body looked young and beautiful—it looked like my body. And then she let herself fall toward the ocean, and as she fell I called out to her, and I knew she heard it: 'I love you,' just as I always say just before we hang up the phone. And I was so glad she heard it, and that was the end. I wish it could be exactly like that."

Well, as I reproduce that message I see that there are a couple of things that may appear unseemly, the main one being the suggestion that my mother's death could be a relief. But perhaps you'll understand it, given my mother's preoccupation with making a graceful exit. At the time, it was hard to imagine she would heal, even though the doctor said she would. She'd broken her bones with her own weight. It was very difficult to watch her in pain like that. It probably also seems a little weird that I described my body as "young and beautiful." Well, that's embarrassing. But one of the things I liked about talking to Sami was that his Asperger's meant he didn't really play by the rules of social decorum. He would just say things without beating around the bush, like that he knew that he was gifted at music and sex, and he was terrible at hugging, and he was highly intelligent and socially inept. In explaining the fact that he'd managed to have a love life despite his extreme social awkwardness, he said, "Well, I'm relatively good-looking, maybe that helped." That was probably a bit of false modesty, in fact, but it gestured toward the obvious. So it seemed natural to respond with similar candor.

For some reason, I guess a combination of dancing, genetic disposition, and all that moderation, my body hasn't really changed much since I was a girl. After my pregnancy, my belly button migrated about half an inch south. My right breast has a little dent in it from a surgical biopsy I had a few years ago (benign), but you can't really see the scar. My mother lost her whole right breast when she was younger than me. Her cancer metastasized, but she's been in remission for many years, and now that's the least of her worries. My hands in the hand dance sort of looked like my body—I mean, they moved the same way. I'm quite sure that the image of my mother's youthful body arching back gracefully like that came from the gesture in the hand dance. I wished I could give her that.

In the same message in which I told Sami about the dream, I also mentioned that my friend Arto had sent me an article about a pickpocket. "He doesn't actually steal for a living," I said. "He's a conceptual artist or a performance artist. He tells people this is what he does, and he always gives back the things he takes. He's a magician, but it's more complicated than that. He says of the people he steals from, 'My goal isn't to hurt them or to bewilder them with a puzzle but to challenge their maps of reality.' This is interesting. Anyway, I wondered why Arto was sending me this article, and I thought it might have something to do with dance, and how I talk about things being dance that don't necessarily look like dance."

I quoted more from the article—a bit where the guy spoke about shaking people's hands. He said he applied a very delicate pressure on the insides of their wrists with his index and middle fingers and then "led" them a bit, the way a salsa dancer would do. He did this to see if they would follow his lead. That apparently makes a person a good mark. He said he was a "choreographer" of people's attention, and he couldn't even explain exactly how he picked up on cues—that it was a neurological peculiarity of his. I wrote, "It's interesting, isn't it? And then I also wondered if Arto sent it to me because of that line about not wanting to hurt the people he steals from, and the fact that the guy tells people he's going to take something from them, and then he gives it back. That's a little like me, the way I tell people that I may take things from them and put them in my art, but if they don't want me to, I won't, and I'll always give it back to them, maybe it will even be a little more precious. That's like me and you. I also did that to Arto. You're kind of irresistible to a pickpocket like me. You have so many precious things in your pockets. :)"

I wasn't just talking about choreographing a dance to Sami's Paganini. I had already told him I thought I wanted to write him into a novel.

A minute after I sent that message I thought, "Uh-oh." I broke my own rule and wrote a second message that day—a very short one: "After I sent you that last message, I thought, 'Hmm, maybe it's not such a good idea to joke with a paranoid person about picking their pockets!' I'm not really a pickpocket! I just take inspiration from you. But I'll give it back if you want it." He said he wasn't worried. He wrote, "I think I know the feeling when someone steals something from you. It's not what you do." Still, I keep asking him if it's OK for me to write about certain things. Later, I began asking Tye as well.

Here, for example, is a story that should be much more embarrassing for me than for Tye, but I'll have to ask him to read it and say if it's OK to tell it. One night I met him and our friend Ani for a drink uptown near his studio at Columbia. Ani is a dancer and also an incorrigible flirt. We actually had a couple of drinks. I'm kind of a lightweight, and I got pretty drunk. Tye offered to show us what he was working on in his studio. He was preparing for his thesis show. The security guard let us in. Tye had put a mattress in the studio, and he was secretly sleeping there, although the guards were probably onto him. We walked past a couple of other studios where some people were working late with their doors open. Tye's space was neatly arranged, with some building materials stacked in one corner, the mattress in another. There were two chairs, a boom box, and a workbench. Tye showed us where he'd hidden his clothes and bedding in a supply cabinet. It was all very tidy. He'd also stashed a bottle of booze in there, and he poured some into three plastic cups. He put on some classical music. Ani bounced around on the mattress and made some suggestive joke about a threesome. I rolled my eyes. Then Ani asked Tye to do some ballet lifts with her. I sat on the workbench and watched. They were both a little unstable on account of the cocktails. Tye explained something about what he was constructing for his thesis project and said he was having a difficult time figuring out how to make a lasting sweat stain on the wall. I suggested he fake it using vegetable oil. He seemed to like that idea.

The conversation turned to some other dancer friends he and Ani had in common and then to a particular one that had made Tye feel really bad. She'd very bluntly told him that she thought he "read" as a woman on stage. Tye found it particularly hurtful that she'd said that about him in performance. He'd had his top surgery, but that was before he'd done any testosterone (eventually he'd start a very low dose). He said he wasn't even going for a "standard" masculine presentation—it wasn't about that—but the implication was that his *art* was failing somehow. That's what hurt. He said, with what struck me as remarkable insight and self-composure for a person in his early twenties, that this woman didn't seem to understand that perhaps the failure was not his, but hers—a failure to see him as he was asking to be seen.

We paused to let that sink in. Then Ani said something gossipy and fairly nasty about the person in question, and the conversation lightened a bit. She turned to me and asked me something about somebody else, an art critic, if they knew Tye's work or something, and I started to answer, and halfway through the sentence, I stammered and stopped. I realized I'd just used the wrong pronoun. I'd called him a her. Tye. I backtracked and tried it again, but the *her* hung in the air like some gaseous abomination I'd just released. I lay back on the workbench with the room spinning around me. I thought I might throw up. Ani and Tye politely plowed ahead with the gossip and acted as though I hadn't just committed the gaseous abomination. It seemed like interrupting them to apologize would just exacerbate things, so I let the room spin for a while. Ani made some more inappropriate jokes, and it was evident she was at least as drunk as me. Tye gallantly offered to put us both in a cab. I stumbled home and crashed.

The next morning I told my son, Leon, about my embarrassing behavior. He was still living with me then—it was the summer before he started college. I told him about Tye's story about that dancer and her cruel comment, and the integrity and righteousness with which he had asserted his right to ask to be seen as he wanted to be seen, and then how *immediately* on the heels of that, I'd misgendered him. Leon listened very patiently. He'd been thinking a lot about what it meant to "read" as a man—in fact, he'd ordered a bunch of books on Amazon about how to do that, in preparation for going to college. (The funniest one was called *She Comes First: The Thinking Man's Guide to Pleasuring a Woman.*) So he heard my story, nodded knowingly, and said, "Well, this story teaches us one thing: a real gentleman—or gentlewoman—never drinks to the point of pronoun slippage."

I love my son.

After a couple of days, I was e-mailing back and forth with Tye about the thesis show, and somehow something about slipping came up, maybe it was that sweat stain or something, and I said, "There's something I've been meaning to tell you about slippage." He was intrigued. He seemed to think it was going to be something dirty. Then I told him about my conversation with Leon. He really liked that. He was very gracious. He said everybody made mistakes, and it was important to have empathy. He also said that he thought the more time I spent with him, the less likely I'd be to mess up with pronouns. He didn't mean I'd get better at looking at him a certain way. He meant I'd get better at seeing him. He was right.

Tye also likes my son—all my friends do. Olivia adores him, and the feeling's mutual, though they tend to give each other a lot of space. I just said, Leon "was still living with me then," but, in fact, he lives pretty close by even now. As in, next door. The fall after the pronoun slippage incident, he moved into a dorm at NYU for his freshman year, but it wasn't exactly the dream of adult living he'd envisioned. There were quite a few drunk guys with dirty socks. After that first year, we decided to divide our apartment, which had two entrances anyway, and he moved back. So he became my neighbor, but we rarely see each other unless we make arrangements to meet on the balcony, which spans his small studio and my one-bedroom. Leon, like me, is a moderate person, but he does enjoy his mild vices. Since high school, he's been an occasional smoker, and I was often on his case about it, but never too much, on account of his moderate disposition. When I was a kid, I also tried to get my mom to quit. Leon and my mom have a lot in common—not just the smoking, but also a dark sense of humor. Also, Leon is not one to suffer fools gladly. I'm the goody-two-shoes of the family. When I was little, my mother once told me she found me "saccharine." Anyway, since Leon became my neighbor, if I want an excuse to meet him out on the balcony, I'll sometimes call him and ask him if he wants to have a smoke out there with me. I never have more than one, and I always brush my teeth afterwards. When this started, I called my new habit having my "family values cigarette."

It's really kind of perfect. A cigarette lasts about seven minutes, which is about the perfect amount of time for an adult person to spend with his mother on a regular basis. Maybe there are other families for whom seven minutes would seem meager, but Leon and I are both solitary types. He likes to read, compose, noodle around on instruments, and learn useful things on YouTube. He likes to go out and hear music with friends and maybe have a lady-friend over a couple of times a week. I like pretty much the same things, except I write instead of compose, and I make uke covers and weird dance videos instead of watching so much YouTube. Leon works as a lifeguard during the summer, and during the school year he studies and I teach.

Sometimes our creative projects overlap. We recorded a uke cover together of a Ryuichi Sakamoto song in Japanese. That was his idea. We did another by Twiztid, also his idea. I got him to make a couple of dance videos with me. We had a beer and rocked out to

Iggy Pop's "Lust for Life." We did another one to a song by Ponytail. When we did that one, he told me afterwards he'd copped some of my moves, and I thought that was so funny because I thought I was copping his.

Anytime anybody suggests that he's a certain way on account of some parenting thing I did, I feel strange. He picked some things up from me, I'm sure, and some other things from a few oddball friends of mine, but Leon seemed to come out with this personality, and I feel like I've been copping his moves ever since, though it's probably gone both ways. I often say he's my favorite collaborator, but I'm not really talking about the uke covers or the dance videos. I mean our relationship feels like a collaboration. I guess in the grand scheme of things, you could call this durational performance art, but it really works best when we keep it under seven minutes, a couple of times a week. Even that will probably seem excessive when he finishes college, though who knows.

Leon is also basically a minimalist. Early in my correspondence with Sami, I said, "My son is a heartbreakingly beautiful multi-instrumentalist who plays classical, jazz, and rock. Men, women, and dogs are constantly falling in love with him. Maybe you know the type. :)" Sami understood this for the mildly flirtatious compliment it was and deflected it by saying that maybe he knew something about that back in the day, but now his charms seemed mostly to work with the dogs. But Leon is not really so much like Sami. He's musical all right; he's the kind of person who can pick up any instrument—banjo or erhu or mbira—and after watching a little YouTube tutorial, he'll play it passably. His piano teachers always said he had a lovely touch. But he's lazy to practice, and he's not really a master on any of his instruments. He gets by largely on his charms. Maybe that sounds familiar.

I mentioned this disclaimer on my website: "Limited instrument. Limited voice. Limited production values. Use your imagination." Well, that was also a slightly coy joke, "Use your imagination," because the name of my conceptual art project was "Naked Lady with a Ukulele." My photo was a cropped shot of myself from the neck down, naked, sitting cross-legged, strategically holding my tenor uke such that it *just* covered my left breast and my sex. I couldn't have taken this shot with the soprano uke—it wouldn't have covered the necessary parts. My hair obscured my right breast. The joke, of course, had to do with the disclaimer: I had minimal assets, but I wasn't afraid to put them out there. Not a very original joke. I think there must be any number of recording artists who have used the word *naked* in album titles the way others have used *unplugged*—to mean acoustic and unadorned. This wasn't entirely true. I've already told you that I overdub, I splice, I fix my most glaring errors, and I'm partial to reverb. (I find it sexy that recording engineers refer to a vocal track with reverb as wet—my partiality may have something to do with this.) But I use that crappy internal mic, and I leave plenty of flaws in. Some of them really please me, like street noises. Actually, car horns often seem to come in at exactly the right moment, right on pitch.

I'm also naked, or almost naked, in some of my videos—for pretty much the same reason. Somehow showing my flaws makes me feel less exposed than if I were to cover them. A very plausible reading of all this is just plain exhibitionism. I wouldn't dispute it, though I kind of prefer the term *shamelessness.* I don't consider Tye to be an exhibitionist at all, although he's also always taking his shirt off.

Well, I already mentioned that after the embarrassing glitch regarding my imaginative capacity, after Sami pulled back and then slowly returned, after he sent me the remarkable suite of piano pieces, and after he admitted to imagining something as well, I made him a hand dance. Not the one like lovebirds, the other one, the one I can't show you. And amazingly, it didn't freak him out. There was no sound on that one either. Or there was, but only breath—three crescendos and a decrescendo: < < < >.

He answered with a voice message. It was very tender and a little shy. I listened to it twice. He was trying to figure out how to respond. He didn't know what to say. But he didn't sound shocked or embarrassed, even. I think he understood it as I meant it—as a dance. When he tried to say how it made him feel, he faltered a little. It was, like many of his messages, mostly phatic. He said "hmm" and "um," and he inhaled and sighed. There was a pause, and then he laughed and said, "I'm not good at this." That recording was so charming—the tone, the hesitation, the breath, the laugh—and, ironically, the most beautiful moment was the one when he said he wasn't good at this. That was when I realized that the voice recordings were music, and I decided to make a dance.

This was the first of the dances to words, the red one.

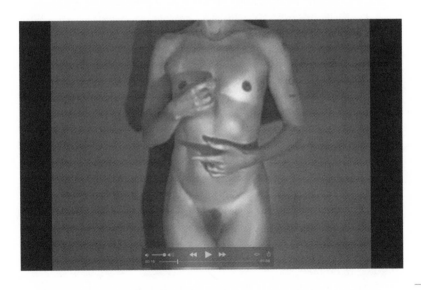

This morning Tye texted me. He was pissed off because some critic was writing a piece about him, and he didn't like the way the guy was talking about his work. He said, "It's so off, Barbara." I said, "You see why I'm going to make you screen my novel for errors? :)"

He said this was entirely different—the guy was talking about a piece he'd only seen a fragment of on YouTube, it was decontextualized, and he was being "reckless" in talking about Tye's transness, like it was a buzzword, and it wasn't just irritating; it was actually hurtful. I said, "Why don't you just say, 'Can I offer you some Track Changes on that?' and then write it the way you want?" He said it would require more than line edits. I said, "I know, but you could delete an entire paragraph and replace it. You can use Track Changes as a platform for guerrilla warfare or conceptual art. I do!"

That's true. That's also not all that original. A few years ago, David Byrne had that project where he made art using Microsoft PowerPoint. Surely you know that Track Changes is the copy-editing command in Microsoft Word. It highlights the deletions and substitutions you make in a text so you can show somebody just how you've mangled their prose, or radically improved it.

Tye said, "There's only one paragraph on me in this piece!" I said, "Perfect! Delete and rewrite!" He said he couldn't give the guy his whole argument, and I said I didn't see why not if Tye's was better. "Plus," I wrote, "it's consistent with ur work. Surrogacy. If u rewrite my novel, I'll try to get u to let me keep a line in that says, 'Tye rewrote all sections of this book concerning him.'"

Tye was not biting. He said, "My whole life is being misread!" I said in exasperation, "I'm telling u, rewrite!!!" He said, "Is it my job to school this guy in a whole fucking decade of trans theory?" I said, "Yup. It's ur job to save the world, mine too, sometimes I don't feel like it and I have a nice coffee instead which is what I'm going to do now. xo."

He apologized for the melodrama, and so much texting. I said, "I <3 marathon texting w u. :)" I don't generally text much. In fact, I have a pretty limited number of texts on my phone plan, which I share with Leon, and toward the end of this exchange I got a text direct from T- Mobile saying "As of 06/22@08:55, you have used

320 of your 400 Txt Msgs and may incur overage before 07/05."
The other person with whom I exchange texts is my sister, regarding our mother. Sometimes those exchanges are a little phatic. Anyway, when I told Tye I didn't mind the marathon texting, he said, "Phew." I said, "I also <3 durational performance art." He said, "What performance art isn't durational?" I said, "Some of mine is tiny! U don't even know what hit u."

After this, I thought it would be interesting to publish a novel in which I asked all of my characters to rewrite the sections of the book concerning them. I could actually print it with the Track Changes visible, so it would say in the margin something like, "Tye Larkin Hayes 6/22/13 08:55 AM—DELETED:" and then show the egregious error I'd committed and he'd corrected. Sophie Calle published a book in which she reproduced the pages in a Paul Auster novel about a character based on her, and she scrawled what she thought all over them. Valerie Solanas also checked a copy of her *SCUM Manifesto* out of the library and scrawled her complaints about the things her publisher made her delete or change all over it, and then she put the book back in circulation.

Maybe you're thinking, "If Tye wants to be understood a certain way, how come he doesn't make art that's a little more obvious?" But we're all misread sometimes, even when we're being obvious. In fact, sometimes it's the worst when we're the most explicit. Sometimes people just can't take in certain information. When I was trying to recall Tye's "Performance for *Women & Performance*," I had a difficult time remembering some parts of it. This may be the moment to explain that my memory is atrocious. Really, shockingly bad. I've diagnosed myself as having PTSD, though people probably overuse the term. It began when that lover of mine got sick, the one who died. I was overwhelmed with sorrow and fear, but I moved through the days as though the world weren't falling apart, and then one day it was like something went *bzzzzt,* a little smoke came out of my ears, and an enormous swath of information just disappeared, like my boss's name and books I'd read and several years from my childhood. And ever since, although I'm a pretty astute conversationalist, literary analyst, and audience member, a couple of weeks after chatting with someone, or reading a book, or seeing a show, I'm likely to retain only arbitrary details—sometimes interesting ones, but rarely the most significant. So when I was trying to recollect that performance of Tye's, I remembered the blood on his ballet slipper, but I couldn't remember where it came from. I thought it was weird that I remembered being concerned about a stain on a shoe but not about the injury that would have caused it. I texted Tye saying that, but he didn't respond. Then I was recounting this to Leon, and as I was recounting it, suddenly a little lightbulb went on over my head. I widened my eyes and said, "Oh my God, there was fake blood." Like, *copious* fake blood, gore continuously dribbling out of his mouth, soaking his shirt. It was extreme. How could I have forgotten that? I texted Tye again. He seemed incredulous, but I told him, "You don't understand the degree of my problem." I was trying to get his sympathy, so he'd cooperate in reminding me of other things. But the truth is, sometimes I like having this problem. It's not just that I seem to have erased quite a few unpleasant memories. Sometimes I think this is what opened up some space on my hard drive for imagining things. Obviously I mean the internal hard drive of my brain, not the external one of my computer.

Tye has been remarkably patient in helping me reconstruct some events and conversations. But this doesn't always go over so well with others. If I forget an intimate conversation with a friend or lover, the person might reasonably assume I didn't take it so seriously. It's been pretty exasperating for Olivia on more than one occasion. My best friend Rebekah is used to it now, but for a few years she'd look at me in disbelief when I'd completely forget a film we'd seen just weeks before. Tye let it slide, my having forgotten the fake blood, but it made me think about why I would retain the small stain on the shoe but disregard the bleeding. I guess the obvious thing would be to suggest that it was too traumatic a scene to hold on to, but I really don't think that's the answer. It was obviously fake—he kept stopping what he was doing to have his assistant give him a new capsule to bite down on. People were laughing. I think I didn't worry about the shirt because I knew theatrical blood would come out in the laundry, but you can't wash ballet slippers.

When I was talking to Leon and suddenly remembered the blood and told him about it, he asked, "Do you think Tye's work is a cry for help?" I said, "Oh no, I think Tye is a pretty happy person." I probably said it too quickly. There have been other times when I thought the laughter at a performance of his was disconcerting. That text he made for the crit ended with a line that was utterly heartbreaking, but it was delivered with such a lack of emotion it seemed vaguely comical. I mean delivered textually—I don't know how it was delivered by the person who read it out loud, but it's hard for me to imagine they would have suddenly gotten all dramatic.

The line might have been about suffering sexual abuse by his father or it might have been a metaphor for having suffered a more abstract abuse of power on the part of his father or it might have been a metaphor for having to bow down before the power of the patriarchy. You may be wondering how a person could make any of that sound vaguely comical.

The blood from the mouth made much more narrative sense to me when I went back and poked around to see what I'd missed in the performances that preceded "Performance for *Women & Performance*." Just a month before, Tye had done that "Dog House" piece at Judson Church. I'm now going to do something that Tye derided in that critic: write about a piece I never saw, other than a fragment on YouTube. In it, Tye is partnered by a woman dancer. She grasps him from behind and while holding him appears to stab him repeatedly with a sword. The music is a single, intense note held for a long time. You see their backs, and the slow, repeated shoving of the sword under Tye's arm. Finally Tye goes limp and falls to the ground, and then the woman drags and hoists him, first onto a piano bench where he slumps over the keyboard, then over a small, carpeted platform by the altar. There was no fake blood, but it occurred to me that maybe the blood came much later, a month later, in another piece entirely, when it wouldn't appear melodramatic, just weird, and maybe vaguely comical. You could also surmise that the blood had more to do with the last line in the text from the crit. Or maybe it was all the same thing.

I also had an exchange with Sami about blood from the mouth, but it was anthropological in nature. It was during that period when his phantom limb pain was getting worse, and he was recounting the various therapies he'd tried, to no avail. He said he was apparently too smart to be tricked by that mirror technique. I told him about an essay by Claude Lévi-Strauss in which he tells the story of a Kwakiutl shaman named Quesalid. I said, "Quesalid thought that shamans were a bunch of charlatans, tricking people into thinking they had healing powers, so he went into training to become one, just to expose how they were fooling everyone. So an older shaman taught him a trick, which was to put a little tuft of feathers into his mouth and then to pretend to suck the sickness out of someone's body. Quesalid was supposed to bite down on the inside of his cheek so he would bleed, and then he would pull the bloody little glob of feathers from his mouth and say, 'Look! I pulled this sickness out of your body. Now you're going to be fine!' Well, Quesalid did this, and the people he treated started feeling better. But instead of exposing the trick and telling people they were being naïve, he decided to really become a shaman, because it seemed he was very good at it, and people kept getting better." I told him that a friend of mine in Brazil had done Reiki on me once, and it seemed to work, and I thought either this friend had a very special innate capacity, or else she'd been well trained. After that I would jokingly sometimes offer Reiki to somebody, even though I'd had no training whatsoever and didn't really believe I knew what I was doing. But weirdly sometimes it seemed to work—Olivia would even ask for it sometimes if she had a headache or sore muscles—and if I could, I'd try it on him, even though effectively I was offering him something like my version of a fake glob of bloody feathers.

Speaking of allegations of fakery. A few weeks after the first dance to words, somebody accused Sami of posting sound files that he hadn't actually created. This person had sent him a very aggressive message through his website. This was evidently another classically trained musician, and he went to the trouble of tracking down some YouTube videos of other pianists who had performed a couple of the Beethoven sonatas with similar phrasing to Sami's. None were identical, but the guy seemed to be implying that Sami had pilfered some unsourced recordings by established musicians and claimed they were his own.

That's a harsh accusation, but you can almost understand how a person could have this suspicion. If you didn't know his story, it did seem a little incredible that one person could be making all that music, on so many instruments, in so many styles—plus singing like that, gorgeously. Never mind that he was so handsome. If you didn't know about his social difficulties, you'd be hard pressed to figure out why he wasn't famous. I confess, when I first encountered his website, these questions occurred to me. I even joked to Sami at one point, "i told my best friend i suspected you might be a 400-pound german hausfrau with an enormous stash of pilfered MP3s and a shoebox of some guy's old photos." It's true; I did say that. Sami said, "Oh my, is that what I sound like?" He meant in his e-mails—this was before the first voice message. Well, his voice put the hausfrau image to bed, and when he started playing my requests, like that version of "Águas de Março," he dispelled any doubts I might have had about his musicianship. His accuser didn't have the benefit of these exchanges. Still, the aggression with which he went after Sami seemed pretty excessive. He was threatening to "expose" him.

Needless to say, it freaked Sami out. He sent me a written message that sounded very anxious. The word he uses when he gets like this is *tensed*. This is when he appears to lose his sense of humor, and sometimes he can sound quite confused or even dissociative. The guy's anger seemed to have triggered some childhood memories. People were often angry with Sami during his childhood—particularly his father.

When he was telling me about his family's story, Sami sent me photographs of both his parents. His mother looked kind of conservative, although he said she'd been a hippie when she was young, which must have been how she ended up traveling to India where she met his father. In the photo, she had carefully arranged dark hair, a well-made navy blue dress, and slightly stout, manicured hands with a wedding band and a rather heavy jeweled ring. Her eyes were shining, and she had nice eyebrows. Sami said she had been a great beauty when she was young. She had remarried after Sami left the house. He liked his stepfather all right. He said that Günther had been particularly supportive after the accident. Sami said he and his mother had argued a lot through his adolescence, and even today she was always pointing out his flaws and telling him he needed to work on things. But he acknowledged that it couldn't have been easy raising him. When he was overstimulated as a child, he'd scream and thrash around. Adolescence presented its own difficulties.

Sami's father was stunning. His hair was gleaming white, still thick, and his gaze was penetrating. His skin was creased, but his features were perfect. He had Sami's perfect mouth. He wasn't exactly smiling, but he had a look of satisfaction. His shirt looked expensive. The photograph looked expensive. Everything about him looked expensive.

After he left Sami and his mother, he'd gone back to India, where he also remarried—a Hindu woman—and had two more children. The boy was studying finance and the girl was just sixteen and she was pretty and sociable and liked to dance to Bollywood music. Sami had gone to visit a few times, and he called Gaurav and Kalyani his brother and sister. He seemed to have some brotherly affection for her in particular, but he confessed to taking mild pleasure in the fact that neither of them showed particular talent at anything. Sami's father beat him regularly when he was a child. His leaving was precipitated by a horrific scene in which Sami called his father an asshole, and then his father hit him until he stopped moving. Sami said, "I think it scared the shit out of him."

I was thinking about that metaphor I used a few pages back, of opening up space on the hard drive of my brain, and I remembered a kind of funny but also poignant incident involving the woman in or near Winnetka, Illinois, who is my name doppelgänger, barbaraandersen64, and the question of storage space in her heart. It was toward the end of last summer, and the only explanation for this incident I could think of was that she was typing up a draft of an e-mail she was planning to send to her daughter, and she sent it to herself, except she forgot to type in the digits, so the draft went to me. In this message, Barbara said she wanted to reach out, and she hoped that she and Meghan could put their differences aside. It had been a tough summer, but it was water under the bridge, and she hoped that Meghan could go back to college in a positive frame of mind, thinking about being safe, happy, and productive. She said, "We don't have to have contact if you're not ready for that. I understand, and I love you. I just want you to know I will always be there for you, and you will always have a space in my heart. Love, Mom."

I told my best friend, "I'm too embarrassed this time to drop her a message saying, 'Oops—remember to type your digits! Good luck with Meghan!' The draft should be in her sent folder anyway. Actually, if I were to write her, maybe I would suggest a minor copy-edit. I think 'a space in my heart' should really be 'place.' 'Space' sounds too much like cubic footage in a storage facility. It might just further piss Meghan off." Of course, I didn't write Barbara that. She seemed to be handling things pretty well, and my little copyedit probably wouldn't have made any difference in the relationship anyway.

When Sami writes about difficult topics like being beaten by his father, he often falls asleep. The first time this happened was in July, when he was telling me about Gaurav and Kalyani. Talking about them provoked some ruminations on his dad. There was an abrupt stop in the text, and then, "---snip---," and a new paragraph beginning, "Thinking about my family is always exhausting so I fell asleep while writing." In August he was writing about his neurological issues and he said, "My right hand is moving almost constantly, as if I was playing the piano, actually this is why my right hand is very quick. When I get nervous my hands will turn into birds and try to fly away. It's a bad manner, the kind of behaviour I've been beaten for when I was a child, my mother still," and then, "---snip---." Out cold. When he wakes up, he's generally OK, and he changes the topic. When he told me this, it struck me that narcolepsy wasn't a bad way to handle emotional overload. It even happens on occasion in his recorded messages.

Sometimes he'll leave in a big section of the sound of him breathing, evidently passed out on top of his headset. It's another of those things that would be comical if these gaps weren't preceded by reminiscences of traumatic events. Apparently he even occasionally passes out in social settings if things get too intense.

That incident with the accusatory cyberstalker just sort of blew over. While he was in the middle of it, he sent a couple of tensed written messages that sounded a little paranoid and confused, and he said apologetically, "Sometimes I'm in this state, I guess you need to know," but a few days later, after the guy backed down, he sounded like his old self. Not long after, though, he sent me a very disturbing voice recording. All of Sami's voice recordings come with titles— "Morning Talks," "Tuesday Palaver," "Late at Night," "Me," "Lunch Break," "In a Chatty Mood," "A Bit Stoned." This one was labeled "Nightmares and Confusion." It was eighteen minutes and four seconds long. Sami sounded disoriented and anxious. He said that he'd awakened from a nightmare and he wanted to talk to me to see if he could calm himself down. He stammered a bit and was speaking more quietly than usual. He kept sniffling, and there were a lot of pauses. I could hear him lighting a cigarette. I don't believe I've mentioned this yet—Sami smokes quite a lot. You can hear it in his singing voice. It produces an appealing vocal quality, but he has to be doing a number on his lungs. I'd already told him I worried about how much he smoked, but I backed off when he told me his mother was also always harping at him about it. Anyway, everything about this recording—the nervous way he spoke while fidgeting with his matches, the strange pauses, his slightly choked delivery—made me uneasy. And then, in a disjointed, barely coherent narrative, he explained how he had gotten into this state. Apparently, he went with Farrokh to somebody's house party, they'd drunk a bit of wine and smoked a bit of weed, and they ended up jamming—Farrokh on percussion, Sami on piano, and somebody else on bass. He got quite hammered, and a woman offered to drive him home. When they got to his house, she went in with him and evidently pressed herself on him in the bedroom. Sami didn't want to be rude, but he didn't really want to be having sex with her. He passed out. She must have been pretty drunk too, because when he came to, she was snoring. He whispered to me, "I—I—I don't want to be with that woman in my bed." He said, "I wanted to be with you. I, oh. I wonder what you will think about me." There was a very long pause.

Then Sami told a story. It was a very, very sad story from his childhood. It involved a piano teacher of his who would touch him while he played and tell him he was a very good boy. He said it felt good, but it was confusing. He said, "I often was told that I'm good when I . . . um . . . when I, uh. Did it. And that was never, um, feeling right." He breathed, and he sniffed. "I can never send this. I never told. I'm sorry. I'm just confused. I. Um. I shouldn't talk when I'm in this state. I'm so sorry. I love you. I'm crazy."

I thought, "Oh my God." I'd sent him that hand dance. What the hell did I think I was doing?

I sent Sami back a loving message, as a friend. It began, "Hello, Sami. I love you. That's the first thing I wanted to tell you because you said, 'I wonder what you'll think about me.'" I explained that I hadn't heard his message the night he sent it because I'd spent the night uptown at Olivia's, and I only had my phone, and since the sound file was big, the phone just told me "Message truncated due to size." I listened to it when I got back home. I said, "I hope I didn't make you worry that I didn't answer sooner. It didn't frighten me when I heard it, and maybe I think too highly of my abilities to make people feel calm, but I wish I could have been with you because I think I could have calmed you down."

I said that his story made me think it must have been very hard for him as a child to have an adult take advantage of his vulnerability and make him think he had to be sexual in order to be loved, especially in the context of the one thing that made him feel special, which was his music. I apologized if I'd confused him with my videos or anything I'd said. As for his own apology for sounding crazy, I said, "I'm not afraid that you're a little off your gourd, Sami. Do you know that expression? It's a funnier way of saying crazy. My father was too; I'm used to that from when I was very small. The funny thing is that when you're confused, it makes me feel simultaneously very maternal and also like you're like my father—but as I told you, sometimes children take care of their parents, and sometimes I have an impulse to take care of you that way as well."

Sami had told me that sometimes Kakay seemed to feel protective of him, and it worried him, but I told him it was all right; children are often wiser and stronger than we give them credit for. That was true about my father. He was totally off his gourd.

By the next morning, Sami was sounding pretty buoyant again. He told me not to worry about anything I'd said or sent. He said his memories of that piano teacher were confusing, but also kind of tender. And he made some jokes about avoiding smoking so much weed and taking home strangers.

I may be making Sami sound more naïve and inexperienced than he is. He's been with a lot of women. When he met Sabine, he was already sleeping with somebody else, a friend of Farrokh's cousin he'd met at a party. He thought of her as a friend, but when he told her about Sabine, she got furious and kicked the door off a refrigerator. That was the end of that. He also had an old friend from his conservatory days, a cellist named Bronislawa, who would sometimes visit him to play duets, and they'd generally end up having sex before she left. Sami mentioned that very matter-of-factly once, a month or two after Sabine had left. I worried that he might be missing the physical intimacy, and he said, "Oh, it's OK, Bronislawa and I had sex after we recorded that Mendelssohn yesterday." Apparently this had been going on every once in a while for many years. They never really spoke about it or anything else particularly personal. After they were done playing, they'd just take off their clothes and do that, and then she'd go. He said nobody knew, and that she was a really good cellist and a lovely person despite the fact that they didn't talk much. I'm not sure if it was a language thing or if she was just reserved.

There were other things. One time Juliane heard about some brief love affair he'd had with a friend of a friend. Somehow it got back to her. She lectured him about promiscuity and said she thought he was being a terrible example to Kakay, although Kakay didn't know about any of this. Sami liked being nagged about this almost as much as he liked his mother harping at him about the cigarettes. Myself, I was more worried about the smoking.

Around the time of the breakup with Sabine, I received an e-mail from Lauren Berlant at the University of Chicago. The bottom of the e-mail identified her as the "Directrix" of the LGBTQ Studies Project at the Center for the Study of Gender and Sexuality. We knew each other a little from professional situations. I'd approached her after a wonderful talk I'd heard her give at NYU, and we exchanged ideas about shifts in political and aesthetic intensity in certain kinds of art after the advent of effective HIV therapies. I told her that she'd made a cameo appearance in my last novel—sort of like Graeber. That must have made her curious, because she ended up reading it. This e-mail was an invitation to speak in a lecture series she was organizing on "new queer writing." She said the series would be focusing on "experiments in remediating history, subjectivity, evidence, and criticality from a perspective fed through a creative understanding of erotic attachments." She said she thought it might be particularly interesting if I could do some kind of workshop in addition to a public lecture. She estimated the kind of honorarium and travel arrangements the center could offer, and copied the administrative staff person with whom I'd be communicating about this, should I choose to accept the invitation.

I was really excited to receive this e-mail. I sometimes referred to Berlant as "the smartest woman in the United States of America," and I thought it would be fun to hang out with her in Chicago. I wrote her back that I'd be delighted to do something, that an honorarium was the least of my concerns, and that a workshop could be very interesting. I'd been thinking about "inappropriate intimacy."

I thought I might try to get other people onto my love spam band-wagon. Maybe I could teach them how.

I just realized, this was right around the time that Sami's ex was worrying about him being a "bad example" for Kakay. Obviously, I was a lot more dangerous than Sami. Here I was, scheming to take my show on the road.

Berlant seemed to like my inappropriate intimacy workshop idea. We tentatively planned for a visit in December. She asked me if I'd be interested in reading a piece she'd published in the journal *Cultural Anthropology*. It was called "A Properly Political Concept of Love: Three Approaches in Ten Pages." She'd written this in response to a piece by Michael Hardt in which he meditated on the phrase *for love or money*. His essay had proposed that by putting the two things side by side, love and money, maybe we could come up with this "properly political concept of love." In response to the challenge, Berlant resisted a little the idea that we hadn't already tried to conceptualize love politically, and then she said something that didn't sound so very ideological on the surface: "Maybe I should say what I always say, which is that I propose love to involve a rhythm of an ambition and an intention to stay in sync, which is a lower bar than staying attuned, but still hard and awkward enough."

That was a pretty compelling definition of love. I thought about the dance I'd made to Sami's phatic language. You might say it was a very literal attempt to stay in sync. Choreographically, I suppose it doesn't seem interesting just to try very hard to align one's movement precisely with musical time—although it gets a little more interesting if the tempo is highly irregular. Or slightly irregular. Anne Teresa de Keersmaeker made a famous set of dances to Steve Reich's "phase music"—his minimalist compositions with very subtle shifts in tempo. In "Piano Phase," two pianos are in sync, playing a repetitive motif, and then they shift slightly and fall out of sync. Two dancers spin in a similarly repetitive and simple pattern, each perfectly matching the time of one of the piano lines—so the temporal disjunction of the music simultaneously becomes visible. The choreography is all about precision. Obviously it requires a tremendous amount of concentration, but you wouldn't think it would be particularly emotionally evocative. Surprise: it is.

Writing this made me think about subtle shifts in time and trying so hard to be careful while I was listening with Tye to that metronome.

All this time, I was continuing, in a somewhat haphazard way, to pursue my conceptual art project with the ukulele cover tunes. Requests were arriving in dribs and drabs. I'd sometimes target particular victims, but often I'd just hear some pop tune on the radio at the grocery store and feel like doing it, and then I'd find some friend to send it to. I made a few for Olivia—"Something Like Olivia," "Nice Girls Don't Stay for Breakfast," "On a Good Day." I made a couple for Leon too. "Beautiful Boy." "This Must Be the Place." I did a nice version of "Mad about the Boy" for Sami. I covered his cover of "I Will Always Love You." That was pretty funny.

Sometimes I'd try something a little more unusual—like my Pussy Riot cover. It was on August 17, 2012, that Nadezhda Tolokonnikova, Maria Alyokhina, and Yekaterina Samutsevich, three members of the performance collective, were sentenced to two years at a penal colony, ostensibly for "hooliganism motivated by religious hatred." Samutsevich's sentence would later be suspended. As a feminist who wrote about performance, I was really absorbed by this case—as was everybody, it seems. Again and again, I watched the YouTube video documenting their action at the Cathedral of Christ the Savior. If I already told you my rapping skills are below average, I can barely begin to communicate my deficiencies in the genre of punk screed. My timbre is closer to that of Blossom Dearie than Nina Hagen. Still, I thought I'd give "Punk Prayer" a try. Doing it in Russian was out of the question, but it was easy enough to find an

English translation online. I figured out the chords on my own and laid down a couple of vocal tracks to simulate the liturgical harmonies of the intro and also the alternation of the husky growler and the high-pitched shrieker on the screed section of the original. It was pretty bad, but I had fun trying.

I don't mean to sound like I was taking their situation lightly. I was as distraught as anybody to learn of the outrageous sentence. I read the women's closing statements from the trial, and I could hardly believe how smart they were. If I'd known how to get in touch with them, I would have sent them my cover. Obviously it wouldn't have been about getting them to listen to my appalling attempts at replicating their punk screed. But maybe it would have been heartening for them to know that somebody was listening hard enough to figure out the chords.

I decided to knit myself a balaclava. I got some beautiful forest green organic wool from a yarn store in the East Village, and I looked up instructions for making a vintage "ski mask." When I finished, I found that I'd really exaggerated on the amount of wool I'd bought. There was a ton left over. Sami had mentioned to me that green was his favorite color, and he'd recently told me something about the special sock he wore inside the silicone liner of his prosthesis. I offered to knit him a different sock, something more personal. Actually, I asked him if he'd like me to knit him a "thigh cozy."

I like to knit things for people. I think about them while I'm knitting, and I handle the yarn with my fingers, and I always feel like if they're wearing the thing I knit for them, somehow it's kind of a way of having physical contact with them, even if we're far apart. Over the years, I've made Leon tons of socks and scarves. I made Olivia wrist cuffs to keep the wind from going up her sleeves when she bikes.

I didn't tell Sami this idea about touching without touching. I just asked him if he'd like me to knit him a thigh cozy. He liked the idea, although he said he wouldn't be able to wear something that bulky with the prosthesis—the special medical sock was very thin, seamless and close-fitting. But he thought it would be nice to wear a green wool cozy around the house when he took the prosthesis off. He gave me his thigh measurements. He said he liked to call his stump "Fred" and he called the prosthesis "Ginger." Fred's circumference was "about seventeen inches at the end (formerly above the knee) and twenty-two inches in the middle . . . nine inches is a perfect length."

That was a funny, cheerful message, the one with Fred's measurements. It arrived on October 18. But a couple of days later, the neuroma began to give him a lot of pain. He sent me a note saying, "Hey Barbara, the past two days have been both boring and exhausting. I'm feeling drowsy all the time and sleeping the day away. I try to drop some lines whenever I'm awake, but my concentration is gone and being awake means to feel pain. Maybe I should rather talk, but I think I don't sound too good. I think this evening my mood has reached the base line. Please excuse me, I'm too tired to write today, maybe I'll talk a bit when I had my next shot and have slept a little. Hugs, Sami."

That made me feel pretty helpless, but it helped a little to begin knitting the thigh cozy.

It was around this time that I contacted Tye to ask him if he might consider giving me a couple of ballet lessons. I had this idea about the Paganini on the ukulele. You may have forgotten that I'd promised Sami I was going to dance to it. Sami himself hadn't exactly been asking about it. But I hadn't forgotten. I knew I wanted to practice something in preparation. I'd looked at a few YouTube videos of some ballet techniques, and it seemed to me that maybe what I wanted to work on were my petits battements. There was a great little video of Romany Pajdak doing these on pointe. Romany Pajdak is a principal artist with the Royal Ballet.

In the video, you just see her legs. The most popular comment notes that she has really nice arches. I knew I wasn't going to get up on pointe, but I thought maybe Tye could get me a little bit more up to speed. I told him we could do it at my house, and he could name his price. He said he'd be glad to give me lessons, though he didn't tell me what he'd charge. He was a little busy for the next few weeks—he was working on a new project, and he'd recently started working at a restaurant—but we agreed to check in later to schedule something.

In the meantime, I thought I'd work on another dance to music. I wanted to think a little bit about what it might mean to practice. I was also thinking about that essay by Lauren Berlant, and what she'd said about love being an aspiration to be in sync, even if only for a moment. I had a practice tape of Thelonious Monk learning the beautiful old Tommy Dorsey standard, "I'm Getting Sentimental Over You." A former colleague who wrote about jazz had given me this recording years before, and ever since, it had been something of an obsession. Actually, he gave it to me for Leon. It was during a period when Leon was learning to play some Monk compositions on the piano. My colleague thought he might like to hear what it was like when Monk himself was learning a tune. The recording is really extraordinary. There are several takes, each increasing in mastery, and also in length. But to me, the most extraordinary take is the very first one. Monk's wife was apparently recording this on an old reel-to-reel recorder at their house. The first take cuts in halfway through the tune, and Monk doesn't even know at first that the machine is on. At the end of it you can hear him telling his wife, OK, go ahead, and she tells him she's already recording.

Basically, that first take is just him figuring out one stumbling little run. It's full of hesitations, like he's trying to decide if this is really what he wants to do. He does it over and over. It's so awkward you can't believe it, but it's the awkwardness of concentration.

By the time Monk gets to the last take, he's all over that piece, he's a kid in a candy shop—that take is almost half an hour long and he's having a ball. But I love the first one. I love hearing him think about the song, and what he wanted to do with it. I wondered if I could dance in sync with that. I wanted to let Sami know that despite my technical weaknesses, I understood what it meant to practice and really learn a piece.

I tried it a lot of times. I made some mistakes. But there were moments when I managed to be in sync, if only for a moment.

Part II

SEPTEMBER 2012 CAME, WHICH MEANT CLASSES WERE STARTING up again. I was teaching a doctoral seminar on advanced readings in performance studies and the course I mentioned on theories of the fetish. I love teaching that course. The readings are intense— plenty of Freud, Marx, and Lévi-Strauss, plus the feminist, queer, antiracist, and postcolonial critiques and extensions of all that— but I borrow a pedagogical strategy from the kindergarten set: show-and-tell. Each week I have somebody bring in an object they feel has some sort of performative power and talk about it. That may sound infantilizing, but the theory really gets interesting when it's attached to a close reading of the poetics of something palpable and particular. As for the doctoral seminar, well, that's pure pleasure. Our doctoral students are very smart.

There were extracurricular goings-on as well. Just as the semester was starting up I got an e-mail from somebody at the Department of Russian and Slavic Studies. They wanted to organize a panel about the Pussy Riot case, and because it was so topical, they wanted to do it immediately. They asked me if I'd like to participate. It was going to be held at the Jordan Center for the Advanced Study of Russia. I felt a little sheepish, as I'm really not an "advanced student" of Russian dissident art or even, as I mentioned, punk rock, but they thought it might be good to have somebody address the question of performance art as medium for political protest. I said sure, and I began cramming.

It turned out to be a slightly more intense gig than I had anticipated. They also invited two Slavicists, a graduate student who had helped translate Pussy Riot's closing statements, a well-known cultural theorist, and Katrina vanden Heuvel, the editor of the *Nation*. The panel was being live-streamed. The in-house audience was already big. The organizers screened the infamous YouTube video, and then each of us made a brief statement about our understanding of the action at the Cathedral of Christ the Savior and the significance of the ruling. The Slavicists gave some historical context to the relationship between church and state in Russia, and the reason Pussy Riot had chosen to target the patriarch as well as the president. The translator spoke about the eloquence of the women's closing statements. The cultural theorist talked about the internet, social media, and the new ways we effect political change. Katrina vanden Heuvel gave an account of Putin's increasingly heavy-handed repression of dissent.

I compared Pussy Riot's performance to ACT UP's "Stop the Church" action in Saint Patrick's Cathedral in 1989, and made an argument for an alternative reading of "Punk Prayer" as an authentic act of faith, counter to the charges of religious hatred. I wondered why a feminist prayer couldn't be taken seriously as such. I referenced a few feminist performance artists that had been cited by Pussy Riot as sources of inspiration. And because I'm fairly shameless, I mentioned my uke cover.

I was surprised by the questions that came from the audience. Obviously, nearly everybody felt that the severe sentencing was a travesty, but quite a number of people seemed to think it was a bad idea to conduct a political protest in a house of worship. And there was even greater resistance to the suggestion that what Pussy Riot did in there was "art." I was glad to have attempted the uke cover. I went on to a purposefully and obnoxiously long-winded explanation of the structure of the song, the liturgical harmonies (lifted from Rachmaninoff's *Vespers*!), and the effectiveness of the alternating vocal timbres in the screed section. Nothing like hitting somebody over the head with liturgical harmonies when they're getting all gatekeeper-ish about art. But what I was really thinking was, "Good grief, what would these people have made of Miguel Gutierrez teaching 'DEEP Aerobics' at Judson Church?" DEEP stands for "death electric emo protest." That was a religious experience and some of the better art I'd seen in, well, ever. I ended up in a threesome with two sweet hippie contact-improv types, feathers stuck to our sweaty foreheads, slow-dancing to "How Deep Is Your Love?"

Later I did a cover of that song. I put it on a set list called *Disco Finger Lights*. I guess that was my embarrassing disco phase.

At the end of the panel, Katrina vanden Heuvel asked me if she could print my piece in the *Nation*. That was shocking. I said sure, and I e-mailed her the text when I got home. It ran right away, and then almost immediately, I started fielding other invitations to talk about the sentencing. I told Olivia and Leon they should address me as "Dr. Pussy Riot." There was a big event planned at the NYU law school with the defense team, who had come to meet with human rights advocates to get more publicity for the appeal. I was invited to ask a question. I took along my balaclava. I wasn't really thinking I'd wear it—that seemed a little theatrical—but I liked the idea of having a prop. There was an enormous crowd for this discussion, and it was being recorded. The defense team and those of us who'd been invited to speak with them were led to a lounge area for introductions. One of the lawyers, Violetta Volkova, saw my balaclava, thrust out her chin, and nodded approvingly. But then she called me over and said, through a translator, "It's nice, but it's too hot. Maybe in Siberia you could wear that, but not in Moscow. You know, the girls, they don't knit theirs. They just take a stocking or a T-shirt and rip out the eyeholes and the mouthhole." I wondered if I should have felt a little embarrassed about my organic yarn and my pattern for a vintage ski mask. I'd done some decorative cable stitching around the mouth.

The event at the law school opened with an invocation of sorts by Karen Finley. Karen is my friend, and I love her unequivocally and passionately. She read a poem that repeated the word *pussy* about fifty times. She kept saying *pussy* really loud. This was in the main hall of the law school, which is one of those exquisite rooms with chandeliers and leather chairs and a big fireplace and portraits of older white guys all over the place. There was a slightly awkward transition, and then someone introduced the lawyers. One of them, Mark Feygin, did most of the talking. He was somebody you might describe as charismatic or possibly a blowhard. He looked like he could be a gangster. I found him handsome. He had a very expressive sneer.

Mostly his point was that Putin was squelching dissent, the charges were trumped up, and the appropriate punishment according to the statute on the books would have been a minor administrative fine for disrupting a religious service. I tried asking my question about a feminist prayer being an act of faith, and that went over like a lead balloon. Somehow, both faith and feminism got lost in the shuffle of legalities and a more generalized despair over Putin's strategies for clamping down on the opposition. Somebody else asked about art, and Feygin wasn't having that either. He dug the fact that Pussy Riot was going after Putin, but he shrugged about the "idiotic choreography, in my opinion." That got a pretty good laugh.

I really loved the choreography. If you watch that video, there's this amazing moment when one of them prostrates herself before the altar, just as the security guards are coming in for the kill. Yekaterina Samutsevich had said in an interview, "It was an act of feminist art and should be treated as such." I'm not sure why people had such a hard time with that.

These Pussy Riot panels weren't my only extradepartmental activities in the fall. In the same week as the law school event, I had signed up to give a class at the Free University, which was an offshoot of the Occupy movement. The project had been dreamed up at a CUNY Graduate Center General Assembly as a strike action in opposition to tuition increases, but they opened it up to anybody who wanted to share some kind of useful or even maybe useless information over the course of a week in Madison Square Park. There were people lecturing on the carceral state, on open-source currencies, and on rhizomatic communication and distributed direct action. There were people teaching yoga and screen-printing radical slogans on old t-shirts. Olivia was also participating. She offered them either "Tips on Urban Cycling" or a seminar on Brecht (they went for the latter). I was giving my first workshop on inappropriate intimacy—this provoked some eyeball rolling on Olivia's part, which seemed for a minute like it might escalate, but we both dropped it and agreed to schedule our courses on different days. The description I sent the organizers for the website read, "This year, I initiated an experiment in stimulating a sentimental gift economy. This involved spamming people indiscriminately with handmade, individually crafted ukulele covers of sentimental songs. Recipients ranged from an obesity doctor in Illinois to the anarchist anthropologist David Graeber. I'll let you know what happened." Given this crowd, I figured dropping Graeber's name might spark somebody's interest.

The first communication I received from the organizers after I offered them my workshop began, "Hi Barbara! We're excited that you've signed up to join us for the Free University, 9/18–22/2012. All information about the event (FAQs, schedule, updates, location, etc.) can be found at our website: http://freeuniversitynyc.org. You will be notified of your assigned location within the park by Wednesday, 9/12/2012." They also asked for a short description of my course and a Twitter handle if I used one. I was supposed to make my own poster board sign with the title of my class and my name. I was also welcome to sign up to help with the cleanup. This was signed, "Jen for the Free U NYC."

I didn't really know how my description would go over. I was pretty sure there would be a fair amount of autonomist political theory. As I said, the Graeber name-drop was hedging my bets. But Jen wrote me back very sweetly, "This session is so neat. I'm going to post it up on Facebook since you don't do Twitter." I said, ":) let me know if you have a request for a ukulele cover tune." She wrote back immediately: "Rainbow Connection—Kermit :)." I said, "on it. meanwhile, i have another kermit cover," and I attached it. It was actually a cover of Andrew Bird's French-language cover of Kermit's

"It's Not Easy Being Green." I'd made that for Sami because his favorite color was green and also because he'd often remarked that it wasn't easy being different, which in his case didn't actually mean being a frog but being an Aspie. Jen wrote back almost right away, "Thank you!! The team here is lovin' it!"

I thought it was sweet that these young activists weren't ashamed to show their attachments to *Sesame Street*. Also, when I looked up the lyrics to "Rainbow Connection," I found them very moving. Unfortunately I can't reproduce them here in their entirety, on account of intellectual property issues, but you could look them up or maybe your memories of childhood are more intact than mine. I believe I can get away with reminding you of a few fragments anyway, like, "Rainbows are visions, but only illusions, and rainbows have nothing to hide." That's a kind of confusing but provocative line: something that's illusory has "nothing to hide," except that Kermit then suggests that maybe the illusion *does* point to something real, presumably a pot of gold, obviously metaphorical—some kind of riches, but what kind? That probably depends on what you're looking for. The people who want to hold on to the possibility that an illusion could somehow lead to actual riches are "the lovers, the dreamers, and me." Which is interesting because it moves from eros to some more abstract possibility—a dream—and finally to something entirely private—the unspoken object of Kermit's desire. It seemed pretty clear that the "team" at the Free University was thinking along political lines. I'm not so sure what utopianism means to Kermit. He tells us, somebody "thought of that" and somebody "believed it" and look how far that's gotten us. But it's not really clear if he means nowhere, or here.

It's tempting to say something about queerness, on account of the rainbow imagery and a vague reference to "young sailors," but that feels a little cheap.

The words that seem strangest and maybe most beautiful to me are in the odd line that occurs just so the modulation can take

BARBARA BROWNING

place. I generally dislike modulation—it seems like such a blatant attempt to ramp up the emotional impact. Sami dutifully did the ramping up in his Whitney Houston covers, but it always makes me feel ridiculous. Still, if you just look at this line as a weirdly unselfconscious comment tossed into the song, it's affecting: "All of us under its spell, we know that it's probably magic." It's a little like that story of Quesalid.

Well, I started all this to tell you about my workshop. I showed up a little before my slot, which was an hour long. I took a seat on one of the folding chairs in my assigned location and set up the little poster board I'd brought. It said "LOVE SPAM—Barbara Andersen." There was an information desk set up where potential students could read about the course offerings. It was breezy, and so I weighted down my poster board with a couple of small rocks next to my chair. There were a few other empty seats nearby. Fortunately I'd brought a book, because I was sitting there all alone for quite a while. A very nice young man from the information desk stopped by to ask me if I needed anything, and I said I was fine and confirmed that I was where I was supposed to be. There were a couple of well-populated discussions that were starting up and a couple that were ending. Some of these were regularly scheduled CUNY grad seminars that had been moved to the park for the day in solidarity with the idea of free education. I didn't feel too bad to be sitting there by myself—I can often recuperate what might appear to be wasted time by thinking of it as conceptual art. But actually, after about twenty minutes, two young women approached me and asked if they could participate in my workshop. We looked around to see if anybody else might be joining us, but when it was clear that this was it, I said, "OK, shall we begin?" I asked them who they were, what they did, and why they'd come. They said they both worked in food service, and they'd read about the event online and thought it might be interesting. I said who I was and asked them if it was OK if I read something to them. They said sure.

What I read was basically the first several pages of this novel, which I'd recently written up and published in the *Brooklyn Rail*. I sent it to the editor there at the suggestion of the editor of my last two novels, Eric Obenauf. I got back a friendly message from the publisher of the *Rail* saying, "Hey Barbara, I much enjoyed the piece and would like to run it in our May issue. I'm hoping that Eric mentioned that, like crime, the *Rail* does not pay. Is that OK? Cheers, Ted." I said, "How great! Of course it's OK," and I attached a cover of "Crime" by the Tiger Lillies, which has the memorable refrain, "Crime, crime, crime doesn't pay—except when the debt collector needs to be paid." Hello, Graeber.

After I read the *Brooklyn Rail* piece to my two students, I told them a little about what had happened since my exchange with Dr. Mel, including the incident with "Les Anarchistes" and Graeber's take on what it means to say "thank you." I also let my students know that for reasons of discretion, I'd altered a few details in telling that story. I said that Winnetka was a fictionalized location, as was Dr. Mel's name and website, as you may have discovered if you attempted to Google him. These were close approximations of his real identity and location.

My real name is not Barbara Andersen.

Sami's real name is not Sami.

Tye's real name is not Tye.

Once in a while I invent entirely fictional characters.

That day in Madison Square Park, I didn't have to prod my Free University students much to get them to apply the Dr. Mel story to their lives. They jumped right in and began talking about weirdly intimate encounters they'd had, particularly while waitressing. We talked about the gender politics of affective labor. We compared notes on Silvia Federici. But mostly we exchanged personal anecdotes. They were really smart and charming. When our time was up, we embraced. They said, "Is it OK if we stalk you on the internet?" I said, "Oh, by all means!"

That was the good news. In less good news, Sami's neuroma was really bothering him. That's a terrible understatement. He was in exquisite pain. There were more of those brief e-mails, but he'd increasingly send voice recordings because it was too exhausting to write. In the fall he gave up his place in Berlin. He just wasn't able to work and it didn't really make any sense to keep an apartment there. He'd have the occasional good day, but it wasn't something you could count on.

You may be wondering about Sami's financial arrangements. I had sort of figured this out for myself, and maybe you have too, but when the subject of letting go of studio-session work came up, he made it explicit. He wrote me, "Hmm, I think I might be rather a man of means than a starving artist, I've once been a quite well paid sound engineer and I had an accident and loss of earnings insurance (wanna have one? :)) and got an injury award from the one who ran me over with his SUV, to park illegally on someone's leg is quite expensive. I'd get by without doing serious work, I just have to work when I have special expenses . . . my counterpart's insurance had to come across with quite some dosh because I lost my leg and had some other serious injuries, and the doctors confirmed I'd have to live with pains for the rest of my life and I have that smart mother who knows everything about investment (formerly known as the girl who lived in a fuckin ashram) . . ."

When people wrote him to ask what kind of piano he used in his recordings, and when he answered a Bösendorfer, they'd always ask how the hell he managed to get one of those in a home studio, and he'd make the inevitable joke about having paid an arm and a leg for it, or rather just a leg—he got a pretty good deal.

You may have noticed the slightly churlish tone Sami used in referring to his mother. This came and went. Sometimes he spoke appreciatively of her help. They'd had a lot of friction during his adolescence, and it seems they got stuck in that mode of relating to each other, even now, well into Sami's thirties. She'd helped him through the accident—I already mentioned that Günther was especially kind then—and she also helped with Kakay. The problems seemed to arise when she'd get on his case about his idiosyncrasies. He said he'd find himself spacing out sometimes when she was around, and she'd start clapping her hands to get his attention. She'd also go after him to do more physical therapy—not for his leg but for the twitching and hand-flapping that tended to happen when he was anxious. She often told him, "You don't want people to think you're an idiot, do you?" I'm not sure if she actually said that—that sounds pretty brutal to me. But maybe she did. That's what he heard, anyway.

As a mother, sometimes I felt for her. Sami was her only child. Imagine having a child that couldn't cuddle or even look you in the eyes. Leon and I spent so many hours staring into each other's eyes when he was breastfeeding. He used to reach up and stroke my jaw. Anyway, imagine that, and then how terrifying it must have been to be left alone with Sami when he was having all that adolescent rage on top of everything else. He acknowledged all of this. He didn't blame her for kicking him out. It sounds like it was better for everyone—somehow he was more comfortable with Farrokh's family. Farrokh's parents pretty much left him alone.

Sometimes, though, Sami would tell me stories that made it hard for me not to judge his mother. I'd try not to because people so often judge mothers harshly, and I was only hearing Sami's side of the story. But that thing about clapping didn't sound so good. Also, sometimes she'd have parties and expect him to play piano to entertain the guests. He'd do it, but a little begrudgingly. Sometimes he'd prepare a piece that he knew might perplex or even perturb her guests—like a David Rakowski étude. Rakowski's music, if you don't know it (I didn't) is, as his label puts it, "teeming with ideas." It's not exactly relaxing. Well, all of this might fall under the umbrella term *perfectly normal family dysfunction*, but the worrisome part was that when he was little, she didn't protect him from his father.

As I got to know Sami better, he gave me more of that story, but it came in very small dribs and drabs, because as soon as he began talking or writing about it, he'd pass out. That was typically what triggered those weird spaces in his voice messages where you just heard breathing against the headset. In his written messages, thinking about his childhood often led to a dissociative passage, like this one he sent after I'd written from an academic conference in Puerto Rico. I mentioned something banal about lying by the hotel pool. When he turned to that in his response, he wrote, "OK, I'll write on but maybe it's gonna be weird, my head's too small, there're inside thoughts and outside thoughts, at the moment I'm not capable of most of the inside stuff. I wonder what the use of lying by the pool is, somehow I think I know it, but right now I'm wondering. Have you ever had the feeling that something is trying to get inside your head and another thing is trying to get out? It's crawling down my spine and then I can feel the belt on my back and this thing is in my spine and in my head and trying to get out. I didn't like to take off my shirt"

That paragraph didn't end with any punctuation. It was followed with a "---snip---" and an explanation that he'd passed out for about two hours.

On October 22, 2012, a trough of low air pressure appeared in the western Caribbean. It picked up speed pretty quickly, and by the evening it got a name: Tropical Storm Sandy. Then Hurricane Sandy. It was moving north, and on October 24, it touched down near Kingston, Jamaica. It killed just one person there but left practically the whole island without electricity and did about $100 million worth of damage. It also hit Haiti, where a lot more people died because the infrastructure was already so tattered from the earthquake two years before. About two hundred thousand people lost their already precarious shelter. Over the next couple of days, the Dominican Republic, Puerto Rico, Cuba, and the Bahamas also got slammed. For a minute, Sandy seemed to be letting up, but then she got angry again, and early on October 29, she hit the Jersey Shore. By the time the storm was over, she killed nearly three hundred people and caused $68 billion in damages.

I realize it's weird to use a female pronoun. This is the convention, although in recent years they've taken to switching back and forth the genders of the names and pronouns for storms. Sandy happened to be female.

October 29 was a Monday. During the day here in New York, it seemed a little threatening, but I'm an optimist, and I didn't really think it was going to be too bad. The gym was closed due to the hurricane watch, and I got the bright idea to run the stairs here in my building. I live on the fifteenth floor, out of seventeen. I went all the way up and down about five times. That was in the late afternoon. In the evening, Leon and I met out on the balcony. By that time, the rain was coming down hard, sideways actually, and the trees in the courtyard below were being buffeted from all sides. They looked like frenzied women whipping their hair around. We put on some Ryuichi Sakamoto and danced to the wind and the rain. It felt great. Then he went into his house, and I went into my house, and after a little while the lights started to flicker. When they went out, I took Leon a flashlight and a couple of candles. I came back here and decided to record a uke cover of "Stormy Monday." I did it by candlelight on battery power.

I figured things would be back to normal by the morning, but they weren't. What's worse, I seemed to have done something to my left foot running all those stairs, and now the elevators weren't working. Nothing was working. Lower Manhattan was very eerie.

Olivia offered to let us stay at her place—Inwood was pretty much spared except for a few fallen trees—but Leon liked the idea of camping at his house, and I didn't feel right staying so far uptown. Partly I wanted to make sure Leon was OK, but also I have a pretty high need for alone time, and though I think Olivia's offer was genuine, I worried about what would happen if she started to feel cramped. The university had a generator running at the gym, so I could shower there. There was another generator set up at the business school, and they'd let you in with an ID to check e-mail and charge your devices. I'd hobble up and down the stairs.

By this time, I'd consulted the internet and diagnosed myself as having plantar fasciitis. I thought it was interesting that there was an etymological link between the pain in my heel and fascism.

That week was depressing. The worst of it was the memories of 9/11. The worst of 9/11 wasn't even 9/11. That was horrible, of course, but so much of the death and destruction came with what was to follow. One could have predicted this on the day the planes hit, but the extent of the repercussions took a while to sink in. This is true of every catastrophe, but we seem to fixate on the moment of the blow.

There were some comical moments during the Sandy blackout. One day our friends Jean-Christophe and Cooter came to get us, and they drove us to their house in Brooklyn. Jean-Christophe was Leon's piano teacher for a while, and he lives with his boyfriend, Cooter, in a big apartment with high ceilings and stuffed birds all over the place. They have that funny kind of video game with a motion sensor that shows a cartoon of you as you move around in front of the screen playing games or doing exercises. We drank a lot of wine and ate gumbo and danced around looking like cartoon characters on this big screen. Cooter is from the South, and he's very adorable, like a baby. Jean-Christophe is handsome, and he has a heavy accent and a handlebar mustache. He left early because he wanted to drive a generator he had out to a friend's place on the Jersey shore. Why did he have a generator? Your guess is as good as mine.

Cooter's childhood friend Nikki was at their place—she's blond and busty and kind of trashy on purpose. And there were two butch lesbians named Dara and Smack, and a Norwegian guy named Torvald, who is sometimes Jean-Christophe and Cooter's third lover, and another shy, quiet guy named Jonathan, who dis-appeared in the middle of the party and then returned all dressed in drag as "Roxy Contin," completely obscene and not shy at all. Leon started to get bored, so he went into the music room to play piano, but the rest of us danced to "She's a Bad Mama Jama," and I forgot for a little while about the mess the storm had made and how much my foot hurt.

I ended up making a uke cover of "She's a Bad Mama Jama." I also covered Prince's "Darling Nikki" because Nikki asked for it.

After about a week, things were almost back to normal here in the city, but the situation on the shoreline remained grim. I had some friends who were driving out every day to distribute sup-plies and check in on sick or vulnerable people. I understood from them—and eventually even the press would confirm this—that the Occupy people seemed to be doing a much more efficient job than the Red Cross at distributing aid. Believe it or not, Olivia was mak-ing trips out there on her bike to check on old people.

I just checked the internet for any recent updates on the after-math of Sandy. I'm writing this passage on June 27, 2013. There was a brand new one: two days ago, on June 25, they added a forty-fourth casualty to the list here in the city. Five months after the storm, they found this guy's body in his trailer in the Rockaways. Apparently he was a loner, and nobody noticed he was missing. They took another three months to determine that this was a Sandy fatality. The medical examiner said several clues pointed to the storm as being the cause of death: a five-foot-high watermark in his trailer, a calendar open to the month of October, and some prescriptions he'd had filled just before Sandy hit. Nobody claimed his body, so they buried it in a potter's field.

I should mention this: Olivia was very generous throughout that Sandy ordeal, even though I opted not to stay with her. She'd bike down and check on me every few days, and she'd rub my sore foot.

We'd make love. But there was a kind of melancholy between us. Both of us felt it, but it wasn't clear if it was the generally depressing situation or if there was something wrong between us. One afternoon I found a little haiku she'd written on a Post-it note, stuck to the refrigerator. It read:

I'm not the person
who should tell you what to do.
I just rub arches.

I just realized I should really be saying more about Sami's musical productions. Just shortly before the storm hit, I sent Tye a violin track from that *Aufgaben* set list. It was an old recording from Sami's conservatory days, and at the very end you can hear the audience erupt in ecstatic applause, but it's cut off almost immediately. Sami says he finds applause extremely disconcerting. In fact, he almost never plays publicly at all anymore. He does those small chamber performances at his mother's place, and when he's feeling well, he can occasionally play an informal gig among friends, but he never does formal recitals or concert performances anymore. Even when he posts the old recordings from his days as a student, he always cuts them off abruptly just when the cheering begins.

The track I sent Tye was Sarasate's "Gypsy Airs (Zigeunerweisen)," with piano accompaniment. I wanted to give Tye an example of Sami's virtuosity. The Zigeunerweisen is one of those pieces that Sarasate seems to have written just to show what he could do. It's technically only one movement, but it's divided into four sections—Moderato, Lento, Un poco più lento, and Allegro molto vivace. Even the Lento section is extraordinarily demanding. It has all this ricochet bowing and staccato volante. By the time you get to the Allegro section, he's tossed in a bunch of double stops, crazy spiccato runs, and left-hand pizzicato. You can't believe one person can be playing that many notes. But the thing about Sami's playing on this kind of piece is that the technical difficulty does nothing to diminish the emotional force. In fact, the more challenging a piece is technically, the more richly he plays it emotionally—it's entirely counterintuitive and different from most any musician I can think of. Often technique seems to evacuate, at least to some degree, the humanity of a performance, but with Sami it's the opposite. I find it extraordinary. I thought Tye might understand that.

He wrote back, "Oh God. That's exquisite." Then he told me that next he was going to listen to something else I'd sent him in a different message—a uke cover of a Bowie tune he'd told me he liked. I said, "Uh-oh, from the sublime to the ridiculous."

Then I wrote Sami and asked if he knew that expression. He said, "Du sublime au ridicule, n'y a qu'un pas—that's Napoléon Bonaparte about his Russian campaign . . . yes, I know this proverb, how couldn't I, it pretty much describes what I am ;)."

I guess that would be one way of putting it.

Sami never liked applause much—it always came as a surprise because when he played, he was so focused on what he was doing he'd forget there was an audience. But it only really became unbearable to him after what happened in New York. That was the one other memory that would make him fall asleep, besides his father's beatings. Because he passed out whenever he thought about it, it took a while for me to get that story, and I still don't know everything that happened, though I have an idea. After Kakay was born, after his marriage fell apart (these two events happened in pretty rapid succession), Sami decided to "shoot for the moon" and come to New York. He'd already completed his conservatory training at the Hochschule für Musik in Cologne, and he won all kinds of prizes. Sami never wrote or said to me the name "Juilliard," but really, what else could it have been? He did say something about meeting Itzhak Perlman.

In fact, for a minute I wondered if he'd come here to be a pop star. You may think I'm kidding, but it's only because you didn't see the shirtless portrait Minoo took of him back when he was in a metal band with Farrokh. And you didn't hear his grainy baritone. There was a line in an Angel Olsen cover I did—it went, "I love the way your voice is sex." That would pretty much describe it.

But no, he didn't come here to become a pop star; he came to play the violin. That much I know. And he loved New York, and he lived in Greenpoint, Brooklyn (pre-gentrification), and his program was very competitive. He played all the time and didn't sleep very much at all and one day he played for a big audience and at the end they began to applaud and the noise was overwhelming and terrifying and it was like when he was a child and he flipped out and started screaming and thrashing around and they took him to a psychiatric ward and he had to be sedated and he got kicked out of his program and his mother had to come and take him back to Cologne. This was the most he ever told me in a single message: "It's over ten years since I played my last concert. I think I'm still not ready to talk about it, cause what happened while I was performing and afterwards was quite traumatic. If I hadn't freaked out I'd probably be famous today, it's kind of pointless to talk about it, I'm not sad it didn't work out that way. Thinking about it puts me to sleep. I wanted to kill myself after it happened."
---snip---

Tye also has narcolepsy.

I had a student in my fetish seminar that fall who announced on the first day that he was a witch doctor. People were going around the room and explaining their interest in powerful objects. When it was his turn, he said he'd trained as an apprentice under a very important hoodoo doctor. These were the terms he used, "witch doctor" and "hoodoo." He told us all he realized that we might not believe in the power of witch doctors but that it didn't really matter whether we believed him because his clients paid him very good money to do what he did, which just went to show how powerful his hoodoo was. You may think this was just an indication of the naïveté of his clients, and you may think that this was a superficial thing for him to say, but this guy was, like I said of Burt Bacharach, a fucking genius. Seriously, he was fucking smart. That line about "good money" was so great.

Let me explain. When it was his turn for show-and-tell, he brought in a tiny bottle of dirt from Billie Holiday's grave in the Bronx. I had assigned some readings from Wyatt MacGaffey's excellent *Religion and Society in Central Africa: The BaKongo of Lower Zaire,* as well as parts of Zora Neale Hurston's *Mules and Men* and Robert Farris Thompson's *Flash of the Spirit.* All of them talk about graveyard dirt as an effective component in various matter-poems, also known as *minkisi,* charms, or power objects. My student took minor issue with Thompson's use of the term *goofer dust.* He spoke quite authoritatively about the use of dirt in Palo Mayombe, and then he produced the little vial. He said, "I bought this. It's dirt from Billie Holiday's grave." I think pretty much everybody was thinking, "Damn, this guy went up to the Bronx, and there was some huckster sitting next to Billie Holiday's cemetery plot charging people an arm and a leg for tiny bottles of dirt he probably dug up from his own backyard." Oh, an arm and a leg. Actually, that would make sense here too. The logic of the power of graveyard dirt is metonymic: it's supposed to absorb the power of the flesh buried in it. Anyway, I must admit that I myself at first understood him to be saying he'd paid "good money"—that is, a lot of it—to get that dirt. But he then explained how the price was determined. He went to the cemetery late at night and asked Billie how much she wanted, and she told him, and then he tossed the coins backwards over his shoulder and took a pinch of dirt. His money was good because Billie wanted it, and she wanted him to have the dirt.

But "good money" also means a lot of money. That's also what he meant when he talked about what his clients paid him. That's how he was paying the crushing tuition fees for his graduate degree. This, too, goes to show that this guy was a fucking genius.

Are you wondering how Tye paid for his MFA? The one he said they had to pay through the nose for? He did a lot of things. He babysat. He worked at bars and restaurants. He did some things for people that they couldn't do for themselves and some things for people who just didn't want to do them for themselves. He did some things for good money, and he did some things for free. Some things he enjoyed, and some things revolted him. His displeasure did not necessarily correspond to the payment he received.

On December 19, 2011, I went to see Tye perform at Judson Church. It was a Monday night. On Mondays in the fall and winter, Movement Research curates free performances. Usually there are four choreographers presenting. The work is experimental and, in keeping with the history of Judson, often stretches the parameters of the notion of dance and/or choreography.

When Tye and I were speaking recently about which performances of his I'd seen and which I hadn't, he asked me if I'd seen the one in which he constructed a replica of the altar in the church. He was referring to this piece, but at first I didn't understand that. Most people would not have described "Call Home" as the piece in which Tye constructed a replica of the altar in the church.

Here is how I would have described the piece. It seemed to me to have three movements. Keep in mind that at these Movement Research concerts, there are four artists presenting, so everyone is operating under time constraints. I believe the time allotted for each was about fifteen minutes. Tye's piece was set to the climactic part of the score from the film *E.T.*—the part when the kids on bicycles suddenly fly into the air. He'd looped the music right at the climax, as he sometimes does. He came in with a bunch of building materials and procured a volunteer from the audience—a middle-aged guy in a green sweater. Frankly, he didn't look like a typical audience member for Movement Research. He looked like a regular guy. He had a pretty normal haircut. With this guy's help, Tye started hammering together some pieces of plywood.

They effectively made a wall about four feet tall. It went across the floor of the church, and the center section projected further out than the sides. If I think about it in retrospect, I can see that this projection corresponded to the projection of the altar at the back of the church, but its primary function in the performance appeared to be to partially obscure what would go on in the second and third movements of the piece.

Because of the anxious, climactic music, and because of the time constraints and the evident hurry with which Tye was working, you thought the big challenge of the piece was going to be getting the goddamn wall built before the time was up. So when the construction was complete, there was a smattering of laughter and applause. I think it had taken maybe ten or eleven minutes. Then Tye took his volunteer behind the wall and they appeared to be discussing something. Because the music was so loud, they were speaking into each other's ears. They seemed to come to some sort of agreement. Then the guy pulled some money out of his wallet and counted out several bills into Tye's hand. Tye counted the money, got down on his knees, helped the guy unzip his trousers and remove his belt, and proceeded to give him a hand job. Because of the height of the construction, you couldn't actually see that if you were seated, but you could have guessed it, and a lot of people in the audience stood on top of their chairs so they could get a look. I was pretty far in the back, so I didn't actually see it, but from all the gasping and nervous laughter, it was pretty clear what was going on. It was later confirmed to me. The *E.T.* sound track was still playing at a fever pitch. Now I guess we were all wondering if they were going to finish the hand job before the time ran out. I think it went on for about three minutes, and evidently at least Tye was satisfied, because at the end of that, he stood, counted out some cash, and gave it to the guy. Tye later explained to me that the guy paid him two hundred dollars for the hand job, and Tye paid him a fifty-dollar performance fee. That seemed fair. Anyway, after that transaction, the guy took a seat off to the side, Tye removed his shirt and pants, and, still partially obscured by the wall he'd built, faced the audience with a look of concentration and proceeded to do an astonishing number of chugging grandes pirouettes à la seconde. This lasted for about a minute, during which the crowd whooped and hollered enthusiastically. Then it was over.

Perhaps you can see why the architectural details weren't what stuck in my mind. To Tye, structural details are very important. It was also significant that he gave the guy a hand job, *not* a blow job. Tye is very interested in thinking about manual labor—that is, what we do with our hands.

Tye's very interested in the kinds of economic transactions that make art possible or impossible.

Tye is actually more interested in that than he is in Yvonne Rainer.

It's also good to think about why he called this piece "Call Home." And what it meant when everybody laughed nervously that night at Judson. It was funny, and it was catastrophically sad.

A couple of weeks after Sandy, I also made a hand dance. The one at the beginning of this section. It was my two hands, alone—one person—even though it looked like two lovers. I like that about my hand dances. I also like to record harmony with myself sometimes on the covers.

One of the first ones I did like that was "Just the Two of Us," which was kind of a joke, and also Sami once requested "Twisted," which is by Annie Ross, but I arranged it the way Joni Mitchell did, so at the end when the lyrics say, "Instead of one head, I've got two—and you know two heads are better than one . . . ," I split into two voices, as if I had two heads.

Well, I shot this hand dance again in my bedroom, which is red, but I reversed the colors in iMovie so it looked blue, and I sent it to Sami. He liked it, but he told me something about colors, about the associations he had with certain colors, and this blue was OK, it was a kind of sky blue, cerulean blue, which he said didn't bother him, but there was a particular blue, what we would call royal blue or electric blue, that he really couldn't bear to look at. It made him very anxious. He said he smoked Gitane cigarettes, but the color on the pack made him anxious. He couldn't look at it or he'd get tensed.

I'd been thinking about when he got tense like that, what provoked it, and how he said his hands would start flapping around uncontrollably, and his voice would become constrained, like he was choking on it. He described it as something embarrassing, the spastic sort of behavior his mother was always telling him he needed to learn to control so people wouldn't think he was an idiot. But, in fact, when he'd sent me that very anxious message—the one when he was stammering, the kind of dissociative one when he'd passed out in bed with a strange woman and woke up in a panic—I worried for him, but I didn't find it ugly. That wasn't the only message like that. He'd had a similar episode in September. Because of the neuroma, he'd been taking more morphine than usual and smoking kind of a lot of weed.

He'd try to lay off all of this if Kakay was coming over, and if he really had to be on medication, he'd ask Farrokh or Minoo to come over at the same time, or he'd call Bina, the woman who did housekeeping for him a couple of times a week. Still, Juliane, for obvious reasons, didn't want Kakay around any drugs at all, and she and Sami had an argument about it. Sami got defensive at first. He wrote that he was sick of her treating him "like a freakin addict" and that she couldn't understand what the pain was like and that he was always careful to have another adult around if he was in a bad way, but if she kept Kakay away from him, he suffered, and what was worse, Kakay did as well, which made him even more anxious. One week Sami decided not to take anything at all—I think it was almost out of spite, just to show Juliane how impossible it was, what she was asking of him—and the pain was intolerable, and he flipped out. He called his mother and also Juliane, and then he recorded a voice message to me that was really alarming. He later told me that his mother showed up at his house that night with a friend of hers who was a doctor, and they had to sedate him, and then he was back on medication, and Juliane nixed any visits from Kakay at all for a few weeks.

But what I wanted to tell you about was his voice in that message. I realize that this may sound shockingly insensitive, to talk about Sami's vocal patterns in a message that was about his excruciating pain—and not just his physical pain. The even more heartbreaking part of the message was about the panic he was feeling and his agony about Kakay. Still, there was something so moving about his attempt to control himself. Usually, his speaking voice was so musical. I've said that already—musical and sexual. It was like every other instrument he'd mastered. He joked about it sometimes. Once, he'd been arranging a little weekend vacation rental at the shore for himself and Kakay, and the innkeeper tried to tell him there wasn't a room available, and he used his most seductive bass-baritone and finally she caved in—he was that good.

But even if the anxious messages weren't seductive, they also weren't ugly, and they certainly weren't grotesque. I tried to tell him that. I quoted André Breton: "La beauté sera CONVULSIVE ou ne sera pas." I told him I was sure when his hands were flapping like that he wasn't the monster that he said he was. There was something else about his voice like that, when all his technique flew out the window, and he was so naked. I think you could only call it dignity.

After that difficult episode had passed, I waited a little bit and thought about it some more, and I listened to his voice message, a lot, and then I made him another dance. I did it in front of a royal blue curtain. I lit it harshly. I wasn't at all sure what he'd think. I was nervous to send it, but I wanted to show him I was trying to understand what it felt like. I also wanted him to see the dignity I heard. I tried to make myself as naked as he was in that recording. I stood with my feet apart. You could see my sex. I wanted him to see me without shame so maybe he could see what I was hearing in his voice. I knew it might be terrible to say what I heard was beautiful. I told him I was sorry if he hated it.

This was the second dance to words.

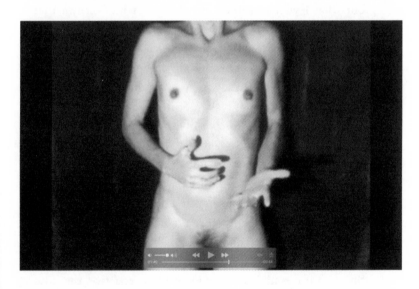

Sami said that's exactly what his hands looked like.

He said he loved the dance. Of course his response was different from his response to the first dance to words. I think the first one may have shocked him a little when I initially sent it, but even if you weren't so into Mauss or Judson, and even if you weren't accustomed to seeing a lot of weird naked performance art set to scores with an attenuated relationship to what most people think of as "music," you still might find that dance beautiful. I mean both the movement and Sami's voice. I think it made us both feel beautiful. This one really wasn't what you'd call "flattering" to either of us. He said it was difficult for him at first—difficult hearing his own voice—but he said he loved it. He kept saying he found it "impressing." From him, this meant a lot. I know I already told you that he could be pretty charitable with his compliments—he'd called my Frampton cover sublime. Um. But "impressing" seemed to mean something very different—like he was recognizing some sort of technical mastery in it, as though I'd approached a language that he and not many others spoke. I think he meant this. I mean, I think he was being sincere when he told me he was impressed by the dance.

It's true I worked very hard to make it. I listened to his voice over and over. I made a loop of it, and I practiced it for days. The night I made it, I filmed myself dancing it over and over. By the end I was drenched in sweat.

I wanted to give him something more beautiful. I made another hand dance, one of those that I really can't show you. It's too bad, because those really were maybe the best dances I made for him. I made this one straight on the computer. When I sent it, I said, "I was going to say something about how I filmed it on Photo Booth so it's a mirror image, and then I thought the reason to say that was you might otherwise think I'm more dexterous with my left hand than I am, and then I realized that if women make love to themselves or to another woman with both hands, it's like playing piano—the left hand is more for the bass notes and the right hand plays the high notes, faster and with more dexterity. Isn't that interesting? I suppose it's different if you're left-handed." I'd never thought of it that way before.

He said he also loved that dance.

I hadn't forgotten about the Paganini. I asked Tye again about the ballet lesson, but we were both a little busy, and we put off scheduling it again.

When Tye and I spoke about that performance in which he dragged the young woman back and forth across the gallery floor, he was surprised that I'd thought she was a dancer, that I couldn't see she really couldn't walk on her own. I said I thought that she was developing a technique—a technique of ceding weight completely, counterintuitively. It's a counterintuitive idea of technique. He understood why I might be interested in this idea, but he said that he thought that the reality of her disability made this piece "better art." The reason still had to do with technique. Tye really does help his collaborator once a week. That is, he goes to her house and assists her in taking care of herself. This is one of the forms of labor that he isn't paid for. He didn't say, "It's difficult." You could see that that night, at the performance. He was performing the same activity with his collaborator's sister that he usually does with her. It was difficult for the woman—I mentioned the red marks on her skin where Tye had gripped her in order to hoist her around—but it was also visibly difficult for Tye. He's strong, but that's a lot of weight to bear, and he was sweating a lot and breathing heavily by the time he'd finished that segment of the performance. He told me that, in effect, he'd been training for that performance every time he went to his collaborator's house and helped hoist her from her chair to her bed. Performing that action over and over in the gallery was like doing that astonishing number of chugs à la seconde at Judson Church.

Tye did a performance in November 2010, before I knew him, in a chapel in an abandoned convent at St. Cecilia's Parish in Greenpoint. I just read about that one. It was called "WILLY." Depending on your attachment to ballet, that may sound like a reference to the

Wilis in "Giselle," the vengeful spirits of girls who died before their wedding days. Or it may just sound like a silly word for the male sex organ. In this performance, Tye executed the entire mad scene from the ballet. He did it repeatedly, starting at seven in the evening. The plan was to perform it to the point of complete exhaustion. Once again, he'd taken into account the chapel's architecture, including a stone altar and stained glass windows. He lit the space with softboxes on photographic stands. He had bottles of Gatorade and a bucket to pee in off to the side. By the end, he'd bloodied his socks inside his sneakers.

There was another performance I didn't see that came shortly after "WILLY." It was called "Duke," and this one was at Dance Theater Workshop. Some reviewer seemed to think the title referred to John Wayne, which would be in keeping with the seemingly masculinist resonances of "WILLY," but could also be a reference to "Giselle," because in the ballet, Giselle is in love with Duke Albrecht of Silesia. He's already engaged to somebody else, but he strings Giselle along under a false identity. When she finds out, she dies in his arms. Then the vengeful Wilis go after him, but Giselle saves him. Sorry if you know all that.

Well, in "Duke," Tye began, shirtless and in padded football pants, moving a bunch of painted planks of wood around the stage, with the help of another of his serial collaborators, Michael Mahalchick. Mahalchick is very tall and heavyset. He has long frizzy hair, a long frizzy beard, and man-breasts. I don't know him, but he looks sympathetic. I mean that in the French sense—he looks sympa, like a very nice person.

In this performance, Tye would bend over and pick up a plank of wood, and Mahalchick would pick up Tye and the wood from behind and then move them to another spot where Tye would dump the plank. Sometimes their interaction looks supportive and tender. Sometimes it looks a little violent and possibly sexual. At one point the two of them faced each other across an expanse and wept. At another point, two other people walked across the stage and unceremoniously knocked Tye over while he was pushing the wood around with a push broom. Finally, Mahalchick assumed the languorous, side-lying position of the dying Albrecht in "Giselle," and Tye leaned over him, repeatedly performing Giselle's tender, protective gesture of forgiveness, evacuated of normative gender assumptions, and apparently—or maybe not—of sentimentality. There was nothing silly about it.

Remember this tableau. It's going to come back.

Late in the fall, my mother took a turn for the worse. I'd gone to see her when she was hospitalized, but after a while they said there wasn't anything more they could do for her there, the bones would just take a while to mend, and it would be best to have a home health aide come in and check on her at home. My sister helped her with the transition. We consulted with each other about home health care, and Carolyn set it up so somebody would come in for a few hours a day to prepare our mother's meals and make sure she was taking her medications. She was able to get to and from the bathroom with a walker, and she could sit and watch TV for a while if she wanted to, but mostly she was supposed to just lie in bed. As you can imagine, she was pretty miserable. We'd call every day, and I arranged to visit every other month. My sister was driving into town every weekend. Our mother's friends in the building were taking turns making short social visits every day.

One day in November, I got a call from Carolyn saying our mother had fallen on the way to the bathroom, and she was going back to the hospital for a while. This was just two days before I was going for one of my visits. We agreed that I'd stay at our mother's place even though she wasn't there. I had a key. On the day that I arrived, I got a taxi from the airport and let myself in to her apartment to drop off my stuff before heading to the hospital. There was a big ashtray on the coffee table, overflowing with cigarette butts.

That was a little shocking. I know I already said she was a smoker, but it had been years since she smoked like that, that much. She'd quit for a long time, and in recent years she'd really been doing it very sparingly, on the sly. In fact, there were signs around the retirement community saying, "This Is a No Smoking Residence." I knew there were a few other closet smokers in the building. My mother had told me that on Thursdays, her friend Adeline from down the hall would come over for a glass of Chablis and a smoke. But that ashtray gave you the impression that she'd been sitting there like a smoke stack. She must have been really anxious or really bored.

When I got to the hospital, she wasn't just anxious and bored— she was also very uncomfortable. Fortunately she hadn't broken anything this time, but she was bruised, and her pelvis was still very sore. She was insisting it hurt more than ever. She was frowning and grimacing, and she kept saying, "I don't understand. I'm not getting better. I can't stand this pain, and they're not doing anything." When her doctor came in, he was very understated. Dr. Billington. I'd met him before, during my last visit. My mother liked him a lot because he was calm, and he appeared to listen to her. When the nursing staff told him that the pain meds didn't seem to be sufficient, he put his hand on my mother's arm and said, "Elaine, we're going to get your pain under control." She looked him hard in the eyes, then shut hers and passed out. He put her on morphine. She could have fifteen milligrams every four hours, if she asked for it. They wrote that on the dry-erase board near her bed.

You can imagine who this made me think of.

I'd brought along my ukulele on this visit. I thought maybe she'd like me to sing to her in the hospital, and if she were feeling up to it, maybe she could even sing a little harmony. We'd once recorded "Bye Bye Blackbird" together. That was on my virtual album *Plays Well with Others* (duets with friends and family members). On this visit, she was clearly in no condition to sing or even to put up with my saccharine warbling. But when I got back to her apartment that night, I recorded a cover. It was for her, though I wouldn't show it to her, and it was for Sami. I did send it to him. It was Marianne Faithfull and the Stones' "Sister Morphine." While I was on that opiate kick, I also recorded Lou Reed's "Perfect Day."

I just made myself cry like a baby, listening to my mother on "Bye Bye Blackbird."

You're not going to believe this, but it's true. Tye just texted me that he went to visit his father at his house for the first time in twelve years, and his father gave him two hundred dollars cash.

Remember the thigh cozy I was knitting? I finished it around the middle of October. I made it with a cable stitch to keep myself entertained. It was very well made. I was a little uncertain about how much to taper the end. I had one photograph of Sami's leg without the prosthesis. It was shot from behind at the beach: him and Kakay simultaneously doing a handstand. That was sweet. But there was a little motion in the photo, so it still didn't give you a very clear picture of the shape of the end of his stump.

Sami said his stump didn't bother Kakay in the least, but that Juliane thought it was disgusting when he'd take off the prosthesis in front of other people. Maybe it just broke her heart.

Anyway, as soon as I'd finished knitting the cozy, I asked Sami for his mailing address, and he apologized but said there was a little problem, which was his paranoia and social phobia, and it was nothing personal, but it always sent him into a panic when anyone asked for his home address. There are a few things that set Sami off, and I'd already learned not to take them personally, so instead of trying to reason with him, I suggested a couple of alternatives. He'd mentioned a little café that had good cake where he liked to go with Kakay—the Café Elefant. They had board games, and sometimes they'd go there and play one. The proprietor was nice to them. I suggested I send the cozy to Sami care of the café. He could ask the owner to look out for it, and he could pick it up there one day when he went to have cake with Kakay. Or I said maybe Farrokh wouldn't mind if I sent it to him, and he could deliver it. Sami found both of these ideas humiliating. He said no, it was unreasonable for him to be afraid to tell me his address, and please have patience, he just had to get over his superstition or neurosis or weirdness or whatever you might call it. I said OK. I'm pretty patient.

There was still a little tension between me and Olivia, but I couldn't put my finger on it. It's funny I just used that expression, because she felt it too, but in her elegant way, she was telling me—exactly—how to put my finger on it. We were lying on my bed, and she brushed the hair from my eyes and said, "Go on, I know you want to touch the soft part." Well, that was sexy. I waited for a second, and she said more.

Then she explained—it was a poem. She'd written me a triolet. She writes a lot of them. Maybe you know what that is: eight lines of only two rhymes, where the first line is repeated, completely, in the fourth and seventh lines, and the second line in the eighth. Imagine. It's very compressed. Well, Olivia gives herself a little room by using off-rhymes. But she's also a lover of technique.

> Go on, I know you want
> to touch the soft part.
> Don't tell me that you can't.
> Go on, I know you want
> to. Relax. I don't
> bite. I promise, it won't hurt.
> Go on. I know you want
> to. Touch the soft part.

I did.

Early in the fall, Lauren Berlant had contacted me again about that workshop at the University of Chicago. She asked me what I thought I might do. She mentioned that somebody great had just been there in the same series, and the lecture was a success, but the workshop part had been kind of a flop because the person half-assed it. I don't know if she used precisely that terminology, but something along those lines. When I read that I thought, "Holy crap, the smartest woman in the United States of America is inviting me to give a workshop—I'd better not half-ass it." I decided to seriously overprepare.

I wrote Lauren back asking if she could get me the e-mail addresses of all the workshop participants one week in advance. I wrote up an assignment that I wanted to send them:

> Sometimes I like to provoke my own writing by working across media: I make a dance or a song or a poem, and then build a story around it to give it a context within which it makes sense. Or the narrative I'm constructing becomes an occasion to make a performance. It gives me a chance to play with myself (I mean this in the Winnicottian sense, but the sexual innuendo is also intended, as I think there's maybe inevitably an erotic component to the process of art-making). But it can also be done collaboratively, which is nice. When the initial creative act has an intended audience of one, it presents the possibility of immediate and inappropriate intimacy. Don't worry, that's good. In order to get the ball rolling, I'd like for workshop participants to e-mail me a little something a few days in advance of our meeting. You can choose:
> • a dirty haiku
> • a photographic storyboard with four frames, no words

- a video of an interpretive dance ("dance" can be broadly construed)
- a piece of flash fiction (three hundred words or less) involving public transportation
- an a cappella cover of a song you love
- a voice mail apologizing for something

Lauren wrote me back, "I don't understand the prompts, and I'm afraid others won't either. You want us to make art and send it to you? LB" I said, "That's funny you found that hard to understand. I thought it was easy—maybe you're too smart! Yes, I guess you could call any of those things art. The idea was for each person to make something—a dirty haiku, a voice-mail apology, a video-tape of him- or herself dancing around, a story about somebody on a bus or a train . . . People would send these to me, and then I would respond, and maybe it would keep going . . ." I'd actually originally thought I could matchmake among them and have them respond to each other, but that seemed like a lot to ask in advance of our first meeting. Also, I kind of liked the idea of forcing myself to produce a bunch of weird art in a hurry like that. When I told Lauren I thought my proposal was pretty straightforward, she said, "I think you overestimate how easy it is just to mediate oneself." I assumed "mediating oneself" was what I was calling masturbation.

I sent out the assignment, but as the day of my visit approached, nobody had e-mailed me anything, except Lauren (a very short story about a weird ballroom dance enthusiast she met on a train—it was sad and a little surreal). I sent another message to the registered participants saying, "hi friends—if you have a haiku or interpretive dance or voice-mail apology or something, please send soon! don't worry, it can be a super quickie—this is just an experiment! thanks, b." I sent that two days before my scheduled talk. The next afternoon, I flew into Chicago and went to the nice corporate hotel where they'd booked me a room. Some things started to dribble in: several dirty haikus, a split-screen interpretive dance by a guy named Fred, and an e-mail from a doctoral student in ethnomusicology who said she'd *just* heard about the workshop but she'd love to participate if there were still room.

Somebody had given her the list of prompts, and she said if necessary she could run over to one of the practice rooms and record something, but maybe I'd accept a recording she'd previously made—not really a cover, per se, but a rendition of Schubert's "Heidenröslein." This woman was an opera singer—a coloratura mezzo-soprano! In the recording, she was singing with piano accompaniment, and the melody was pretty jaunty. She trilled her *r*'s, and she had a very robust vibrato. Her name was Natali Pandit.

I checked all this out in my nice corporate hotel room and quickly got to work recording a cappella songs for the authors of the dirty haikus. I'd take an image or concept from somebody's poem—say, bondage—and type that into Google with "lyrics," and then bingo, I'd find some weirdly appropriate pop song. I'd play the song into my head on earbuds and record myself singing along. These recordings were even more naked and eerie than the uke covers, though I made them wet with a little reverb. I wrote Fred two poems, and then, because I was having fun, I made a diptych of two found videos based on the imagery in the poems based on his dances. One side showed a guy doing a hip-hop dance in a sheep costume; the other side was a woman demonstrating the "drinking bird" yoga maneuver. I Googled Natali's Schubert and saw that it was based on a Goethe poem. When I read a translation of the poem, I was kind of shocked because it was quite obviously about a violent rape and retribution (the imagery was of a rose begging not to be plucked and then pricking her rapist with her thorn). It was so weird that the melody was so jaunty! Then I found out that the German metal band Rammstein recorded a related song, but much darker. I did an a cappella cover of that for Natali. That one was uncanny.

By this time it was getting late. I decided to make Lauren a dance. Her story was about a conversation she'd had with a guy on a train in Manchester, England. Even though I'd asked for a piece of flash fiction, I intuited that this was a true story. When I later asked her about that, she looked at me like, "Duh." I don't know if she thought that was obvious because she only ever wrote non-fiction or because the story was so strange. Life, as the cliché goes, is generally stranger than fiction. In the story, Lauren had been reading *I Love Dick* on a train, and she laughed out loud, which prompted a little man to ask her what she was reading. Actually, she called him "a tiny small man." He told her about his failures in love and his enthusiasm for competitive ballroom dance. He was an anesthesiologist. Before he got off the train, he told her she seemed special (indeed, she is), and he gave her a charcoal sketch he'd made of a house with a chimney. She tried to dissuade him, but he wanted her to have it.

My corporate hotel room had an enormous window overlooking a big parking lot. There were skyscrapers in the background. I turned out the lights in the room. I pulled up an instructional ballroom dance video on YouTube and stripped down to a pair of boy-cut underpants. I bunched my hair up in a rubber band. I thought maybe if I filmed myself from the back in the dark like that, in silhouette against the depressing lights in the parking lot, I might pass for the tiny small man practicing his cha-cha-cha. It was pretty bleak and lonely, all right. I'd thought maybe I could pass myself off as a man because of that last dance to words. I really didn't look like a woman in that one. I mean, I did if you looked at my sex, it was obvious, but the rest of my body in that harsh light looked so scrawny, breastless, and hipless. I showed it to my best friend, and that was the first thing she said, how weird it was that I looked so male. But even with those boy-cut underpants, in this one I looked like a woman, even following the instructor's directives for the man's steps. I still kind of liked it. It was ridiculous and sad.

I sent everybody their art, and I went to bed.

Back in June of 2011, Tye presented "Duet with Thomas von Frisch" at Abrons Arts Center. I went with Olivia. She'd never seen Tye perform before, and I'd been talking about him. There was also another artist billed that evening. Ostensibly, the pairing of the two had to do with "nonnormative masculinities." I think Tye wasn't entirely sanguine about the way his work was being framed by the curator of the event. The other performer was working out something about being an alpha male, which it seems he felt he wasn't. He had his parents move through the audience, cutting bits of hair from the heads of volunteers (Olivia and I let them have a little of ours), and then the guy glued this hair to his body. His parents looked pretty ill at ease, though who knows, maybe they were acting. Then the guy lost disastrously in a boxing match with an opponent whose head was a screen for projections of various people who had emasculated him (a former girlfriend, a gym teacher, and so on). There was something with a dog. I think the dog's hair perhaps was also cut. I remember feeling bad for the dog, I'm not sure why.

Tye's piece was, as the title indicated, conceptualized as a duet. Thomas von Frisch is a quantum physicist. Tye met him through a queer and trans scholarship foundation, and things developed from there. He's generally pretty game, as you will have noticed. Tom enjoys the arts.

He's a dance enthusiast, among other things. In fact, shortly before the performance, he told Tye he unfortunately couldn't make this one because he had tickets to a ballet he really wanted to see that night. I believe that the original concept involved some balletic lifts, some lecturing on quantum physics, and some maneuvering of heavy physical detritus from a prior performance.

Because Tom wasn't there, Tye had to narrate what he would have been doing, had he been there. Tye also had to accomplish all of the moving of materials by himself, so it was even more grueling than it would have been. I don't remember exactly what the architectural configuration was of the materials in question. There was also a section in which Tye repeatedly performed a ballet move.

Relative to the alpha male performance, which one might have characterized as slightly histrionic, Tye's was very unassuming. I suppose if you were unfamiliar with his work, you might have thought, "Oh well, I picked a bad night to see Tye Larkin Hayes perform, his partner didn't show up." I may even have thought to myself that night, "Hmm, too bad for Olivia. I kept talking Tye up, but this is pretty understated." But there's something very poignant about performing a duet with somebody who isn't there.

I only just made the connection to my hand videos.

After my workshop at the University of Chicago, I went out for a drink with Lauren Berlant. Actually, she doesn't drink. She had a seltzer, but I had a glass of wine. We were in a hotel bar—not the one in my hotel, someplace downtown. We talked about our parents and our sexual histories and our writing, and I told her a little about Sami and about the dances I'd been making, and I said I wanted to write a novel about him and that I worried sometimes about the ethics of it, not just the novel, but the dances, everything, because even though I kept asking him if it was OK, he was, as he kept telling me, autistic. What did it mean to keep pushing all this intimacy on somebody who'd announced that he had severe social phobia? Lauren said there might have been a time when she would have worried about autistic love, but now she thought maybe all love was autistic.

I'll have to check with her to see if I can quote her on that. It might be the kind of thing she'd say in a hotel bar but not in a book.

I quoted the line to Sami, but he disagreed. It didn't make him angry, and his reservation wasn't like Tye's when that critic just started flinging around the term *trans* without considering what it really meant to somebody like him. Sami just said that loving was the one thing that in fact made him feel like he *wasn't* autistic—it was what allowed him to have moments of feeling connected to someone else, not, as he often put it, sealed up in his bottle. But I told him that what I understood her to be saying was that maybe all of us are more trapped in ourselves than we like to pretend, and love is simultaneously what makes us want to get out of the bottle and what makes us feel how stuck in it we are.

He got what I was saying, but he seemed to prefer a more optimistic view. I mean of love, not of autism. Still, a few days later he posted a long and complex guitar meditation called "Love Is Autistic."

The next day, I had some time to kill before I went to the airport. I took a little stroll down Milwaukee Avenue and wandered into a vintage store. They had some artisanal perfume, and I put a little on my wrist. It was called Silent Films, and I really liked it. There was another called Realism that I also liked. You could buy a little set of tester flasks of these perfumes. I needed to choose a third scent, and I chose Jackal. These little testers came with short explanations of the general impression each scent might make, as well as its notes, aspects, and ingredients. I'm not sure what the difference is between a note and an aspect, although *note* sounds musical, while *aspect* would appear to be visual. Silent Films was the one I thought smelled most like me—not my natural smell, but maybe the way I ought to smell. The description was poetic, if not exactly obvious: "Like an uncanny image of the body, a mercurial impersonation—almost as if in a mirror, or projected on a screen . . ." Its notes were vetiver, vanilla, leather, and smoke. Its aspects were mysterious, powdery, brutal, nostalgic.

Realism had notes of a crushed stem, soil, herbs, hay, and citrus. Its aspects were green, sunshot, and blooming. Jackal was earthy, animalic, dark, and vast. It had, among other things, "the bitter, magnetic smell of money."

Shortly after that trip to Chicago, my friend Arto came to New York. You may have guessed that I mean Arto Lindsay, the musician. I met Arto years ago, when I was living with Leon's dad. He played percussion in Arto's band for a minute. If you aren't familiar with Arto's music, you should be. He's known both for his shrieking, dissonant noise guitar and for his delicate, bossa-inflected vocals. He's a composer and a subtle, perceptive lyricist. He often combines seemingly opposed sensibilities in a single song. Arto also likes to collaborate with visual and performance artists, sometimes on parades. I'd written about one of these in my last novel, and I think I may have offended him a little by describing the performance as "disturbing and confusing." I didn't think this was an insult. A lot of my favorite art is disturbing and confusing. Hello, like Godard. I sent him the passage thinking he might like it and didn't hear from him for a long time. I won him over again, though, when I did a very sentimental uke cover of one of his songs. Actually, Leon had requested that one. He loves Arto's music. So do I—both when it's tender and when it's disturbing and confusing.

Arto grew up in Brazil, where I also lived for a time, and he moved back there a few years ago. At the end of November, he came here to play a gig at the New Museum, and I went to see him with Leon, and the next day Arto and I met for tea. First we stopped at a bookstore and poked around a bit. He bought me a copy of *Antwerp* and I bought him *Leaving the Atocha Station*. Then we went to sit down and talk. I told him some of the things I'd liked about his performance at the New Museum. He'd played solo there, and Leon and I were sitting up in front so we could see all his pedals, and we could even hear the scratchy, weird sounds of the ends of his guitar strings rubbing against one another as they were sticking out of the tuning pegs like messy hair. I asked him about his current projects, and he asked me about mine, and then I told him about my dances with Sami, and I asked him if he might be willing to help me with one. I explained about the dances to words, and the dance I'd done to the Monk practice tape, and I told him I wanted to make a blue dance to music, one that would correspond with the anxious dance to words. I wanted to know if he'd be willing to give me a guitar solo for it.

He was very interested when I told him about Sami. Most everyone seems to be—it's quite a story. I asked him if he wanted to see the dances to words, and he said yes. The tearoom where we'd gone had a small table in a narrow hallway, which is where we were sitting. I gave him my iPod and he put the earbuds in his ears and hit play. First he watched the red dance to words and then the blue one. I was pretty nervous. I'd asked Sami if it was OK for me to show them to my friends, and he said of course, they were art. It was hard for him to hear his voice in that blue one, but even he could hear it was music when he watched the dance. He hadn't shown Farrokh or Minoo—I don't know if he was protecting himself or me or if he's just more discreet or modest or shy than I am—but he didn't mind if other people saw them. Anyway, I felt fine showing them to my best friend. Rebekah's a writer and a filmmaker, and we show each other pretty much everything. She watched them with the dry eye of a critic, and when they were finished, she looked at me and told me she thought they were the best thing I'd ever made. She said this without an ounce of sentimentality. Not Arto. When the second one finished, he pulled the earbuds out of his ears, put down the iPod, reached across the table, and kissed me on the top of my head. I think he had tears in his eyes. I'm not sure if they were for Sami or for me. It was awkward, and I didn't know

where to put my face. He said he'd send me a sound file after he
got back to Rio.

I'm very fond of Arto.

In December Sami was still having a lot of pain. His messages were
often fairly incoherent. In one of them he included a little poem
he'd read:

> **A**lways
> **U**nique
> **T**otally
> **I**nteresting
> **S**ometimes
> **M**ysterious

I wrote him back:

> **S**incerely
> **A**ffable, though
> **M**uch of the time
> **I**ndisposed.
>
> **M**aybe
> **O**ut to lunch . . .
> **H**ow
> **A**re you
> **N**udnik?
>
> "**Z**zzz . . ." uh-oh,
> **A**sleep again.
> "**Z**zzz . . ."
> **A**nd then,
> "**I**'m back, sorry . . ."

I meant *nudnik* affectionately. Sami's middle name in this novel is Mohan. His last name is Zazai. I guess you figured that out.

There had still been some of that nice organic wool left over after I finished the balaclava and the thigh cozy, so while I was waiting for a solution to the paranoia problem, I made Sami a little cap, and then I crocheted him an iPod cozy. After I'd finished those, I brought up the topic of sending a package again, but this time I suggested a new plan: I researched mailing stations where a person could send things, and I discovered that DHL had something called "Packstations" for just this kind of situation. Well, they didn't specify "paranoia" on the website, but it seemed you could send a package for whatever reason to one of these Packstations, and the recipient could pick it up there. Sami again groaned a little about how embarrassing it was to be so crazy. Also, this would require him to set up an account with DHL. He said if I were just patient a little while longer that maybe he could send me something. They'd make him include his return address at the post office, and because he was also a neurotic rule-follower, he'd be forced to write his return address, and then I'd have it. Besides, he said there weren't any Packstations very close to Von-Ketteler-Straße. I said, "Sami, did you just tell me you live on Von-Ketteler-Straße?" He said, "Yes, I tricked myself. ;) It's number 11." Bingo.

I made up a little package with the pieces of knitting, and I put a small plastic deer in there too. I took the tiny tester vial of Realism perfume and tucked it into the iPod cozy. I thought Sami might like it because the scent was so green. That little slip of a description that came with it said it had a "particularly precious" ingredient called "hay absolute." I looked up *hay absolute,* and, indeed, it seems it's very pricey on its own. There are different ways of extracting scent from things—you can get an essential oil, for example, or an essence, but an absolute is a very pure thing, and since you can't actually express any oil from hay, it seems that getting the scent of it is a pretty arduous process. Well. I wasn't sure if Sami would like it, but I thought he might. I also thought it would be nice to know at least what he smelled like.

I took the package to the post office at Eleventh Street and Fourth Avenue. There was a long line because of the upcoming holidays. As I was standing in line, I saw a sign explaining what kinds of things you couldn't send via airmail: obviously really hazardous materials like lighter fluid and firearms but also alcohol, perfume, prescription drugs, and tobacco. Hmm, perfume. But my flask was so tiny, and it was all wrapped up in the iPod cozy, plus the package was sturdy and all taped up. I couldn't imagine the tiny vial would break open, and if it did, there were just a few drops in there—they'd surely evaporate right away. When I got up to the window, the clerk looked humorless. She weighed my parcel and looked me dead in the eye: "Any perfume in there?" I looked her dead in the eye and said no. She put the necessary postage on the package and tossed it into a bin.

Despite the time of year, it wasn't a Christmas present. Obviously I love gifts, but I'm not a big one for Christmas. I mentioned that my mother was an atheist. My father was a lapsed Catholic and also a staunch secular humanist. Jesus and the Virgin Mary would only visit him during his psychotic breaks. We did the usual pagan business with the tree and all of that when I was a kid, and if she had her druthers, my mother would still like us to be with her for the holidays, but I think that's mostly because other people expect that. Leon has no interest in Christmas whatsoever—or practically any holiday. He likes to say that Mother's Day was invented by the Nazis. I think this is a little inaccurate. Anyway, I have to concur with his disdain for the commercialism of various official days of celebration.

Because I'd been traveling to see my mother every eight weeks or so, it just didn't happen that I'd be going to see her for Christmas.

Besides, in her condition, it wasn't like there was going to be a lot of partying. Leon was on break from school, so he planned a road trip to New Orleans. Olivia was going to Montana to see her niece. I thought I'd just spend the break writing comments on my students' papers and maybe doing a few uke covers and a dance video or two.

Perhaps you've begun wondering if Sami and I ever discussed the possibility of meeting in person. In fact, we did. I don't remember who raised the possibility first, but once in a while we'd say something like, "Well, if we ever meet, you'll notice that I have a tendency to"—fill in the blank. You can probably imagine some of the tendencies. Sami's mostly involved convulsive movement or oddball conversational patterns. Mine involved certain predictably moderate habits of sleeping, eating, and exercising.

Sami, for his part, having been raised in a Muslim household, also had no attachment to Christmas—in fact, he found it alienating and depressing. Kakay still expected a celebration, but it was mostly with Juliane's family. Sami participated only peripherally. So when it became clear that Leon's apartment would be empty, I mentioned it to Sami and told him that if he had a hankering to see New York again, he'd be welcome to crash next door. I asked Leon if that would be cool, and he said sure—he's not very territorial.

It seemed perfect. I knew it would probably be a mistake to have Sami stay at my place. I have a guest bed, but he sometimes had those freak-outs, and when he was overstimulated, he really needed to be alone. I already mentioned that I need alone time. There's an upright piano at Leon's place and a ton of other instruments. I thought it might be nice to hear Sami playing through the wall. Sami got sort of excited about the possibility. He was still in contact with a few friends here. He even began the process of applying for a visa, but as the winter progressed, it became clear he was not in any condition to travel. Part of me thought this was just as well. I think maybe Sami thought so too. He'd say he was anxious about my coming face-to-face with his awkwardness and social phobia, but he would have been justified in being anxious about facing my own peculiarities, which I won't point out if you haven't already noticed them.

I did give Leon a quick call on Christmas Day. He was couch surfing, and he complained a little about the hygiene of his housemates and how slow things were in the Quarter on account of the holidays. I also called my mother. Well, I was calling her every day anyway. This call wasn't so very different. I don't remember if it was one of the ones where she was kind of lucid or if it was one of the ones where she was mostly moaning. Even the morphine didn't seem to be resolving her pain. Billington decided to try putting her on fentanyl. When Carolyn told me this, I said, "Oh, I have a friend who's on fentanyl. It's pretty strong. Maybe that'll do the trick, fingers crossed."

My sister and I were, at this point, in constant communication. We were both doing internet research on various aspects of our mother's condition—not just the physical ones but also the financial ones. Our mother had been extremely judicious in planning for this stage of life, and she'd squirreled away significant savings. Still, Medicare had caps on benefits, not all the hospital expenses were covered, and home health care was obviously going to deplete her resources pretty quickly. It made you wonder what happened to people who weren't as judicious—and fortunate—as my mother.

I should pause to explain something about my sister. She's a little older, and we weren't particularly close growing up. She married very young, which surprised our parents. Her marriage collapsed, and she subsequently moved to a rural area with another boyfriend. Over the years her politics had gotten more and more right wing. Our mother, as I've mentioned, is a lefty. You may already have situated me somewhere on the lunatic fringe, or maybe you think I've got my bearings just right. Carolyn is the only one of the three of us who's fearless about broaching political topics when we're all together. She goes at these topics with the keen resolve of an ardent sports fan. This is possibly a healthier attitude than my own morose stupor when faced with political arguments I find unconscionable.

Well, we disagree about a lot of things, but this experience with our mother had really cast her in an entirely new light to me. She and I had both raised our sons as single moms, and you might have thought we'd have bonded over that, but I guess while we were doing that we were both so busy we didn't stop to think about it. But watching how capably and generously she was responding to our mom's situation really gave me pause. When I'd apologize for not doing more of the heavy lifting, she'd shrug it off, saying she was closer and she knew if I were in her place I'd do the same thing. In fact, I would have tried, but I don't think I would have been nearly as good at it. She could be a pit bull with insurers and other bureaucrats on the telephone. She was firm but also appreciative with the medical staff. When our mother would testily grouse about some nurse's ineptitude, my sister would scold her for being so judgmental and remind her of how difficult their work was. When our mom was loopy on meds (sometimes she'd even stick out her tongue or give somebody the finger), then Carolyn would really tell her off—rightly.

Carolyn had some misgivings about Dr. Billington. He seemed nice enough at first, and my mother was clearly enamored of him, but his office wouldn't always return my sister's calls in a timely way, and when she asked questions, she sometimes found Billington's tone a little condescending. Geriatrics was not even his specialty. She mentioned these concerns to me, but we agreed that given our mother's fragile state, she should probably have a consistent care team, at least until she got through the worst of it.

In addition to medical power of attorney, our mother had also given Carolyn control over her finances, and frankly, that was probably also good thinking and not only because she was closer than I was. My relationship to money, as you may have noticed, is a little mystical. If you're spending down your life savings, you probably want to have a pit bull in your corner.

Leon's politics are a lot like mine. Olivia's are even more extreme, or at least they were for a time. In the eighties, she lived in a queer intentional community in Virginia called Twin Oaks. Maybe she would have stayed indefinitely, who knows, but she had some kind of very intense breakup with another woman who was living there, and that's when she came to New York.

Whenever I'd try to talk about politics with Sami, he'd say he was uncomfortable with all "isms," and the only thing he really understood was music. He certainly had feelings about racism, having experienced plenty of it as a brown person in Germany, and he'd express despair and confusion when there were terrible stories in the news about violence against women or shocking economic exploitation. I'd say, "Sami, take my word for it, you're a feminist and a communist. That just means you abhor the mistreatment of people on the basis of their sex or class." I have a pretty expansive idea of what constitutes communism and feminism, but I don't think they're like those of the critic who exasperated Tye with his expansive idea of what constituted *trans*. Maybe it's strategic naïveté—a way of flipping around "If you can't beat 'em, join 'em" so it becomes, "Just tell 'em they've already joined you." Graeber also has a pretty expansive definition of what he calls "baseline communism," which would be what happens when you grab the check at a restaurant because you know you make more money than the person you're dining with. You may think that's bourgeois politesse, but, like Graeber, I'd prefer to call that communism. Eventually Sami conceded to being a communist and a feminist. It may just be that I wore him out.

After I wrote the story about lying to the United States Postal Service about the contents of my package, I got a little nervous for a minute that they might come after me. It's interesting, what it means to confess to having committed a crime in a piece of writing. Well, this is a work of fiction, although obviously I fudge what that means sometimes. There's a moment in *Mules and Men* that I always like to point out to my students—a place where Hurston seems to be admitting to having committed a crime. And it's not just sending perfume in the mail. She claims to have been an accessory to a murder! *Mules and Men* is ostensibly nonfiction. It's folklore—an ethnographic account of her training in hoodoo, and also storytelling. But Hurston also fudged the distinction between fiction and nonfiction habitually. Anyway, the passage I wanted to tell you about is the story of Muttsy Ivins's enemy. While Hurston was training under the hoodoo doctor Anatol Pierre, a shady character named Muttsy Ivins showed up and offered to pay Pierre to get rid of his lover's husband before the guy got rid of him. Pierre didn't like Ivins, but he was willing to do the job for two hundred and fifty dollars (what my student might call "good money"), which Ivins begrudgingly promised him. Then Pierre set Hurston, his apprentice, on the case, procuring various materials for the spell. She had to get a beef brain, a beef tongue, a beef heart, and a live black chicken. Pierre took a piece of paper and wrote Muttsy Ivins's enemy's name on it nine times. That was inserted into a surgical slit in the beef heart, and they sutured it with some steel pins and put it in a jar of "bad vinegar." There was some more writing (soaked in whiskey), a little effigy, some burned and bitten candles, and something gruesome involving the chicken and a black cat. There was a fairly long waiting period for decomposition, and then they put the beef brain on a plate with nine hot peppers "to cause insanity and brain hemorrhages." They slit open the tongue and put the guy's name in there, closed it with a pack of pins, and buried it with all that other stuff. Pierre told Hurston they had to keep some black candles burning over the tomb for ninety days. He told her, "No one can stand that." Pierre slept by that mess until the ninety days were up. The passage ends: "And the man died."

If you read the whole thing, you find out that Muttsy Ivins's enemy already had tuberculosis, which is probably as good an explanation as any for his demise. Also, it's pretty clever, the way she ends it. She doesn't say, "So the man died." She says, "And." This shows you something interesting about narrative, which is that if two events are juxtaposed in the telling of a story, you assume a causal relationship. That's actually related to the way that objects become powerful in hoodoo. That's what I was saying about graveyard dirt: it absorbs the meaning of the things next to it (that was the business about an arm and a leg). In figural analysis, we call this metonymy—the association of two things because of their proximity or contiguity. A synecdoche is a kind of metonym also—a part for the whole. Like an arm or a leg. Zora Neale Hurston was Anatol Pierre's right hand. But back to narrative, which works similarly: linear narrative juxtaposes events in a way that tempts you to make a causal connection between them. Or maybe it really makes things happen.

Remember how I told Sami very early in our correspondence that things I imagined in my fiction often ended up coming true? You'd be surprised how often that happens.

Early in January, I got another one of those draft e-mails from barbaraandersen64. I found it distressing. It wasn't clear to whom she was writing. This time it seemed like maybe she was writing to herself, just to keep it together. Another way of putting this would be that it seemed like she was trying to compose herself. The message began abruptly: "I stay in this relationship for the sake of the children." She said she was all they had to hold on to, that "he" had left them just as damaged as she was. She said he catered to the kids when it increased his sense of worth, but otherwise he couldn't care less. She acknowledged that she herself experienced some sense of value when she was able to be supportive to the children. Then there was a noirish line about the business of the apartment in Back of the Yards just being a "threat." She said, "I don't think he really did it." She wasn't sure though. Maybe he'd "done it," whatever "it" was, and he was waiting for the right moment to break it to everyone. "I don't know—he does not tell me. He would have to tell the kids, though, so at some point more will be reviled."

This message freaked me out a little. I showed it to Leon, and he said, "Wow, well, wait and see. Maybe more will be reviled."

I don't mean to be making light of Barbara Andersen's situation.

When I was six and my sister was eleven, our mother decided to divorce our father. She was still in love with him, but when he was depressed, he'd try to kill himself. When he was manic, he'd drive very fast with us in the car. It wasn't a safe environment. I mentioned those visitations from the Virgin Mary. Once, he swerved the car to avoid hitting her. When he was well, he was extremely charismatic. He was also very handsome.

The new semester began. I was teaching a course called "Performing Fiction," and I was supervising the MA thesis group. I also had some off-campus gigs lecturing about voodoo dolls, dance on film, and, of course, Pussy Riot.

I say "of course," and yet already by late January some of the excitement about the group seemed to have waned. Actually, if you kept up, which I tried to do, you found out there were some discouraging internal disputes. Tolokonnikova's husband, Pyotr Verzilov, had been at that NYU Law School panel, along with their adorable little daughter. He spoke eloquently about their case to the media, and Yoko Ono presented him with a peace prize. But shortly after that, Tolokonnikova and Alyokhina issued a really angry letter saying that Verzilov was "fraudulently" passing himself off as their spokesperson, and the only person who should represent the group was a girl in a balaclava. Verzilov was flummoxed.

It was slightly less surprising to me to learn that there was also conflict with that original legal team. In November somebody discovered that Feygin had attempted to register *Pussy Riot* as a trademark. It seemed he'd done that back in April, and nobody knew about it. All three of the lawyers from the original defense team ended up withdrawing from the case. They also got into a kerfuffle with Samutsevich. She said Feygin and the others had illegally held onto some of her documents. She wanted them disbarred. Feygin countercharged on Twitter that Samutsevich was part of a "defamation campaign" organized by Putin's cronies.

At first, when Samutsevich had gotten off in her appeal, Tolokonnikova and Alyokhina expressed only joy for her. She said she was going to use her freedom to continue to promote their cause. But eventually Tolokonnikova also ended up getting really angry at Samutsevich for not writing her enough in prison. She said, "That's it, to me she is already dead. There will be no more talk of collaborating after this." That one made me really sad.

January had been a very bad month for Sami. He continued to post music every few days—mostly Bach, which, as I mentioned, helped him calm down. But our personal communications made me worry. There was one very disconcerting e-mail in which he wrote, "Maybe you'll think this is stupid, maybe you'll hit me"— and then he fell asleep. Why in the world would I hit him? Then there was a terrible voice message in which he kept stammering and saying how sorry he was, though he didn't owe me an apology or even an explanation. He said, "Sometimes it's like it's happening, it's like it's happening today, and I get so dizzy, and frightened. I'm—I'm—I'm—I'm sorry." There was a long pause and a lot of breathing. "I was not always, um, I wasn't always like this. I, um—I—I—I couldn't remember. It all started. Um. Hmm. It all started when Kakay was born. And I—I—I, uh, I couldn't, I was, I was, I was afraid. Um, I, um. I—I—I—I was. Hmm. I was afraid that I—I—I—I would, um, I—I would be like, um, like, um—um—um. I'm really sorry."

It seemed clear that the physical pain of the neuroma was triggering the painful memories, but I was also beginning to worry about how much medication he was taking. Juliane was too. On a relatively calm day, he told me he was aware of how complicated it was, trying to balance his pain regimen. He wrote, "Well, I know that morphine isn't good for me, anyway there's virtually no alternative when the pain is really bad. I've tried a lot of things in order to find a better solution, smoking weed helps as long as I don't have violent pain, and acupuncture shows some effect as a preventive therapy. But sometimes I need some heavy medication to get by, I need to withdraw twice a year at least, I do it whenever I get the feeling that morphine starts to rule my world, and for the time remaining I live with my addiction. I think I act rather responsible, I rarely drink alcohol and I eat well and I take care of my body. You don't have to worry. It's very sweet of you you'd like to take away the pain, I wouldn't want you to take it. I get by, I can handle it and it doesn't really put me down. Anyway your tenderness makes me want to kiss you. Most tenderly, Sami."

I'd said I wished I could just take it away from him for a while. I did. He didn't mean that kiss in a sexual way. Some people eroticize pain, whether by force of will or natural inclination, but Sami's not like that. When he's in pain, that's the last thing on his mind, and his usual aversion to other kinds of touch is exacerbated. I think that kiss was pretty abstract, even if it was tender.

At the end of the third week in January, they performed a microsurgery on his neuroma. Very shortly thereafter it became clear the surgery had failed.

My mother was also doing pretty badly. They'd moved her from the hospital to a nursing home. This was ostensibly a temporary situation. She wasn't sick enough to remain in the hospital, but it wasn't safe yet to have her at home, even with a visiting home health aide. There was just too high a risk that she'd fall again. When I went that month to visit her, they had a big sign on the door of her room saying "Fall Risk." She was supposed to call a nurse anytime she wanted to use the bathroom so that somebody could help her get there. But when she'd wake up in the middle of the night, she wouldn't remember to call the nurse, so she'd try to get to the toilet on her own. This would set off a really loud alarm, and somebody would come running. The alarm was terrifying, and my mother'd get even more confused and end up shouting obscenities at the nurses.

My mother was sharing a room with a woman named Margery. Margery was younger than my mom, but she weighed about four hundred pounds and was far less mobile. In fact, every time she wanted to use the bathroom, they had to bring in an enormous hydraulic contraption to hoist her out of her wheelchair or her bed, and then they'd transport her to the toilet, and then back again. It involved strapping a big canvas belt around her back and under her arms. Her ankles were very swollen and purple. When they'd hoist her, she'd moan in agony. Even though my mother can be pretty acerbic, and even though she was going through her own pain, she really felt for Margery. Who wouldn't? Margery also was concerned for my mother. Even though Margery's physical condition was direr, she could see how confused and disoriented my mother was when she woke up in the middle of the night. This didn't mean Margery wasn't bothered by all the alarms and cursing, though. In my mother's more lucid moments, she'd acknowledge that she was the roommate from hell. She'd frown and sigh and shake her head about that.

When the nursing staff was overburdened and Margery was already in her wheelchair, sometimes I'd offer to push her down to the dining hall at mealtime. She was very appreciative. Her breathing was shallow, and her voice was thin as a reed. She'd say to me,

"You know she's not in her right mind, don't you?" She meant my mother. She didn't mean it maliciously. She just wasn't sure if I understood. I'd say, "It's very difficult, I understand."

No one here can love or understand me.
Oh, what hard luck stories they all hand me.

After a while they moved Margery elsewhere so she could get some sleep. A couple of weeks later, my sister texted me that Margery had passed away.

I recorded a lot of uke covers around that time, just to keep myself from getting too blue.

I put out a call for requests, and I got some good ones. A friend's teenage daughter asked for a song from her favorite cartoon ("Daddy, Why Did You Eat My Fries?"). It was by Rebecca Sugar. Somebody requested Rihanna's "Birthday Cake." That one came out surprisingly well. As you know, I have a thing about cake. A pretty theatrical person I met told me he was crazy about Adriano Celentano, a cheesy Italian pop star, so I did "Mi Fa Male."

Although these are all pretty silly songs, my renditions sounded weirdly melancholy. The truth is, all my uke covers sound melancholy. Besides, despite their silliness, there were some inherently sad things in the songs themselves. "Mi Fa Male" says it right in the title: it hurts me. Rihanna's "Birthday Cake" was a duet with her abusive ex, Chris Brown—that's disturbing. And then there are the words to "Daddy, Why Did You Eat My Fries?": *I bought them, and they were mine. But you ate them, you ate my fries, and I cried, but you didn't see me cry.* When I sang that, I thought Rebecca Sugar might also be a fucking genius, but it may have been my emotional state.

When I'd mailed that package to Sami, they estimated that it would arrive in a week to ten days. I waited a couple of weeks, and then I asked him about it, but he said it still hadn't arrived. I figured maybe things got backed up over the holidays, but a week later I asked again, and it still hadn't gotten there. Sami was pretty doped up during that period, so he wasn't getting particularly worked up over the whereabouts of the thigh cozy. Once, he told me he'd asked his neighbors if they'd seen anything, but they hadn't.

I began to think it hadn't been such a good idea to leave that flask of Realism perfume in the package. Maybe the postal service had dogs sniffing international packages now. I didn't really think they'd come and arrest me—I figured if they found contraband in a package, they'd probably just throw it out the way they throw out liquids if you don't follow the protocol when you go through airport security.

It didn't make me too sad. I went back to the yarn store and got some more organic green wool. There were a couple of adorable pierced and tattooed young women working there. They were both knitting. I didn't want to buy too much again, so I picked up one large skein and asked them if they thought it would be enough to knit a tubular item, about twenty inches in circumference and about nine inches long. One said, "Yes, I think you should have enough. Um, what is it you're making, if you don't mind me asking?" I said I had a friend with an amputation, and I was making him a thigh cozy. She nodded and said, "Oh sure, I think that's enough yarn." I said, "I made him another one, but it got lost in the mail. I don't mind, though. You know how it is with knitting: it's never the thing itself that matters—it's the process of making it." Both of them knew exactly what I meant.

On Valentine's Day, which was a couple of months after I'd given that workshop at the University of Chicago, I received an e-mail from the opera singer, Natali Pandit. She thanked me for getting so many ideas percolating in her. She said, "I checked *I Love Dick* out of the library and also *How to Be a Person* (wait, is that actually what it's called?), and the checkout guy with whom I always have awkward conversations (because he mumbles and says things like 'what's going on?' which always takes me a while to register, translate & respond to) and I gave each other weird looks, hehe." I had recommended these books, though she'd misremembered the title of *How Should a Person Be*. Then she said, "I'm thinking about performing Handel's 'Lucrezia' naked. I think it works . . . but I need to think about it more . . . Here's a poem (below) I found in my drafts box just now. I never sent it . . . but I am sending it now!! :)" Needless to say, it was erotic.

I said to Olivia, "I think I may have created a monster." I meant it warmly. I realize it was probably massively presumptuous of me to assume any credit whatsoever for Natali Pandit's monstrosity.

That was the good news. But something really terrible happened that same day, though I wouldn't read about it in the paper until the next morning. Oscar Pistorius shot and killed his girlfriend. I didn't mention it to Sami. I was sure he'd find it upsetting.

Sami mentioned suicidal ideation very early in our correspondence. He said he'd always assumed he'd die young anyway and that he didn't find the idea frightening. There were many times he felt he'd rather be dead, especially when the pain was unbearable, but after Kakay was born, he decided that killing himself simply wasn't an option. A person might surmise that his heavy smoking was one manner of arriving at a mercifully early death through a kind of socially acceptable bad habit, but we all know people who manage to smoke heavily into their nineties. Anyway, after he told me that he sometimes longed for death and certainly always contemplated it without fear or aversion, I told him that I could understand that—I didn't find it strange. He was glad I understood. I guess some other people had told him he shouldn't really go around saying that kind of thing.

My grandmother died an agonizing death from breast cancer when my mother was thirteen. She has terrible memories of her mother's groans and the little bell she'd ring to call the nurse when the pain was unbearable. This surely influenced my mother's feelings about the right to die. She had Hemlock Society materials around the house for as long as I can remember. That organization later merged with another and became Compassion & Choices, which is obviously a more euphemistic tag. Derek Humphry, the founder of the Hemlock Society, was very pragmatic. He wrote the classic how-to book for self-deliverance, *Final Exit*. Despite the name of the society he founded, hemlock was not actually at the top of his list of methods. The recent updated edition includes a new suggestion involving helium and plastic bags, which is convenient because you don't need a prescription.

My father's repeated attempts at ending it all were through exsanguination, that is, opening his veins in a warm bath. My mother had to clean up after a couple of those. You would think that pills would be people's method of choice, but here in the United States, almost 54 percent of suicide attempts are through the use of firearms. My mother and I are great champions of gun control, while Carolyn is a staunch supporter of the NRA. But surprisingly, my mother announced to us over Thanksgiving dinner a few years ago that she herself had briefly (and legally) owned a gun. The idea was just to have it on hand in case she found herself in unbearable pain and needed to get things over quickly.

Eventually, though, she felt too weird about having a gun in the house, so she called the cops and asked them to take it away, which they did. She didn't tell this story with any particular melodrama nor comedic swagger. She was just saying that it happened. It was a little awkward. There we were, my sister, me, and both our sons, eating turkey and listening to this story. I was kind of dumbfounded, but Carolyn just dryly hacked, "Oh Mom, you wouldn't have shot yourself. You're too tidy for that. Think of the mess!" It's true; our mother is a very fastidious housekeeper.

When she started having severe pain and they put her on the meds, I realized that all that reading and planning were really for naught. Once it gets bad enough that you'd really want to do it, you're too confused and disoriented to remember what your plan was. That was a depressing revelation.

In a lucid moment, when she asked Billington to give her a DNR bracelet, he quietly lectured her about how precious life was, and then he told her that doctors weren't supposed to hand those things out unless a person was clearly at imminent risk of death, which she wasn't.

Once, Sami wrote me, "When I die they should write 'I've been sound and smoke' on my tombstone, actually it has to be in German cause 'Schall und Rauch' is a metaphor for 'nothing' or 'unimportant,' in English it's 'smoke and mirrors,' but sound and smoke have no limits and no borders and therefore I'd love it."

Toward the end of February, my mother lost her mind entirely. It was devastating. My poor sister. They'd begun calling her in the middle of the night from the nursing home hoping she could talk our mother down from a shrieking fit. During the worst one, she thought she was in the hospital to have a baby. She was screaming that she was in labor, and it was time to push. A couple of times Carolyn had to drive there at the crack of dawn the next day, but there wasn't a lot she could do, except consult with the staff and try to get Billington on the phone. He was phoning in prescriptions for antipsychotics, but when we researched these online, there seemed to be some counter-indications for the elderly. The truth is that our mother had had a couple of very small strokes in recent years, and we'd noticed mild confusion and memory loss since then, as well as an increase in the grouchiness that had always been, as the saying goes, part of her charm. I don't mean that facetiously. She was a salty old broad. It was charming.

When those little strokes were taking place, she'd have a spate of linguistic misfires, and in addition to gibberish, she'd toss in a few Tourette's-like obscenities. So it's not as though her current symptoms were completely new—but they were now unrelenting and pretty horrifying. The only good news was that she kept passing out. When I got there, my sister and I just looked at each other, speechless. We really hadn't anticipated this. When we weren't together, we were sending each other those phatic texts. There were sad emoticons frequently. I was trying to figure out which assets I could liquidate in order to help with the costs of what would surely be intensive, long-term caretaking. At the end of my March visit, I felt guilty leaving, but when I was with her she was mostly unconscious, and when she'd wake up, she thought I was Carolyn.

During those weeks, I was sort of on autopilot in my classes. Surprisingly, autopilot seemed to be working pretty well—in fact, I think my students felt like things were going swimmingly. Even my public lectures were fine. I'd just sit down in front of the computer and write them, and then I'd deliver them, and afterwards people would tell me I'd said something smart. My colleagues were very supportive. They knew what was going on, and they'd offer to pick up the slack, but I seemed to be holding things down on my own. Olivia gave me a lot of space. She'd been through something similar with her dad a few years ago. I'd tell Leon what was happening, and he was calm and sympathetic. He'd listen and pat me on the back, and sometimes he'd make some kind of joke about how in the future if I were ever in really dire straits like my mom, I could count on him to give me the old heave-ho off the balcony. He'd say, "Don't worry, Barbara, the next time you forget a word or a name or lose your keys or your reading glasses, it's alley-oop for you, right over the guardrail!" I'm constantly losing my reading glasses. Leon's called me Barbara since he was about nine.

Sami was also really not well. I told him I wished I could do something. I asked him if he minded having someone touch his hair when he was in pain. He said that was one thing he liked, he wished I could do that for him, it might make him feel better.

It was almost spring break. Because of all those trips to see my mother, I had a lot of frequent flyer miles. Miraculously, when I looked on the American Airlines website, it didn't seem hard to get to Cologne. I could use my miles, and I'd only have to pay some taxes on the ticket. I could go for four nights. I asked Sami if he wanted me to. He said yes.

I knew I couldn't stay with him—he said he had a guest room, but he already wasn't doing so well, and I didn't want to add any pressure. I thought I'd stay someplace cheap and just go by his place a couple of times. He said, "Maybe we can record some music together. :)" I wasn't sure that was going to happen, but I thought perhaps we could talk a little more about our collaboration and the dances and also the novel I wanted to write. If he was in pain, I thought I could just scratch his head a little. Maybe that would help.

I found a cheap little studio to rent in the Belgian quarter. The guy who usually lived there was named Max, and we exchanged a couple of friendly e-mails. He was going to stay with his girlfriend while I was there. He offered me tips on how to get there from the airport and things to see in Cologne.

All of these plans were very last minute.

I told my sister that I'd be in Europe for a few days but that she could reach me by text or e-mail if there was an emergency. I said I was going to be doing research. This did not feel to me like a misrepresentation.

I have an old friend from college named Abner Berg. He's now a highly regarded professor of constitutional law. I don't have a lot of friends like that—mostly I seem to know kooky musicians and poets and performance artists and the people who write about them. But Abner's also interested in those things. He himself is an enthusiastic, if somewhat sloppy, honky-tonk pianist, and he likes to debate things like censorship law in relation to the provocative performances of some of my friends, like Karen Finley. He has a little crush on Finley. I read some of the articles he publishes in law journals, and he reads my fiction.

I also like to ask him about intellectual property law. That's not his area of expertise, but he's happy to share what he knows. It's an interest of mine partly because of my communist tendencies but also because of that Lewis Hyde question of where artistic productivity comes from. People have a tendency to talk about appropriation as a postmodern phenomenon that's been facilitated by digital technology, but it's been around forever. Olivia loves to write centos, which are poems entirely constructed of lines from other poets. The form originated in the third century AD.

I find it interesting to consider the legal arguments regarding intellectual property, even though it ultimately goes so much further for me, into the realms of metaphysics, ethics, and aesthetics. All that said, I tend to investigate the law and obey it. And then think about it. Technically, all the uke covers infringe on intellectual property, except for the public domain ones. But because I never charge any money for them, I'm unlikely to be challenged, and the worst-case scenario would be a cease-and-desist order, telling me to take down a post, which I'd do. I always credit and tag the composer, and if I'm copping the phrasing of another musician's interpretation, I tend to note that as well. Most uke noodlers would call that bending over backwards—sort of like what I do with my characters, always asking if they're OK with what I'm writing.

Every few months, Abner and I will go out for a drink and talk about these things, and sometimes we'll go hear music together. A couple of days before my trip, we got together, and he asked what had been going on with me. I told him a bit about my mother, and he was very sympathetic, as his own mother has had some cognitive issues in recent years. Then I told him about Sami. I explained about his extraordinary musical gift and his difficulties expressing emotion, and I said we'd been collaborating, and I was thinking of writing a novel about him, and, actually, I was about to go to Cologne to visit him.

Abner didn't have quite the reaction some other friends had when I told them about Sami. That is, he found it an interesting story, but the next day he wrote me a quick e-mail saying, "last weeks' ny times magazine story about paul frampton, which i just read, and last year's events involving the notre dame player manti te'o, make me a little concerned for you! i shouldn't be, right? but like a doting friend, i am, a bit. xo abner."

Maybe you know those stories. Paul Frampton was a sixty-eight-year-old British particle physicist who met a beautiful Czech bikini model online. Her name was Denise Milani. Frampton and Milani had a very intense correspondence. He suggested they speak on the phone, but for some reason she was never able to. They did chat on Yahoo Messenger. She told him she was tired of being ogled in her bikini and was ready to settle down, but she wondered if an intelligent man like him could ever be proud of somebody like her. He told her of course he could. She finally invited him to meet her in La Paz, Bolivia, where she was doing a photo shoot. There was some confusion with his ticket. He missed a connection, and by the time he got to La Paz, she'd had to go to Brussels for another shoot, but she was sending him a ticket to meet her there. He needed to make a connection in Buenos Aires. There was just one thing—could he please pick up a bag she'd left in La Paz? No problem. Some guy delivered the bag to his hotel, but it was empty. He wrote Milani, and she explained that it just had sentimental value. He filled it with his dirty laundry and got on the plane to Buenos Aires. There was more confusion about his ticket. He finally got frustrated with all the mix-ups and decided to go back home to Chapel Hill, North Carolina, where he was a university professor. He was hoping maybe she'd meet him there after she finished these modeling gigs. Surprise: he got arrested when the airport security discovered a large amount of cocaine sewn into the lining of the bikini model's suitcase.

Well, the suitcase didn't really belong to a Czech bikini model named Denise Milani. Milani exists; she's a real person, and if you Google her, you find that she's selling a workout tape. She looks really fit. Whoever sewed the cocaine into the lining of the suitcase just borrowed her identity in order to buffalo Paul Frampton into being a mule for their drug smuggling operation. When the authorities contacted the real Denise Milani, she had no idea what they were talking about.

In the *New York Times* article, Paul Frampton is described as something of an "idiot savant." His ex-wife depicts him as having the emotional maturity of a three-year-old, though he's very good at particle physics. He was sentenced to four years and eight months for drug smuggling, but he'll probably be released early, because under Argentine law a foreigner can be expelled once he's served half his sentence.

Apparently this whole ordeal didn't deter Frampton from his dream of living happily ever after with a Czech bikini model. The article in the *Times* ended, "One of Frampton's last e-mails to Denise Milani was written on a pirated cellphone a month into his stay inside Devoto prison: 'I only think of cuddling all day and having sex all night with Denise Milani. How can you prove that you are Denise Milani?'" Wow.

Then there was the story of Manti Te'o. I think everyone heard about that one—Carolyn even mentioned it on one of my trips to see our mom. Te'o played a great season in 2012 despite the death of his grandmother and also the death of his girlfriend, Stanford undergrad Lennay Kekua, who was involved in a serious car accident and then was diagnosed with terminal leukemia. That was a pretty overwhelmingly sad story, except it soon came to light that Kekua was a fictional online persona created by some family friend of Te'o's, a guy named Ronaiah Tuiasosopa. Later, Tuiasosopa would tell Dr. Phil on national television that he was a "recovering homosexual." He said he fell in love with Te'o and then came up with the idea of having this fictional relationship with him online. Te'o, needless to say, was pretty confused by the revelation. He thought Kekua was a beautiful young woman. He'd told his family that he'd actually met her, but he later explained that he'd only said that because he thought they would think he was crazy if he told them he was having such an intense relationship with somebody he'd only interacted with on the internet.

Well, after I got Abner's e-mail, I read about both Frampton and Te'o. It's hard for me to write "Frampton" without thinking of that cover of "Baby, I Love Your Way"—the one Sami thought was sublime. Paul Frampton's story concerned me but maybe not for the reasons Abner thought it would. That is, I understood that he was implying that I was Paul Frampton in this story, a possible dupe for a drug-smuggling thug posing as an Eastern European bikini model—or in this case, who knows what kind of criminal mastermind posing as an Indo-Prussian autistic musical prodigy. But I was at least as uneasy when I read that personality assessment of Paul Frampton, an "idiot savant" with "the emotional maturity of a three-year-old." Sami had repeatedly characterized himself in almost exactly these terms.

I jokingly mentioned the story of the Czech bikini model to him. He thought it was funny.

Olivia actually wrote a cento for me once:

> I asked of my Muse, had she any objection?
> She smiled a little wan and ravelled smile.
> "A little, passionately, not at all?"
> "I know what you're going to say," she said.
>
> A pote is sure a goofy guy;
> A song is but a little thing,
> I am singing to you,
> I am unskill'd in speech: my tongue is slow.

What shall I do with this absurdity—
What should I say?
What syllable are you seeking,
What words are these have fall'n from me?

Whe-ooh, ooh, ooh, ooh, ooh!
Oh, what shall I do? I am wholly upset.
Let's dance the jig!
Let's get our dreams unstuck.

Vivid with love, eager for greater beauty,
I can't tell you—but you feel it.
Let's dance the jig!
Let's get our dreams unstuck.

She bade me follow to her garden, where
She does not mind a good cigar.
She gave a little cry and fell quite prone.
She sang, and I listened the whole song thro'.

You can see why I fell in love with Olivia. That line about being "unskill'd in speech" was obviously another case of false modesty—but then again, it probably also was when Matilda Betham wrote it.

I'd screwed up the courage to tell her about my travel plans. I wrote to her while she was in Montana. I don't know if it was because she was with her niece or out in the beautiful snowy plains or if she was just feeling placid, but she was entirely calm. She told me I'd like Cologne—aside from Berlin, it was probably the most queer-friendly city in Germany.

In the days leading up to my trip, Sami started to sound a little better. He was still on medication, but he seemed a little buoyed by my upcoming visit. He even made a reservation at a restaurant for the evening of my arrival, and he attached a Google map showing the route on the S-Bahn from Max's place to his. But he suggested we meet at the restaurant, which was close to where I'd be staying. He said he already had butterflies, but he was glad I was coming.

That message arrived the night before my departure. I had an easy trip to the airport. I was traveling very light. I'd decided not to take along my ukulele—I'd probably be too shy to play it in front of Sami anyway, although I thought if he were up for a jam I could sing harmony without embarrassing myself too badly. Or I could always dance. But when I got to JFK, there was a little catastrophe. I'd booked my flight through the American Airlines website, but the flight itself was on Air Berlin. There had been a scheduling change on the flight, and because I hadn't booked my ticket through Air Berlin somehow I failed to get word of the time change. It was leaving forty-five minutes earlier than I'd planned. At the Air Berlin desk, they told me there was no way I'd get through security and to the gate in time to board. I had a momentary thought of Paul Frampton missing his connection to La Paz. I tried to stay calm. Certainly it wasn't going to help matters if I freaked out. The Air Berlin people were none too apologetic—they blamed American— and the American people blamed Air Berlin, and they all pointed out—correctly—that I really should have given myself more time anyway. There were lines at both counters, and the representatives were pretty grumpy at first, but when I slathered them all with apologies for my own poor judgment and took them off the hook, they started to offer useful solutions. Finally, we figured out that I could rebook myself on a flight to Düsseldorf the next day and take a short train ride. The Air Berlin representative had lived in Düsseldorf, and she gave me detailed information about where and how to get the train to Cologne, and the train was cheap and went direct from the airport, and American eventually said they'd waive the fee to change my ticket, and it really wasn't such a bad situation.

I quickly wrote Sami saying, "Oops! Change of plans—my flight was rescheduled, and I missed it, but don't worry! I'll just be one day late, coming by train from Düsseldorf, arriving at Max's early in the afternoon on Thursday. Sorry!" He was concerned, but for me, not for him. He felt bad my journey was turning out to be arduous and hoped the airline would pay for my train ticket. They wouldn't, but that was no big deal. Sami said he was nervous but trying to chill. He attached a picture he took, apparently from the computer, of him sitting in a chair looking fidgety. The picture was blurry, and it seemed like he might be spinning a little in his chair. He ended his message, "Are you really coming?"

I went home and wrote Max that I'd be staying only three nights, not four, and I hoped it wouldn't inconvenience him, as he'd arranged to meet me with the key. He was very nice about it. He said the next day he'd be at work, but his dad could meet me, and it was no problem. I texted Olivia and Rebekah and told them about the hiccup in my plans. I had a beer with Leon who was, as usual, unflapped. I went to bed early and thought how comfortable it was to be lying down instead of sitting up in an airplane seat.

My flight the next day went smoothly, and so did the ride on the Deutsche Bahn. It was about noon when I got to Cologne. I rested a bit and cleaned up and then wrote Sami a quick message: "Well, this will surprise you: I lay down and went right to sleep! But then I woke up and took a shower, and I feel fresh as a daisy— but hungry! So I'm going out for a bit to find something to eat. Max just has a sad piece of salami, and I just have your pomegranate seeds." I'd brought Sami some chocolate-covered pomegranate seeds—among other things. I'd probably overdone it with the treats, oops. I'd managed to get a little replacement vial of that perfume—I ordered it on the internet. I even had gifts for Sami's friend and his son. I ended the message, "Well, if you don't write me by tomorrow, I may eat your pomegranate seeds. Don't say I didn't warn you. :)"

I went out foraging and came back with a few staples. Still nothing from Sami. After about two hours, I wrote, "Um, now I'm just a little worried about you. It's OK if you got nervous! Just tell me you're OK so I won't worry. Are you OK? I love you."

At ten thirty that evening, I wrote, "Well, I went out for a long walk. I thought I should go see the cathedral. You were right, it's beautiful at night. Rebekah wrote to ask after you, and I said you were missing, and she was worried, but I said sometimes you had panic attacks and maybe that was all, and maybe tomorrow you'd write, and maybe you wouldn't, but I think you'll be OK. I hope you're OK. I'm a little melancholy. I feel I should dance—maybe I will, I'm sure I won't be able to sleep for a while; it's only 4:30 in New York now. Look, I set out all the things I brought for you." Here I inserted a photo. "That's a real Pussy Riot mask. I thought Kakay might like to have it. And there's your thigh cozy, and a plastic deer, and an origami frog someone made for me once but I thought you should have it, and some tiny pieces of edible gold leaf to wrap olives in, and that weird T-shirt I thought Farrokh might like, and a little bottle of Realism, and of course the chocolate-covered pomegranate seeds I promised you. If you can't see me, can I leave these things somewhere for you? It would be so sad to take them home. Sami, I miss you, and I'm sad, but it's not your fault. But I wish you would just tell me you're OK. Then I'd cry just a little, and then I'd write something or dance something or sing something. Well, I guess I'll try to do that anyway—it's the only thing I know to do. I love you."

What was really weird was that something almost exactly like this had happened in a novel I wrote—that first one that Sami had read. In that novel, my narrator travels all the way to Bamako to meet her secret lover, but he doesn't show up, and it turns out there's been a miscommunication. He tries to warn her to remain in Paris because of an outbreak of dengue fever, but she doesn't get the message and ends up in a hotel room with a mosquito bite and a high fever, severe joint pain, nausea, vomiting, and an oozing rash all over her body. Fortunately, there was no dengue fever in Cologne, and Sami wasn't what you'd properly call my lover. But the setup was uncannily familiar.

After a dose of NyQuil, I had a fitful sleep, and awoke to find the following message: "it's like shouting at you—leave me alone—don't leave me.can't stand me, can't stand this. don't wanna say I'm sorry. this isn't me someone should smash my head so i can make my mind up. not stoned was a mountain that's my world lcocked in there make me numb don't wannafeel it i tried there is noother me no one know me forbeing better deep down inside so much better thats me doin drugs and guilt."

I think you can imagine how this made me feel.

I wrote, "It's ok Sami. I'm sorry I made you feel so anxious. I'm sorry if my writing you now makes you feel anxious. I'm writing you because I want you to know it's ok, everything will be just fine, but I don't think you should be alone. You should call Farrokh. I'll be here at Max's until Sunday morning. If you feel better and you want me to visit you, I will, but it's fine if you don't. If you want to write me and say, 'It's too much, this is too weird, please stop writing me, don't make any more dances about me,' I'll stop. I'll be very sad, but I won't be angry, and I'll just ask you to forgive me. I didn't want to frighten you; I thought you might love it. The drugs come and go, and your fear comes and goes. I'm right here. I'll go if you tell me to or else I'll just entertain myself—it's ok. If you see Farrokh, maybe you can ask him if he'd meet me for a coffee in Brüsseler Platz or someplace else, and I could give him all the things I brought for you, and he could give them to you when you feel better. I really think you should call him, though. I don't think you should be alone. I won't keep apologizing for writing so much. I know you want to be alone, but you don't have to read all this—maybe you'll want to read it when you feel better. I'm sad, but I'm sad because you're sad."

I imagine you may be thinking I am very kind, or you may be thinking I'm a torture artist or that I'm totally off my gourd.

After a few hours, Sami sent a voice recording. His voice sounded strange, and his speech was a little slurred. He said, "I should have told you, that it's so difficult for me to go out, it's so difficult to meet people, I should have told you, but I, it's—it's—it's—it's hmmmm it's—it's like I—I—I want I want to be, but I'm not. And I don't go—go—go out. I just—I just—I just when I have to. I'm—I'm—I'm just I'm too afraid, and I'm . . . I'm mmmmmhmm. I'm too. Afraid. I tried I tried I tried." Then he sniffled; it sounded like he was crying.

I wrote him, "Sami, everything is just fine! I mean me, I know you don't feel fine, but you will again, as fine as you can feel, I promise." I apologized again for writing so much, but I wanted to make sure he knew everything was really OK. I told him I understood that it was too much to hope for us to meet but that I'd still like to go over to his house and just leave my bag of gifts on his doorstep, since I'd come all this way. I asked if that was OK.

The next morning, there was another voice recording, but it was almost entirely composed of the sound of Sami snoring into his headset. I wrote him, "Sami, that was a funny message. I mean, it's not funny, it's sad, but if you think about it, it's kind of funny that you send me recordings sometimes of you sleeping. Maybe it's because you know I love John Cage. The last couple of minutes were like 4'33", just shorter. Sami, you didn't answer my question if I could leave your gifts by your door. Now I'm starting to feel a little obstinate. I think I'm just going to do it. I promise not to look in your window or talk to your neighbors or anything. It's rainy, but it's not that bad, and yesterday I went out in the rain with an umbrella and it was fine—at least it's not windy, and it's not that cold. In fact, I hear some birds singing now. I just checked the weather. Monday it's going to get nice and warm, but I'll be gone, oh well. Tomorrow cloudy but nicer than today. You see? Things always get better. Anyway, I was saying I was feeling obstinate, so I'm going to take the train to your house today. I think I'll get there around two. I won't ring the bell, I'll just leave a bag for you. Surely your door has a doorknob or a handle or something I can hang a bag on. If you want, you can peek out of a curtain and see me. If you want me to ring the bell, you can tell me to and I will, but I think you'll still feel too afraid, and that's OK. Wait until 2:15 or so, and then I'll be blocks away, and you can reach out the door and find the bag. I'll also send you a message saying, 'I left you the bag.' I think I may use a fabric bag of Max's—he has a bunch of them in the kitchen that say 'research now.' I don't think he'll miss one, and I'll leave him a gift. Did I tell you I crocheted something for his father on the train? An iPod cozy—he seemed to like it. Now I just looked up yarn stores in Cologne, and apparently there's one out past your neighborhood a little further north. Well, we'll see, maybe I'll be too tired, but if not, maybe I'll go get some yarn to make something for Max. I would do this anyway, even if I weren't taking his shopping bag. He has about eight of these identical ones, plus some others—maybe twenty all together. Europeans are so much better than Americans about shopping bags. My people love to waste plastic. It makes me crazy. As you can see, I'm getting kind of excited to leave you your gifts. Then maybe I'll get some yarn, come back to Max's, and make him something. And I'll read and try to sleep early because I need to wake up early tomorrow to go to the airport. You should sleep too. OK. I'm leaving soon. I love you."

I'd already left Max's with my bag of presents, and I was sitting on the S-Bahn shooting toward Von-Ketteler-Straße when I got a message that began: "OK, this gets me super nervous." He said that, indeed, the whole situation was funny, at least he was—he was ridiculous, sitting there twitching and jerking around. He said his heart was pounding; he could barely breathe. He didn't know if it was a series of panic attacks or just one long one that he was taking little breaks from. It had started Wednesday night. He said at some moments he felt he needed to cut himself, to cut his hands off, but then he'd sit and look at himself as though he were a stranger, and he felt detached, and he felt no empathy for himself at all.

He asked me not to go to his house. He said, "I suppose it will get worse when I know you'll be close, I'd like to beg you not to do it, beg you on my knees cause it feels like dying." He said if I went there, he'd want to throw a door open, but he'd also want to run away. He said he felt flayed: it was as though he had no skin, and every nerve was exposed. His bones felt broken. It was like every beating was coming back, pounding through his bones. He said his tormenter wasn't outside of himself. It was in him, and this was the problem, the reason there was no escape—except maybe one. "My other me will get up and inject some mercy and then I'll be numb. It makes him furious when I'm away and he shows me that he rules over me, this is when I started to live in my universe. I'm insane. You could say I'm also obstinate, not a little, but a lot, and it's irrational and I know it." He said one day maybe he'd manage to kill himself. He said, "I like the idea of going to sleep and stop the pain." In fact, he'd almost done it on his birthday. I thought, "Oh shit, I didn't say anything on Sami's birthday." I always forget birthdays, and as I said, I don't like to attach gifts to specific holidays—I prefer to give them randomly, all the time. I hadn't thought Sami would need special attention on his birthday, but apparently he did. "It was a sad day and I thought it would be nice not to feel anything anymore, but I just took enough to sleep. If I didn't have Kakay, I'd do it, I told him that giving up is no solution, but I lied to him, it is . . . I don't think there's any sense in this life, maybe some people make sense, but I don't. All I do is pretending and I'm tired now. You are wonderful, Barbara. I'm going to rest my mind and stop the pain now, I'm so afraid. Do you think we come back once we die? I'd like to have another life, everything went wrong right from the start in this life, it isn't fair I think. Please forgive me."

My blood froze. There I was on that commuter train, with my ridiculous bag of treats. I thought, "Jesus Christ. I pushed him over the edge."

I quickly typed with my thumbs: "Sami, stop. I'm on the train now. I'll be at your house in twenty minutes, and now I have to ring your bell because this message is so frightening, and I'm afraid you'll hurt yourself. Who will I call? Don't open the door if you don't want to, but at least shout through the door that you're OK, or I'll have to call a neighbor or someone." I felt so idiotic. I didn't even know what number you're supposed to call when you have this kind of emergency in Germany. What the hell had I done?

Sami wrote, "Don't! I'm OK I have to care for my son so I cannot go away I don't want to end up in some mental ward."

I looked at that. Maybe he'd exaggerated just slightly. I wrote, "Thank you. You terrified me. Don't do that again. Close your eyes and put on headphones. In about fifteen minutes, I'll be gone. I will have quickly left you your things and disappeared. Don't scare me like that anymore. I love you."

The train stopped at the Köln-Stammheim station. I quickly got my bearings. Fortunately it wasn't raining—there was just a slight mist in the air. I'd printed out the Google map, which estimated that my walk would take twenty-five minutes, but I was half-running the whole way and got there pretty quickly. Von-Ketteler-Straße was a quiet suburban street. Number eleven was on the corner. It was painted yellow, and there were lace curtains in the window. Something seemed a little weird. Sami had sent me a photo of the house, but I thought I remembered it being darker, with some ivy on it. I opened the garden gate and walked up the little path to the front door.

There were two recycling bins, some potted geraniums, and a seed catalog on the front step. I looked at the bell on the door. Under it was a small nameplate: "Schuler."

I was confused. I stood there for a second. I looked at the windows. There didn't seem to be any movement. I took my bag and hung it on the doorknob. I walked back down the little path to the sidewalk and stared at the house. What if I'd gotten it wrong? I tiptoed back and retrieved my bag of gifts. I pulled out my phone and wrote Sami, "Is your house number eleven? The door says Schuler."

No answer.

There was a nice-looking middle-aged couple in the front yard next door. They were gardening. I said, "Entschuldigen Sie, sprechen Sie Englisch?" They smiled and said, "Yes, can we help you?" I gestured toward number eleven and said, "Is this the home of Sami?" They looked confused. I said, "Sami Zazai, a young man with one leg? He's a musician." They shook their heads and said there was no one of that description on Von-Ketteler-Straße.

I stood there for a minute, and then I wrote Sami, "Um, are you by any chance a Czech bikini model?" I didn't yet hit send. I began wandering back toward the station, but I got turned around at one point and went pretty far out of my way. I was still holding my phone. I was trying to type with my thumbs as I walked, but my hands were shaking. I wrote, "Your neighbors on Von-Ketteler-Straße never heard of you. I got a little confused. I kept the frog and the mask and things. Maybe I'll leave them for Max. Do you want to tell me anything? I'm not really sad, just a little disoriented because I thought I knew the novel I would write and the dances I would make, but now I think maybe you wrote the novel and choreographed the dances, and I'm a character, which would surely serve me right. Well, I'd like to know who you are and where you are, but I think maybe you won't say. It was still one of the most beautiful years ever, and I think the dances I made for you were the most beautiful dances I ever made, and I'll still make the blue one to music and the gold one to the Paganini, and I'll credit the music to Sami Zazai unless you tell me to credit it to a Czech bikini model. I still love the idea of you."

After a short pause, Sami answered, "I didn't mean to terrify you about wanting to hurt myself, it's just telling the truth for a change cause in fact I pretty much feel like doing it but I also feel like meeting you but there's a big difference between what I'd wish to do and what I'm actually doing." He said he knew it was a "disgusting" way to be; it was fear that drove him, but fear made all animals aggressive. He said his aggression was turned in on himself, but he ended up hurting other people, which just made him hate himself more. He called himself a "bad bad man." It struck me that he almost never referred to himself as a man like that. I don't mean that he had obscured his gender; I just mean that he tended to speak of himself as though he were somehow speaking of a child. He said, "I cannot stand people to come close and I desperately long to be close to someone. I should have told you that it would drive me mad, it would have been responsible but I thought, I wished, I thought please please make me act normal for just some days and explain everything. I'll try to explain. I have to sleep a bit. I'm sorry Barbara, not everything was a lie, and I love you."

It wasn't very reassuring.

I'd stopped feeling apologetic about writing so much. I sent him a long message when I got back to Max's.

"I wanted to write, 'Hello, Sami,' but now I'm not sure if that's your name. Everything is so confusing. Anyway, whoever you are, I made it back to Max's, but it took me forever because I got disoriented on my way to Köln-Stammheim station. I walked very slowly to the train wondering what was real and what was imaginary, and I wasn't sad, really, or upset, just kind of confused and wondering what to do about our collaboration. It's funny, you'd think if anybody could collaborate with a fictional person, it would be me, but even for me this was disorienting. Well. So I got on the wrong train somehow and got a little lost, but finally I made it home, and here it's warm and dry. Are you somewhere in Cologne? Well, don't answer that. Of course, I want to know everything, if you're a Czech bikini model or an enormous German lady like I first said you might be or an elderly particle physicist. If you have one leg or two or three. Did you really make all that music? You don't have to answer that either, or if Kakay's real.

"It's very easy for you to check, but to quote Popeye, I yam what I yam. A naked lady with a ukulele. Leon's real, even though he appears to be a dream, and so are my friends. My lovers are too, except that that kind of love is always kind of illusory—that's what my novel was about, the one you read, that we're always kind of telling ourselves a story when we're in love. But it's true that I loved that person, and he was a great artist, one of the great artists of our time, and it's true that Olivia's an astonishing poet, and that's why it didn't seem so far out of the realm of possibility that I should encounter someone so strange and wonderful as you seemed to be. Maybe you are some of those things.

"I don't always think it's bad to misrepresent oneself. In fact, I wouldn't use that word, and I certainly wouldn't use the word *lying*. But in my case, I always call it fiction. Even in my fiction, if I say, 'This really happened,' then it's true. It really happened. I find this more interesting. And I like being transparent. Or naked.

"I seem to be talking to myself. Before I felt I was talking to you, but I think the thing that makes it hard even to try to talk to you as though you are real is that you went so far as to say you might want to throw open the door when I arrived at your house, but you couldn't, because it was Herr Schuler's house. There were little potted plants and a seed catalog.

"Do you know someone who lives on Von-Ketteler-Straße? It's a pretty street. The neighbors seemed nice in a kind of bourgeois way. I don't mean that to sound disparaging. They wanted to be helpful.

"Well, I guess I can't really decide what to do about the dances or the novel until you give me another story. I'm afraid I won't believe it though, and it will be so hard to make it work. Hmm. Does the novel break in the middle? What happens to Sami? I don't want you just to turn out to be fictional. That's so predictable. It's what Abner thought—this kind of thing happens all the time, and the internet is crawling with Czech bikini models. The curious thing is the music. I feel certain you recorded 'Águas de Março,' and if I listen to it now, I'll just feel like I love you again. Tell me the Paganini is also you. And the Rachmaninoff. Well, that I could let go of, the Rachmaninoff. But the others would break my heart a little if they weren't you.

"I don't know what to say about your voice messages. In a way they matter less, if they're true or not, because the dances were all about finding technique where there seemed to be none. So it would almost make sense if they had artifice. It's so confusing. I wanted to give you something beautiful.

"I'm not sure if you gave me beautiful things. I think so, but the most beautiful thing was that you made me want to make things for you, so I guess I should still say thank you, Du bist so wunderbar and all of that, though it feels kind of weird to say it, and it may take me a little while to get used to it.

"Will you tell me something honestly? You said today you were aggressive, though before you said you weren't. Are you? I kind of need to know how dangerous you are. That's a silly question to ask a person who says he lives in a house he doesn't live in. Oh well.

"I wish you would tell me everything."

I spent my last night in Max's bed tossing and turning. I had a dream that Leon and I were in a freight elevator, and it was falling, and somehow I knew I'd be OK, but I was worried about Leon. When I woke up, there was a message from Sami. He said he'd meant to send it in the evening, but he fell asleep while writing it, so he was sending it when he woke up, at dawn. He said he was sorry

I got confused and lost. He wasn't a bikini model; he was only what he'd tried to tell me: a freak with some talent and a lot of paranoia. He said, "I didn't intend to start loving you, but you're very wonderful, it's hard not to love you. Also it's the most beautiful thing I've felt for a long time. So I didn't stop it. Well, you didn't ask if that was fictional, but I thought maybe it's important. Well, for me it is crucial in a way, and maybe it's even very logical for someone like me to love someone who lives on another continent, far away, that's very safe." He reiterated some of the things he'd always held about his existence: he was a musician, he lived in Cologne, he'd been married once for a year, he had a son, he had Asperger's and an anxiety disorder, he stammered when he was nervous, emotionally demanding situations put him to sleep, he lost half of his leg in an accident three years ago, since then he'd had a problem with opiates, he'd fucked up each and every relationship he'd ever had, everybody loved his music and when he was making it he felt free, he wanted to open a door and let me in, he couldn't because he was too afraid. There was one revelation, a significant thing he hadn't previously told me because he hadn't wanted to betray the confidences of others concerned and because he felt his own part in that story was nothing to be proud of. I won't tell it here for the same reasons. It involved a certain lack of judgment but was neither criminal nor difficult to understand, just sad.

He said he was at fault for not communicating the extremity of his paranoia. That's why he'd lied about the address. He said, "That was really a lie, not fiction. If everything else were a fiction then this would be too, but I just lied about that because I was afraid." But he said that, in a way, he now understood that he had kind of turned us both into characters. He said he did very stupid things when he felt under pressure, and he was ashamed to say he'd lied about the address. He thought he'd meet me that first night in the restaurant and explain. He'd really made that reservation. Then everything fell apart.

I said, "I'm sorry I keep asking questions. I should probably just say, 'I'm sorry too, and I should have listened when you said you were paranoid and not made such a long trip because I should have known better.' But I still want to ask you things just so I can understand." I wanted to know if Farrokh and Minoo were real people, and Juliane and Sabine too, and if the photographs were really of him and if Minoo took them. I asked again about the music and if he'd really lived in New York and if the photos of his parents were real and if it was true his father beat him. I asked about the story of the piano teacher who touched him. I said, "Is it fair for me to ask you if any of these things are true, because maybe if you're really this unstable sometimes things seem true to you that aren't? I'm asking because you said you made us both characters, and I'm trying to understand how much was made up. I guess I couldn't really judge you badly for making things up if you did because I'm the one who said that we all do that in love, imagine ourselves and the other person to be characters in a way. So it's really very silly of me to ask you for the truth. Although everything I told you was true. There's nothing I wrote or said to you or sent you that I'm ashamed of, and there's nothing I'd mind if someone else saw; when I was most naked, I was most clothed."

I apologize for the melodrama. I was kind of in shock.

I had to finish that message so I could shower and go to the airport. I ended it, "Maybe we should write, but less. What do you think? Or should I write you when I've finished the dances and the book? I'm not sure. I'm confused. Well, it was still such a beautiful year. I think I still love you for that."

I took the S-Bahn to the airport. It was smooth and efficient like everything else in Cologne. But when I got to the security checkpoint, I saw a sign showing what things were prohibited—like we have in the United States and like that sign at the post office that I'd disregarded when it prohibited my perfume. And there on the sign was a picture of a bottle with a skull and crossbones on it, and next to it was the German word: *Gift*.

My mouth dropped open, because I knew that, but I'd forgotten it—in German, *Gift* is poison. The title of the novel I wanted to write, the novel about Sami and Tye and eros and the economy and collaboration and the experiment that began with the uke covers—that book was, in my mind, called *The Gift*—after Mauss, and Lewis Hyde's reading of Mauss, and Graeber's, and mine. It was meant to be funny, the title, because it's been regifted so many times. Seriously, type in "The Gift" on the Amazon Books page. You won't believe how many people have used that title. And it had all started as a kind of joke, an experiment to see if I could produce a ridiculous surplus of unoriginal gifts of purely sentimental value. Then Sami and I had spent nearly a year giving each other gifts, excessive ones, beautiful ones, and I'd been thinking about his gift, his Inselbegabung, which is wonderful but also a terrible burden. And it was so devastating to think that my gifts, maybe even the beautiful ones, maybe even this novel, might be also poisonous for him, and maybe his gift was also poisonous for me. I'd thought maybe the hazardous thing was the Realism. I could understand that. Maybe the whole thing needed to remain in the realm of the Imaginary. They'd tried to tell me that at the US Post Office. Now the Germans were trying to tell me the dangerous thing was the gift itself.

I was almost sick in the airport, but I managed to get on my plane and get home.

When I got back to New York, Arto had sent me his guitar solo for the blue dance. And despite everything that had happened, I made it exactly as I had made the blue dance to words. I did it over and over, and sweat was dripping off my body. I used the very last take. I'd carefully hung royal blue curtains as a backdrop, and I'd made myself a tutu out of blue tulle. But when I was editing the dance, I couldn't seem to get it to look right. It needed to be more electric. I tried reversing the colors again, the way I had in that hand dance.

Suddenly all the fabric disappeared. The terrifying blue thing was me.

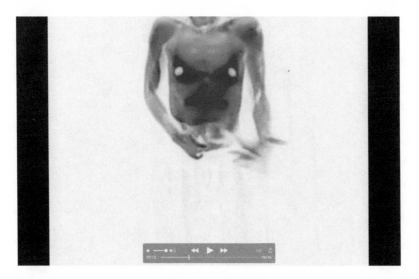

Part III

WHEN I GOT BACK TO NEW YORK FROM COLOGNE, THE OTHER thing waiting for me, besides Arto's guitar solo, was a message from Sami. He answered all of those questions I'd asked in the affirmative. He said that the things he'd told me about himself and his family and friends were true. He also answered my earlier question about aggression. He said he hadn't answered it before because it was so confusing for him to even contemplate it. His aggression was all self-directed—he never even raised his voice with other people. He felt so much fear that it was difficult for him to understand anyone being afraid of him. I didn't need to be afraid. He said, "If you want me to stop writing you and leave you alone I will do it. I will disappear if you want me to. If I have hurt you too much I understand, it was all my fault, it was a beautiful year, I was happy, I'm sorry, maybe I shouldn't love you. Excuse me, I'm getting a little desperate."

I answered, "Sami, old habits die hard. Look, I'm writing you again." I told him my trip had been all right. I got home and saw Leon, who cheered me up a little, and I made a dance (I'd send it later), and I said Rebekah was coming over soon. I apologized again for possibly having provoked his meltdown. I told him about the sign at the airport, the one about the poisonous gift, and I said that when I got home, I looked again at Lewis Hyde's book because I thought I remembered something about that and found a sad quotation there from the poet May Sarton: "There is only one real deprivation . . . and that is not to be able to give one's gift to those one loves most . . . The gift turned inward, unable to be given, becomes a heavy burden, even sometimes a kind of poison. It is as though the flow of life were backed up." I said it was sad because I knew he felt that sometimes—there were things I was sure he wanted to give Kakay that he couldn't. Maybe there were things he'd wanted to give me, and certainly there were things I'd wanted to give him, but couldn't. I apologized again if I'd made him feel afraid.

When Rebekah came over, she really wanted to throttle somebody. To be fair, she wasn't just angry with Sami or even with me. She was also angry with herself. She'd been sort of excited about the idea of Sami and me meeting, because she loved the dances so much. But then when I wrote her from Cologne about what had happened, she told her husband, and he blew his top. He couldn't believe she'd let me go. He said, "That's how people end up hacked into pieces, packed up in ziplock bags in somebody's freezer!" She asked me what Olivia had said, and I explained that we hadn't really talked about it yet. I managed to talk her down from her frenzy, and I convinced her that it was statistically unlikely that I would have gotten dismembered, but she still thought it was a distinct possibility that somebody was "fucking with my mind."

That's an interesting expression.

Old habits die hard is also an interesting expression. When Sami wrote me back, he said it wasn't one he usually liked, since he'd gladly give up many of his own, but he was very happy I still wanted to write him. He said he wasn't even sure if it was my visit that had been the trigger; sometimes it could be just a smell or a color or a sound. Anyway, he was feeling calmer, and he'd spoken with Farrokh (who said what I'd said, that Sami should have called him as soon as he started to panic, but he could never think that rationally when a meltdown was happening). Soon he'd start his drug withdrawal, which was hard, but he knew what to expect as he'd done it before. He was very glad I was home safe and had people with me.

Well, I went to bed that night feeling relatively calm, but the next morning I awoke in a panic thinking, "Barbara, why do you persist in holding on to this fiction?" I wrote Sami a vaguely hysterical message in which I told him exactly that. I said, "If it were all a fiction, it could still be just as beautiful, a fiction based on a fiction, instead of based on something real, so I'm not sure why it matters to me, except there was that one part you didn't answer, and it's the strangest part: why you didn't just say, 'It's not my real address! I'm sorry, I lied because I was afraid!' Why did you say, 'If you come to my door, I'll be in agony! I'll want to throw open the door and say, "Finally!"' But it wasn't your door. That's the most confusing part. Surely you understand that any reasonable person would doubt everything after that. Why do I want to believe you? What difference does it make? If it were all true, how could you show me anyway? I don't even know." As I reread my message it has slightly terrifying resonances with that message Paul Frampton wrote to Denise Milani from the jail in Buenos Aires. "Sometimes I think either way it doesn't matter, and maybe we can still collaborate even if it's completely fictional. Then I think it's too implausible; if no one else could believe it, how could I? As you can imagine, no one else could believe this. Rebekah was very angry with me. I told her I asked you if you were dangerous and you said no, but obviously this wasn't particularly satisfactory to her. I started to think that the only reasonable ending to your part of the story was that sign about the forbidden Gift in the airport in Cologne. It makes me so sad, though, to think that the gift ends up poisonous. It's not the story I wanted to tell. I don't believe gifts are poisonous! At least I gave that T-shirt I brought for Farrokh to Max—he seemed to like it. But who in the world will want your thigh cozy? What did the Schuler family do with the first one that I mailed to their house? That must have been so confusing. Look, you have everyone confused."

Sami wrote back, "I was in agony because the door I sent you to wasn't mine and I wished I could open the door, my door, tell you not to go there because you wouldn't find me! But I failed to do that, instead I panicked. How can I explain if my actions are not rational when I am afraid?" He said he also didn't think that gifts were poisonous, but objects, physical objects, often frightened him. He preferred weightless gifts, the songs and dances and words we'd exchanged. Objects frightened him because in the past his father had used them to control him, or somehow to feel that he'd compensated for the beatings. Sami was afraid of feeling indebted—it was irrational, but it was how he felt.

As for being dangerous, "I was often told that I was bad, inappropriate, ridiculous, a curse, a judgment from Allah, a nul. Should I add implausible, dangerous, and a liar? Would that be more plausible? This is how my story ends?" Then he asked the terrible question: "Was it all about your fiction, Barbara? I don't understand. If you cannot turn it into a story, it's not true? No, I didn't act right at all. I messed it all up, and that's terrible. I have everyone confused and sad, and I'm sorry. I can only beg you to forgive me. But I don't understand if you're talking about your next novel or about our friendship or if it's all the same or if you're telling me that you can't believe me. Does our 'story' end at the airport in Cologne, or is it just your fiction? Am I supposed to end with a forbidden gift sign? Well, I'm still here, but what symbolism. It's almost seductive, what a great ending. If everything is just fiction, do you believe that I love you? I should try to play some music, that would be reasonable. Please tell me if you want me to leave you alone, will you?"

Imagine what I felt.

When I told her, Olivia was surprisingly calm about what had happened. She didn't rub it in—she just listened and thought about it and asked me if I thought he was really capable of suicide. I said if this were all true, and if he were, it probably already would have happened, years ago. I wasn't sure if she was asking that empathetically. I thought for a second that the question almost sounded competitive. But then I told myself that was a horrible projection.

Did I believe Sami or didn't I? If I tried to look at this rationally, it seemed there were a few possibilities. He could be real and in great pain, in which case I'd obviously been the impossibly cruel one to think only of my novel, never mind having overloaded such a sensitive person with all that intimacy. Or he could have been lying about everything, in which case I was a ridiculous dupe. Or he could have been lying about some things, but who knew how many? I had to respond as though he were real, because if he were, it would be heartless to do anything else. But I also had to acknowledge that there was a chance that he wasn't. I had to decide to believe him but to prepare myself for another possibility.

I told him, "I'm sorry I confused you about fiction. Your music is real; if I write a novel, it will be real; and my dances are real. It was a lie when you told me the wrong address. It would have been fiction if you had said, 'I'm giving you this address because you insist on having an address, but it's a fictional address—I can't tell you my real address.' I wish you'd said that. I'm sorry you feel uncomfortable about objects, but I guess I have to accept that. I have no difficulty accepting any kind of gift. The gifts that delight me most are art, especially music. Gifts never make me feel obligated, though they often make me feel inspired, so I make something in response but never out of a sense of debt. I'm a communist and a feminist. I'm kind of making fun of myself when I say that but not really. That's what those things mean to me—to enjoy giving pleasure because it gives me pleasure, never out of debt or obligation. This is also how I feel about sex. All of these things I've told you before."

All of these things I've told you before.

I told Sami I wondered if maybe the degree of his terror when I went to Cologne had something to do with all the fentanyl he'd been taking.

My sister had the same question about our mother, and she was right. After that catastrophic night, the one when she thought she was in labor, our mother was briefly hospitalized and put under psychiatric evaluation. The psychiatric staff reviewed her charts and agreed that she'd been egregiously overmedicated, and they began to dose down all the narcotics. They couldn't make her go cold turkey, but they pulled her off the fentanyl as quickly as they could and reduced the morphine. Her pain was no worse at all, and the cognitive problems improved almost instantly. There was some friction with Billington, who was resistant to admitting an error, but eventually even he apologized to our mother. Carolyn was pretty steamed, but she's not really a litigious person, and she wanted to handle things gently. We agreed that our mother should probably have a new primary physician with a geriatric specialty, but we wanted her to stabilize first. Mostly, it was just a massive relief to see our mother's mind returning.

It was a great relief to our mother as well. She was a little dazed, and she couldn't remember a lot of the things that had happened. Carolyn wasn't shy about letting her know that she'd blown a gasket. Our mother listened to the stories of some of her escapades as though hearing about somebody else. She'd shake her head, her eyes wide, imagining this poor old broad who seemed to have gone to hell and back. She retained some hallucinations from the worst period as though they were memories, but fortunately, she didn't remember the pain.

One day I called her, and she began to tell me about the week she was under psychiatric observation. She had a strong impression that she spent that week at the mansion of some millionaire filmmakers. She said they were very kind to her and that they had held a special screening for her of a film they'd made years ago, starring Dr. Billington as . . . a doctor. She said, "He was very convincing in the role." She seemed to think Dr. Billington was a movie star.

I said, "Well, Mom, I think that probably didn't happen—I was in constant contact with both you and Carolyn that week, and I'm pretty sure you didn't leave the hospital. I don't think you stayed at a mansion." My mother hesitated and said, "Well, of course I wasn't entirely well. I may be a little confused. Maybe it was just a few days, not a whole week . . ."

I said, "Hmm."

After a while, she stopped being confused like this. She'd still forget things, and she'd misplace her glasses, but as I already told you, I do that kind of thing myself all the time.

Two weeks after I'd gotten back, Olivia had what I guess you'd call a delayed reaction. She came over one evening to hang out, and she seemed a little on edge. She said she had a headache. I offered her my famous Reiki—I was kind of joking, but she didn't look very amused. I offered her a beer instead, and she said she'd get it herself. She was in the kitchen, and I was sitting on the couch where I couldn't see her. We hadn't been talking about my trip or anything related to Sami, but I had a feeling she might be thinking about that. There was a pause, and then I heard her yelling, "I just don't know why the fuck it wasn't enough! I was here!" And then there was a horrifying thud. She'd slammed her fist into the counter. It dislodged the shelving below. I suddenly remembered that story that Sami had told me about that lover of his who'd kicked the door off a refrigerator.

Olivia hadn't just broken my shelving: she'd also cracked the fourth metacarpal bone in her right hand. I took her to the emergency room. That was a very hard night. They gave her Percocet.

When I asked Sami if he thought his meltdown might have had anything to do with his own meds, he told me he'd already thought of that possibility himself. In fact, right after I'd left, he'd asked Farrokh to come and clear out his stock of "killer candy" and also the morphine. The withdrawal was excruciating, but he'd been through that before. He talked to Chinonye, and she put him in touch with a colleague of hers who was a pain specialist. When this man heard about Sami's reaction to fentanyl, he was "gobsmacked," and told him they were going to find a better solution. He wanted to implant a thin cannula into Sami's stump so that when the pain was bad they could inject the drugs directly into the nerve. There would be less medication running through his system. Also, he put a little metal pin in Sami's ear, like "permanent acupuncture." This would diminish Sami's cravings for morphine. In fact, Sami said that after they put the pin in, he even felt less like smoking.

During his initial withdrawal period, Sami spent a lot of time throwing up, drinking weak tea, and sweating in his bed. But once he seemed to be feeling a little better, I sent him the blue dance, the one to Arto's electric guitar. I wasn't sure what he'd make of it, but he responded much as he had to the blue dance to words—he found it very "impressing." He hadn't been sure about the idea of "noise guitar," but it moved him, the intensity of the playing. It evoked his own sense of those moments of feeling flayed, exposed, and electric, and once again, he recognized something of himself in my spastic motion—but distanced from himself, he didn't mind looking at it. Even that blue wasn't making him uncomfortable the way it usually did. He said he thought maybe after watching it so many times his associations with that color were changing. It wasn't so frightening. He made a double smiley emoticon.

We talked a little about what it meant, for me to have tried to take into my body the anxiety in his voice, and for Arto to have taken it from me and made it music, and then for it to go through my body again and back to Sami. It was different from empathy; it was taking, and it was giving, but it was confusing to say which was happening when, and that brought us back to conversations we'd had about sex. And Sami sent a tender voice message in which he reflected on that, and then I sent him back another hand dance, the gold one. And I made it again directly on the computer, with the Photo Booth app, and it reversed my hands, so the left looked like the right, and the right looked like the left. Again the two hands were my hands, but they looked like two lovers, and still you couldn't say which was right and which was left, and I told

Sami when I sent it that it was a mirror image because of Photo Booth—I wear my thumb ring on my right hand, not my left hand—but I asked him, knowing that, "Which hand is you?" I got confused when I watched it. And he said the beautiful thing about sex was exactly that: it was confusing whose body was whose, and where one began and where one ended, and I agreed. And a little while later, he posted a beautiful piece of music on his site, an extended improvisation on acoustic guitar called "You."

When I began writing this novel a couple of months ago, I asked Sami if he wanted to look very much as he really does or if he wanted me to change some things a lot or maybe just a little. For example, I could change the side of the leg that he lost from the right to the left. He said maybe it would be nice if I could change that, because if he still had his right leg, it would be easier to drive and to use the pedal on the piano. He could do those things with his prosthesis, but it would be a little easier if we changed things around. So I did that. I wish I could really do that for him.

I thought about having Olivia break her left hand, not the right, so she could at least write with a pen while it healed, if not type. But that didn't make much sense. People punch things with their dominant hands.

After Olivia hurt herself, we took a few days apart, but then went back to our sporadic schedule of seeing each other. The mood was muted but not angry. As for Sami, we also settled back quickly into our old pattern, despite the catastrophe that was my trip to Cologne. Rebekah was less inclined to forgive and forget so easily. She'd make a kind of growling sound every time Sami's name came up. I'd shown her one of the e-mails I'd sent him when we were still sort of flailing and trying to figure out whether we should continue to collaborate and how. It was when I decided to believe him but retain some kind of escape hatch just in case. In that message, I was sympathetic, and I took responsibility for my own lack of judgment, but I told him he needed to get his act together, and he needed to tell me the truth from now on. If he were going to say anything fictional, he needed to call it that. Rebekah approved of the ground rules, but she was going to reserve judgment. So for a while, every time I mentioned Sami she'd add, "If he really exists. Ahem." But slowly, over time, she started to soften. Mostly she wanted to see the dances I was making and talk about the novel. Those, she really believed in.

For his part, Sami told me he'd ordered Rebekah's last novel, as what I'd told him about it made him curious.

He'd also looked at Olivia's translations of Brecht. He found them impressive.

I'm aware I'm not saying enough about Olivia. I'm not saying enough about Olivia, and we weren't saying enough to each other. Maybe it was cowardice on my part, or maybe I thought I was sparing her by being discreet. Maybe she thought she was trying to give me space until that night she exploded in my kitchen. Rationally, when it came to erotic autonomy we were on the same page. But there are the things that Olivia thinks, and the things she feels, and they're not always the same. That's true of all of us, I know. That business about my being frustratingly rational, about not feeling jealousy— that was probably a little disingenuous. It's not that I don't know what it's like to feel left out.

Olivia told me when we met that she had an ex she sometimes slept with—a former student, Elyse, who'd moved in with her for a while. It didn't work out and Elyse moved to New Haven, but they remained friends, and occasional lovers. Olivia was also discreet about that, but when she did talk about Elyse, it made me more uncomfortable if she said something vaguely dismissive or deprecating about her than if she indicated something about their intimacy. Once, I was smoking a cigarette, and she looked at me with a slight smile and asked me if I knew how to do that holding the cigarette with my foot. I said I'd never tried. She said Elyse had shown her that trick. Elyse is a dedicated yogini, so I guess she can do a lot of interesting contortions. Suddenly I had this image of Elyse sitting naked, lifting a cigarette, or more likely a joint, up to her mouth with her toes, her sex splayed open, and I realized how funny but also how sexy that must have been. I'm not lying when I say this: the image made me happy. I liked to think of Olivia looking at Elyse like that. I liked imagining her taking the joint from Elyse's toes, taking a toke, and kissing Elyse's mouth, and reaching down with her free hand and touching Elyse's sex.

But there was one night when I tried texting Olivia and she didn't text back, and then I remembered that she'd said Elyse was in town that weekend and I thought they were probably together. I felt left out. I didn't ask her about it. I was texting her because I was feeling a little sad and lonely that night, because Sami was having a rough patch. That may sound somewhat contradictory, or maybe not.

Olivia didn't want to be angry with me about Sami.

I planned to begin writing this book in the summer, when classes ended. As you can see, that's what I did. I told Sami and Tye too. Back in March, just a few weeks before my trip to Cologne, I'd finally gotten Tye to schedule a private ballet class with me at my house. When he came to give me the class, we spent about an hour and a half talking about his work and about his life, and I told him about Sami, and I played the Paganini for him, and he was amazed. I said I wanted to write a novel, and it was going to be about technique and art and love and surrogacy and gift economies and feminism and communism and the erotics of collaboration. I was making dances to silence and to words and to music, and I showed him a couple of those. And then I said that mostly what I wanted to do in preparation for making the gold dance to the Paganini was to get my petits battements under control, and I confessed that I was a big ballet faker and had very little technique at all. I asked if he could help me get up to speed and if he thought it was even possible. He thought yes. He gave me a little sequence of about five moves to practice, basic barre exercises that would help me work on my lousy turn-out and pointe and speed and precision. I wrote down everything he assigned me. I think we worked on that for about ten or fifteen minutes. Before he left, I gave him a square envelope that had a CD of some of my ukulele covers plus some cash. That was before I knew that he usually charged two hundred dollars for his more shady transactions—he explained that in a later conversation when we were talking about that performance "Call Home." Tye hadn't given me a price for the ballet class, although I kept asking. In fact, I think he only took that envelope because I said it contained the CD of uke covers. I wish I'd known then that he usually charged two hundred dollars for a particular kind of intimate encounter. Well, as I said, there are some things he does for free and some he does for pretty normal hourly wages in the context of manual labor and the service economy. And then there's the unpredictable and generally inadequate compensation he receives for his art. Before Tye left, he said he hadn't really taught me much ballet, and I said that all the things we talked about were a part of the lesson in technique, but he already knew that, and he also understood that I wanted to write him into my novel, and that I'd keep asking him if he was comfortable with the terms of our collaboration. We've been talking about it ever since, and sometimes it's hard to say whose hand is whose. I don't mean that sexually, but in terms of making art.

Later, after I got back from Cologne, we had one more ballet lesson. Tye seemed to think I'd improved a little. That time I slipped the cash into a small gift bag containing the tester vial of Jackal perfume.

I realized when I was writing about Rebekah's reaction to Sami's story that she was a Wili. Not Olivia. That was something else.

Just to leaven that a little, I should tell you that in April I received a brief update from Natali Pandit, the mezzo-soprano. It came out of the blue. She said, "Happy Saturday!! Yesterday, at a dinner where I knew only two people, I managed to give my old business card (from when I used to gig in Toronto) to the nine people there and ask each of them very directly and sincerely to send me a love poem. Ha-ha . . . I felt so great, and I thought of you!"

Speaking of dinner parties, after Tye had to perform "Duet with Thomas von Frisch" without Tom, they had another glitch, but this time it was Tye who didn't show up for something. Tom was hosting a dinner, and he'd invited Tye, and because Tye's vegan, he'd gone out of his way to prepare a special meal that Tye could eat. It was on a Sunday, the day Tye had been meeting for open rehearsals and discussions with the other artists associated with the performance series at The Kitchen. On that particular Sunday, the conversation had been somewhat confrontational. Some of the other artists in the group came down hard on Tye about the way he'd been resisting feedback. It wiped him out, and he wasn't sure he could really handle a dinner party after that, so he texted Tom that he'd gotten "hurt" at the session, implying, of course, a physical injury, and instead went out for drinks with two friends. He felt the "hurt" text was not exactly a lie, though it also wasn't exactly the whole truth. He felt a little bad about it.

At his next presentation to the group of artists, he invited Tom to perform. Tom agreed. Tye told him that the score for the performance would be for Tom to spend forty-five minutes talking about something. Tom said he could do that. He's gregarious, and as a scientist, he's had plenty of experience lecturing. When Tom got to The Kitchen, Tye told him that what he wanted him to talk about was the dinner party Tye had missed. He said Tom should describe in detail who was there, what they brought, where they sat, what they ate, and what they said. He told him to include

Tye's text message, and his own response. Tom balked. He didn't think he could do that for forty-five minutes. Tye said, "Try." He tried, but he ran out of things to say after about ten minutes. It was awkward for the other people watching. Tye was waiting. Tom was starting to get visibly uncomfortable. Tye had never seen him quite like this. Why was he resisting this? Tye said, "Try again. More details." Tye had placed a block of dry ice in the corner. There was a little fog coming off it. Tom was starting to look really tortured. And then a little pissed off. He began to remember a few more details. They were things about how he had prepared a special meal, just because Tye was so particular about the food he ate. But Tye hadn't shown up. There was another awkward pause. Tye walked over to where Tom was and said softly, "Do you hate this?" He said, "Yes." Tye said, "Do you hate me?" He said, "No." Tye said, "Try again." Tom was a gentleman, he held it together, but he was clearly in agony. Finally Tye said, "Describe the double-slit experiment." Perhaps you know this—I didn't. The double-slit experiment was first performed in the early nineteenth century, and it's said to be the precursor to quantum physics—the basic demonstration of the fact that light appears to be transmitted in both particle and wave form. Well, Tom could talk about that for as long as you let him. Tye eventually had to cut him off. Tye then asked him to describe a different evening when Tye and another young artist had dinner at Tom's, and Tom had given them the double-slit lecture. Tom described that. Then Tye asked Tom if he'd be comfortable talking about his experiences as a client of sexual escorts. He said he would, and he did. His description was quite explicit, frank, and unabashed. Then the forty-five minutes were up. Tye hadn't known they were going to cover all those topics. He had really only planned to have Tom talk about the dinner party he'd missed.

There was a line in the "Duet with Thomas von Frisch" where Tye was standing there alone, looking a little uncomfortable, and he said, "Now Thomas would be standing here, describing the double-slit experiment."

Tye told me one of the reasons he liked to invoke the double-slit experiment was because the name sounded so dirty, even though it's just an old chestnut of quantum physics. Maybe you figured that out for yourself.

On May Day, they held another pop-up Free University—this time just outside of Cooper Union, close to my house. Olivia skipped this one. I'd signed up to give my seminar on inappropriate intimacy again. I used the same description I'd used for the last one, but this time I was prepared with my list of possible assignments to give people. When I got there, there was a disconcerting number of New York City police officers standing around, as though something dangerous might happen. There were also some helicopters flying around. That seemed like overkill, though it makes me think they were worried about something a little worse than people being told to spam innocent bystanders with interpretive dances or to request love poems from strangers. The scenario was similar to the one in Madison Square Park: a few other instructors had healthy crowds of students leaning in to glean their knowledge, and I was sitting alone with my sad little poster board flopping around in the wind. But eventually two students showed up again—a man and a woman who seemed to be in their late twenties. She was a graduate student in comparative literature, and he had gone to law school but had recently decided to devote himself to activism. They'd both read a lot of theory, and they were familiar with Mauss. When I started talking about the optimistic reading of gifts and the notion that wealth itself might have some agency and want to move itself around, she said, astutely, that this was interesting but risky, because the logic could also be invoked in defense of the so-called free market. True. That's a problem.

But they were into the idea of the experiment, and the recuperation of the notion of sentimental value. They laughed at my jokes, and they seemed like they might be game to send me or somebody else some piece of handmade art. We embraced at the end, though they didn't ask me if they could stalk me on the internet. That evening I recorded another Léo Ferré cover for David Graeber: "L'été '68." This time he didn't write me back. I think I may have irritated him by suggesting in my note that he take up the question of sentimental value.

About a week after that, I got an e-mail that was intended for the other Barbara Andersen. This one wasn't written by Barbara herself. It was worse. It was written by her therapist. She said she just wanted to go over with me one more time some points we'd discussed on the phone about what it meant to be "proactive" in my separation from my husband, Mitchell. This didn't mean waiting for him to telegraph his next move. I needed to tell him what I expected of him and when, including the date he would be removing his belongings from my home. Barbara Andersen's therapist reminded me that Mitchell had been leading a "double life," and I needed to take matters into my own hands. I popped a message back to the therapist saying, "oops i think you sent this to the wrong barbara andersen, i live in new york," but she didn't write back. I'm sure she was mortified.

That same week, my friend Abner checked in to see how things had gone on my trip to Cologne. He said he'd been a little worried but refrained from bugging me for as long as he could stand it. I said it was kind of a long story, so he invited himself over for a drink so I could tell him. Knowing how suspicious he'd been of Sami, I tried to narrate events as factually as possible, leaving open the various possible interpretations. I didn't want to prejudice his analysis of the "facts" as we knew them, and I didn't really want to look like an idiot, which may have been unavoidable, regardless. Abner was uncharacteristically quiet as I spoke. He's the kind of person who tends to cut you off midsentence with a parenthetical assertion or clever counterargument. But he listened, right through to the horrific "Gift" revelation in the airport and the denouement of the flurry of conciliatory e-mails when I got home.

Abner was not assuaged. In fact, he was even more worried than he'd been before my trip. He had the bleakest possible evaluation of my story. He used the term *psychosis*. I found that rhetorically excessive. While you certainly might call what happened to Sami during my trip to Cologne a *psychotic break* or *episode,* I thought the term was a bit exaggerated for a general diagnosis. Then it suddenly dawned on me that Abner wasn't talking about Sami. He was talking about me.

A couple of days after that, my friend Lun-Yu Wolf came by to give me a facsimile of some of her new etchings. Lun-Yu is a very interesting visual artist, but she's also a psychotherapist. We talked a little about her new series, which appropriated iconic cartoon characters but placed them in tragic circumstances to surprisingly poignant effect—think Goya, *The Disasters of War*— and then she asked me about my fiction. I told her a little about the novel I was about to begin writing, and I showed her the red and the blue dances to words, and she was fascinated and began asking questions, and then I told her about my trip, and that my friend Abner, who was a lawyer, had thought maybe I was psychotic. Obviously, I was looking for a little professional reassurance that I wasn't. Lun-Yu was very nice. She said she had a very good radar for this kind of thing, having had a number of social phobic patients in the past, and Sami's story rang true to her, but even if one were mistaken about that, I appeared to be handling the situation in a rational and grounded fashion. She thought that my friend Abner was probably very good at legal analysis, but she didn't think I should worry too much about his psychiatric diagnosis.

I also told Lun-Yu about that e-mail I got from Barbara Andersen's psychotherapist. Her mouth dropped open. She said, "Oh my God. That has to go into your novel." Actually, when it happened, I thought about it, but I was a little worried about the question of ethics again. But here was a mental health professional telling me to do it.

Maybe you're thinking I should take everything my friend Lun-Yu tells me with a grain of salt. She also told me that day one of her favorite psychoanalytic theorists was Wilfred Bion. I'd never read Bion before, so after she left I read a bit about him, and I found online the complete text of a seminar he held in Paris in 1978. The beginning of this seminar is very interesting. At least it was to me. Bion says that he wants his listeners to imagine a scenario: they're seeing a new patient, a twenty-five-year-old man who comes in complaining of some dissatisfaction in his family life. Bion says he's not sure what family the man is referring to, and asks his age, which the man gives as forty-five. Bion is confused. He just said the man was twenty-five, and then he notices that the patient has wrinkles, and appears to be in his sixties. He asks his listeners to consider this confusing state of affairs and to determine whether they would, under the circumstances, take on such a patient.

He says the question is much like the question of what you would do if you walked into a bookstore, picked up a book, and read the scenario he just described. He asks if you would continue reading this book. Then he says, imagine it's not a book, but a piece of music. Or a building you're in, and you see the way the light falls, you see the colors coming through the window. Do you want to think about the window some more?

I imagine these questions were somewhat perplexing to some of the participants in the seminar. At one point in the transcript, someone in the audience makes an "inaudible reference" to "psychotic experience." Bion calls that a very "cerebral" question, not a practical one to the analyst. He says that analysts shouldn't be blinded by labels, like *manic-depressive* or *schizophrenic*. Rather, they should be asking themselves what kinds of artists they are and whether there's an interesting spark that occurs with a potential analysand that might lead to something productive in the consulting room or, as he puts it, the "atelier." Somebody asks what an analyst is supposed to do if he's not really the artistic type, and Bion says that if that's the case, then the person's in the wrong line of work. In fact, he says, if that's the case, he doesn't even really know what *would* be the right line of work, since a person needs to be an artist in his everyday life.

Then he throws out the term *artist,* which has obviously become meaningless. The point is, he tells them, that reducing things to "scientific" diagnoses or narrow definitions is really the death of things. "You will have to be able to have a chance of feeling that the interpretation you give is a beautiful one, or that you get a beautiful response from the patient. This aesthetic element of beauty makes a very difficult situation tolerable."

Obviously I loved that. I wrote Lun-Yu and told her about the seminar I'd read and how it had moved me. She said, "Oh, that's the 'bad' Bion, from his mystical phase. That's also the part I love best." Apparently sometimes he wasn't quite so wacky.

In the middle of May, I gave another reading. This one was with Sarah Schulman, the well-known lesbian activist and writer. We'd been invited to read from our fiction and then to engage in a conversation on the topic, "What is the queer novel?" I was pretty sure I was getting in over my head with this question, but then again, who wouldn't be? I answered the invitation, "Sure, I'm happy to think about a big, basically unanswerable question like that." Sarah also agreed to do that, though she had the more obvious bona fides to speak on the topic, given the history of both her publications and her political engagements.

I read first, and I introduced the passage by saying a little speculatively that, to me, writing queer fiction was maybe not so much about representing nonnormative sex acts or the people who engage in them as it was about understanding the fundamental relationship between fiction and sexuality. I said that a lot of writing workshops would begin with the old saw, "Write what you know"—that is, if you're of a certain race or class or gender or sexuality, tell people what that's like. But I said I thought it was interesting to assume that you don't know what it means to be, say, a woman or a man. My novel was narrated by a man, but he was a lot like me. He was living in my apartment, eating my food, looking out the window at my view, thinking about some of the things I think about. There was a character in that book that looked a lot like me, but she wasn't the narrator. In truth, I'd cribbed all her dialogue from Walt Whitman. She had a lesbian lover whose lines were similarly copied and pasted from Emily Dickinson. That character wasn't based on Olivia. I wrote that novel before I met Olivia.

I really like the novel Sarah read from. It's called *Empathy,* and she described it as one of her stranger works. There's something unexpected at the end that I found very interesting.

The discussion afterwards was animated and friendly. I'd been a little worried about how that don't-assume-that-you-know-what-it-means-to-be-who-you-are suggestion would go over among people who had made some pretty extreme sacrifices in order to come out as who they were. But it was an open and generous conversation. Nobody hammered me. We talked about the writing process, and Sarah said that while her activism had been, obviously, about engaging with a collective, novel writing was quite a solitary process. I said, "Actually, the book I'm beginning now is about collaboration, and the eros inherent in the collaborative process, which is also the process of writing the novel." It was helpful for me to say that out loud. It also had to do with that big, basically unanswerable question we were supposed to be discussing.

After my mother had gotten back home, I went to visit her, and she wanted to have a little talk about my life. In the past, she'd occasionally confided in me that she worried sometimes about my sister because, first in her marriage and now in what amounted to a common-law marriage, she had so completely thrown in her lot with a man, and in my mother's experience, that could sometimes lead to disappointment, if not disaster. She'd often expressed relief at my own self-sufficiency. But it seemed that her recent brush with mortality had made her start to worry a little about what would happen to her daughters after she was gone. Even though she hadn't exactly been taking care of us for many years, she was uneasy at the thought of leaving either of us without a protector. My mother liked Carolyn's partner, despite their political differences. She said that she found it comforting to think that my sister would have him to lean on if she were to get sick or have any other kind of crisis, emotional or financial. She asked me who would take care of me if something bad happened. Of course, I didn't mention Leon's charming offer to take me out of my misery the next time I lost my reading glasses. But I told her about my friends and the ways they had come through their difficulties with a network of support. I pointed out that, while Carolyn had done the lion's share of caretaking during her own sickness, several of my mother's friends, as well as me and her brother, had been eager to lend a hand, and I said that I found this a preferable scenario to two people fearfully clinging to each other "till death do us part." I pointed out the flaw in the logic of that program: even if you manage to stay together for richer or poorer, in sickness and in health, somebody inevitably gets the short end of the stick and ends up alone, unless you both get old and sick at exactly the same time, in which case, good luck getting the TLC you need and good luck giving it as needed to your sick, old spouse. I said all this much more gently and diplomatically than I'm saying it now. My mother seemed to be quietly contemplating each point, and when I'd finished, there was a short silence, and then she nodded and said, "That's very interesting, what you've just said." That was much like what Sami had said when I told him what I thought about love.

Once, I told Sami that I had thought the blue dance to words would be the most difficult one, but, in fact, it was the one in which I found it easiest to be in sync with him. He asked me what I thought it meant, that it was easiest for me to be in sync with him when he was suffering. I don't think he posed this question as an accusation, although certainly it's possible to draw some very disturbing conclusions.

Tye texted me in June and asked me, "Can you keep a secret?" I said I was very good at that. He told me about a professional gig he'd been offered, as an artist I mean, something very good, but he was supposed to keep it under his hat for nine months. He said if we were to speak about it, we'd have to come up with a secret code name for it, like "white bread" or "Warner Bros." or "World Bank," and I suggested "Whitey Bulger," the name of the notoriously violent crime boss whose trial was just getting underway. Tye seemed to like that. I was really excited for Tye about the Whitey Bulger— not the real Whitey Bulger, the code one. I wonder if you can guess what Whitey Bulger is a code name for. By the time you read this it won't be a secret anymore anyway.

If you do figure anything out about Tye, I wonder if you could be so discreet as to keep it under your own hat. When we first began talking about my writing him into my novel, I asked Tye if he'd like me to use his own name or a fictional one. He wasn't sure at first, and we played around with a few alternatives. For a while, he thought he'd like for my character to assume his full identity, and

I used his real name in much of my first draft. But then he made that trip home, and there was that disconcerting thing about the two hundred dollars, and the whole experience was pretty draining, and afterwards he texted me saying, "I think I need an alias." He had suggested Tye, and I came up with Larkin Hayes. That was because at the end of June, Tye and I were eating together at a vegan restaurant in San Francisco, and I looked out the window and saw a street sign that said "Larkin—Hayes," and it reminded me of Tye's last name. We were in town for an academic conference on performance art, and it just so happened to be the weekend of Gay Pride. Tye and I watched a few minutes of the parade but got a bit aggravated by all the product placement and also so many bridal veils. Tye is even more vehement than I am that gay marriage just feeds into the massive marketing scam that is the nuclear family. Anyway, we went into the restaurant, and I looked up and saw the street sign that reminded me of his name, and I said that, and he also kind of liked it, but worried that if I used it in my book, it would efface his Jewishness. I said I thought *Larkin* sounded plausibly Jewish, and when I looked up *Hayes* on the internet, it said it could be an anglicization of the Yiddish *Khaye* with a possessive *s*. In this case, it would be of Ashkenazic origins. Tye said, "Oh yeah? Cool." So just two things for you to keep in mind: Tye's Jewish—he'd rather not efface that fact. Also, there's someone he'd rather didn't read this book or know it was partially about him.

Sami would be much harder to track down. Because of his paranoia, he's done a pretty effective job of keeping himself well hidden. But if you do figure out who he is, maybe you could be so discreet as to keep that under your hat as well.

Gia Kourlas just wrote a piece in the *Times* about how much intelligent experimental dance is going on downtown these days, and she mentioned Tye's piece in the attic of The Kitchen, the one with the metronome. She didn't describe it, but noted that, as usual, he'd scheduled it inconveniently so that in order to see it, she'd had to give up some tickets she'd bought for the ballet. She said, "No regrets." I texted him and said, "Nice," but he was miffed because she'd referred to him as "Mr. Hayes." He said, "Apparently my father's piece at The Kitchen was pretty good."

Gia, it's Mr. Larkin Hayes.

Still, it's nice she just wrote something vague and suggestive like that.

In the winter, I'd done another reading at a bookstore with two other writers, Kate Zambreno and Matias Viegener. In the question-and-answer period of that one, somebody asked us all if it was ever complicated writing real people we knew into our works. Kate had written a searing, incisive work of nonfiction, which included some details regarding her marital situation. I was going to say that it was forthrightly feminist in orientation, meaning, among other things, it understood the personal to be political. But *forthrightly* is actually not the right term. She told me that while she certainly identifies as a feminist, she felt that this book was ambivalently feminist— that is, she'd allowed herself to flail about things. That, to me, was also feminist. Also, interestingly, she told me that she'd originally intended to write that book as a novel but her editor asked her to write it as nonfiction.

Matias was talking about a book that his press described as "neither memoir nor diary," in which random lists of things he posted on Facebook were strung together. Somehow, out of these lists, a narrative emerged. Like me, Matias had included people he knew. I'd liked this book as well—it gave you the impression that he was a sensitive, interesting person. He also gave that impression in real life. Matias and I answered the question similarly, saying that when we wrote about real people, we thought long and hard about it, considering the legal, aesthetic, and personal ramifications. Kate differed somewhat in her opinion, noting that it was often women who were expected to worry about offending other people. I think we all used the word *ethics*. I've already used that word a couple of times in this book. There's actually a bumper crop of fiction and borderline fiction/nonfiction that references writers' real lives now, maybe because of the ubiquity of confessional prose, often by people who identify queer and/or feminist. But there's plenty of historical precedent, not all of it with this political orientation by any stretch of the imagination. I think I was seventeen when I read Breton's *Nadja*. For better or worse, that book changed my life, not just my writing. Oh, and *The Autobiography of Alice B. Toklas,* which is queer all right, but maybe not all that feminist. And not all fiction that incorporates real people appears to be all that invested in the question of ethics. Like either of the books I just mentioned, for example. Or *I Love Dick.* I love those books, and I'm very glad somebody wrote them, but I wouldn't have written them that way myself. In fact, in the fiction class I was teaching that semester, I kept finding myself advising students to err on the side of discretion or to ask permission of anybody who might be affected.

I think that evening I was feeling particularly tender because it was the period when my mother was doing very badly and also Sami wasn't at all well. I probably said the word *ethical* more than I usually would. Matias was also surprisingly principled that night. I don't know if he was also feeling unusually sensitive. Anyway, a couple of my very smart young students were in the audience, and later they had a little bloggy exchange on the internet in which they talked about the discussion that night, and they were nice about our work and what we'd read but expressed a little impatience with all the talk about ethics, which they thought was a sentimental deflection of what really counted: politics. Well, that made me feel a little old and a little soft and dumb. I understood what they meant—it's the kind of thing Lauren Berlant often says, and surely I ought to know better, but somehow I couldn't help it.

I was feeling tender about my mother and tender about Sami, and I was feeling like if I were going to write somebody into my fiction, I wanted to do right by them.

I always show people what I'm writing about them, even if they're disguised, to make sure they're OK with it.

This event with Matias and Kate was before I got the idea to write a novel in which everybody gets to show their Track Changes on their own characters. Actually, that's not even this novel—it's just a concept, and I'm not really sure I'll do it. I just like the idea.

Now is perhaps the moment to explain something about Olivia. As I said, I sometimes invent characters who are entirely fictional. Olivia is one of them. I had to make her up because someone else found it too painful to be part of the story when she read the first draft of this manuscript. I loved this person and I wanted to do right by her, so I did what she asked and took her out. And much as I love Olivia, she has nothing to do with the person I excised from this text. I was going to say, "Olivia resembles no one I've ever known," except the truth is, she physically resembles another fictional character I once invented—my first lesbian lover. She's also a little bit like me in some ways. I wrote all her poems, by the way, so now you can really roll your eyes about my making claims for her as a writer of consequence. And if I'm going to be entirely honest, I have to tell you that her capacity to blow her top reminds me a little of my mother.

After I read the bloggy critique of my ethics, I wrote to Berlant for reassurance. She said, "I have also written that ethics to me feels like politics in denial, but that's not always true, because sometimes no matter how politically saturated a relation is, it's just about one person showing up for another." Maybe she just felt sorry for me when she said that—but that would kind of prove the point. It would mean even the smartest woman in the United States of America would be willing to err on the side of trying not to cause somebody pain—that is, me. I'm not usually that sensitive to criticism. I was so worried about my mother.

I wasn't really surprised when Tye was invited to participate in the Whitey Bulger. He'd recently had some fairly high-profile performances. There was one that took place just shortly before my trip to Cologne, and there was a follow-up shortly after my return. I went to both of these. They were at Bard, where I'd gone a few times when Olivia was teaching there. Bard is just a couple of hours north of the city, in Annandale-on-Hudson. Tye's work had been commissioned by someone in the curatorial program there. The curators had decided to organize their final work around the idea of collaboration, and each one had paired artists whose work they felt would speak to each other. Tye had been paired with a very famous conceptual artist in his seventies. This artist might also, like Tye, resist the term *conceptual artist,* but his work is so far ranging, I'd have to make a long list to accommodate the diverse disciplines he touches on. I'll call him Tito Vincenti. Like Tye, he's interested in architecture and engaging with his spectators. It did seem to me like an interesting pair of people to put together.

The title of the entire series of collaborations was Less Like an Object, More Like the Weather. The title was taken from something John Cage said about his own collaborations with Merce Cunningham. He was trying to explain that it wasn't always easy to say who influenced whom or where the work of each of them began or ended. Obviously, this is related to what I was trying to say about whose hand was whose. I love both Cage and Cunningham very much.

It was the end of March and still a little chilly when Tye's first performance took place. I just looked at the e-mail I sent him after I got home. It's dated March 25, 2013, and the subject heading is "I haven't been doing my exercises." The email said, "I loved that I left the house at ten this morning and got home at ten at night. The pilgrimage part was definitely important. I looked at everything else and liked a lot of it, and I watched A. von Spach's dance, and I read everybody's statements, including what Tara Critchley wrote in the little book about you and Vincenti. But I didn't know it would be so dancerly. And I'd seen an image of you like that from 'Duke,' though I didn't see that piece. I loved the slow and concentrated movement over the fog. You looked so strong and graceful, and I couldn't stop watching your hands. I've been doing a bunch of videos of just hand dances—your hands were amazing—but then when first one and then a second enormous man came in, that's when tears started streaming down my face, and I wasn't sure if it was the palimpsest of your other performances (osmosis, masculinity, flesh, helping someone move, endurance, trembling—oh, I forgot to mention that during the fog part, I was standing on my tiptoes to see, and my legs were shaking and cramping—that wasn't the part when I cried, but I was wishing I'd been doing the ballet exercises you gave me—oops, sorry, I've been distracted with my mother's situation . . .) or if it was just that I'm a sucker for Romanticism. Well, Romanticism with a difference. But I thought the Romanticism was genuine, even with the difference. Or maybe I'm just really sensitive these days. I loved it so much. <3"

Let me explain a few things. There were other performances and ongoing exhibitions besides Tye's, and Bard had arranged for a free bus to transport people from New York to the college. The bus left Manhattan in the morning and left Annandale-on-Hudson a little after five in the evening, when the museum closed. Except that Tye had made special arrangements for his performance to begin *after* the closing time of the museum, and like that performance in the storage attic at The Kitchen, this one was just illuminated by the dimming natural light, because the museum lights had already been shut down. There was a great deal of negotiation with the museum administration, and special security had to be hired, and they had to shine flashlights to guide the spectators through the space, and it meant that if you stayed for Tye's performance, you missed the free transportation back to the city, and you had to take a bus to the train station, and this whole arrangement was a pain in everybody's ass, and if you were to ask Tye if any of that were intentional, as I did, he would smile slightly to indicate that, indeed, the pain-in-the-ass aspect was part of his conception of the piece, though maybe he wouldn't have smiled like that if I hadn't been indicating that that was one of my favorite things about it. The pilgrimage was really necessary. It was a very small sacrifice compared to the kinds of difficult situations that Tye sets up for himself on a regular basis.

The fog that I mentioned was artificially created and blown across the floor of the gallery space in which Tye was performing. One might have read that as a reference to a famous atmospheric piece made in the past by Tye's collaborator, though Tye was trying to evoke the opening of act II of "Giselle," when the curtain goes up on a fog-filled stage. I should say more about the spatial design. Tye had occupied a large room in the museum. To get to it, you had to walk through a gallery filled with iconic works by politically oriented late twentieth-century artists like Jenny Holzer and the Guerrilla Girls. These works were part of the permanent collection of the museum, and the curators noted the irony of the fact that despite the artists' impulses to question the fetishistic logic of the art market, their art had become part of the museum's "holdings." Well, Tye had constructed two large barriers to blockade the two passages from the gallery of those permanent holdings to the space within which his foggy, ephemeral performance was taking place. We knew from the curator's notes that there was wall text in that space, but we couldn't see it because it was on the side of the wall facing away from us. The barricades Tye had constructed, and which we watched him laboriously push into place, were at roughly eye-level, if you were of average height—hence my comment about standing on my toes to try to see what was going on in there. Tye was assisted in setting things up by somebody who appeared to be Thomas von Frisch.

Can you imagine the scene you could glimpse in that obscured space, if you stood there on the tips of your toes, your legs trembling? There was another looped score, the opening four-chord progression from the second act of "Giselle," held just at that orchestral moment of breathless suspension. And Tye was repeating that graceful gesture of forgiveness. And first Michael Mahalchick lay down before him, his flesh surrendering to gravity, his heavy arm lifted gently, time and again, by his protector. And then after a few minutes, he awkwardly pushed himself to his feet, stepped out, and another very large, fleshy man with long frizzy hair, a Michael Mahalchick look-alike, eased himself into Duke Albrecht's place, and the two heavy men alternated like that for some time. It seemed like it was Tye who was in more urgent need of a replacement. While his movement phrase was subtle, it required putting nearly his full weight on his bent front thigh, and after some time he began shaking with exertion. But he later told me that the switching off of his partner was more necessary than they had anticipated: the fog rolling across the floor made it difficult for the men to breathe. They really couldn't stay there very long. At first, you could see a quiet, concerned conversation taking place between Tye and the Mahalchick look-alike, but nobody realized the guy was saying he was suffocating.

You've already read what that performance made me think and feel.

Some time later, Tye asked me if he could read my message about that performance out loud during one of those working group sessions at The Kitchen, and of course I said yes. I don't know what he did when he got to the heart emoticon, if he said "heart emoticon" or tried to draw it in the air or if he just ended his reading with my declaration of love for the piece. Or maybe he cut it off before that. Tye isn't really one to blow his own horn.

It's probably also important to mention that the famous artist with whom Tye was collaborating failed to show up for this performance. Because of this, there was a delay in the start time of the piece, and Tye not very apologetically mentioned that they were waiting for the guy to show up, but eventually they just decided to start without him.

So as I said, that was just a couple of weeks before my trip to Cologne. And then there was another performance, in the same space, just a few days after I got back. I think you can imagine my psychic state: rattled. Tye had asked me to write him again and tell him my impressions, but it took me a little while to get around to it—in fact over a month. I just tracked down that e-mail. The first line refers to the news about the Whitey Bulger.

"Tye! I was so happy about your text. I'd been meaning to write you anyway, because I promised I'd write about the April 20 performance. Well, that was just shortly after my catastrophic trip to Cologne, and I was still reeling. So I decided not to try to catch the early bus and have one of those pilgrimage trips again but to take the train and a taxi a little later in the day. I told you I thought the pilgrimage part was important when I saw the first piece, and afterwards I wished I'd done it again. The whole thing of waiting, killing time, wandering around, feeling hungry, wondering what you were doing. But instead I took an efficient train and a taxi and got there just a little before you started. I think I said to you this performance felt to me more cerebral than the one in March, where I wept copiously, which is interesting. Because in a way, as you pointed out, the presence of the breastless woman might seem to be an overt invitation to think about trauma, and who knows, maybe it was me just shutting down or needing to experience it cerebrally and not so much emotionally, maybe because I'd been on overload in the days after Cologne, maybe because breast cancer is overdetermined for me (my grandmother died of it when my mother was very young, my mother had a mastectomy when

I was very young, they police my breasts like little time bombs, I have a dent in my right breast from a lumpectomy [benign] and it's always kind of humming like the sound of electric wires in a field, I tend to filter it out). But also in the performance in March, I had this sense of a kind of more imminent danger, not something past but something present. When you told me that your friend was having difficulty breathing because of the effects of the dry ice, I wondered if that was part of it, that you were actually doing caretaking in the moment, not just referencing it through choreography. I'm not sure. Well, also, maybe it was being able to see the wall text and analyze it—something specific to text that made me read the scene more than feel it—I'm also not sure about that. When the ice handlers swapped out, I was vaguely aware of the change but never at the very moment it happened, and I liked that, that it kept slowly dawning on me. You'd told me about meeting her, though you hadn't been sure she'd become a part of the piece. Always with your work I feel I want to know more— all the details are interesting, the family history, her complex relationship to Tom and Jewishness, and her sexuality—I knew some of this as I was watching, and some you told me after. It was good to think with, as the saying goes, but this time the palimpsest felt to me more like a layered narrative than like residual emotion. As I said, it's hard for me to know whether thinking through the layers, rather than feeling them as I did the last time, had more to do with the performance itself or with me. I like feeling, but I also like thinking. I was very absorbed. The very strange thing for me was the end of the piece, when you left and she was standing there, very matter-of-factly, and people began to leave, and they all hovered over the dry ice and held their hands close to it without touching it, and no one looked at her. She was looking down with no expression of emotion at all, and I wasn't sure if she felt what I felt, how strange it was that no one was looking at her— though obviously I was looking at her, or I wouldn't be able to tell you this, but I think even I was looking at her in a discreet way, and I imagine she didn't register my looking. I went outside, and after a while someone came with coolers of the used ice and began dumping the pieces into a rocky pile of leaves. I made a little video on my cell phone of the fog coming out. I wondered why we were all so drawn to the ice—that seemed strange. I had a lot of questions for you, and I still do. It seemed to me a little like a mystery novel, trying to understand the relationship between no breasts, male breasts, trauma, Jewishness, sexuality, age, mortality—and Tito's present absence, which was also on my mind, and fog. And I thought and thought about all this on the way home. Here is the video from my cell phone."

Well, guess who didn't show up again for the April 20 performance. That famous artist, even though his parts in this collaboration were supposed to be "responses" to Tye's performances. This time we were allowed to go into the space, and we could see the wall text. Tye had knocked over those barricades he'd built, and he moved one around so it partially obscured the text. The wall text said

Landing Field: Tito Vincenti and Tye Larkin Hayes
(2013)

March 24, dusk[1]: opening[‡‡]

March 25–April 19: *Antarctica for 2 (Or More, Until It's Too Many . . .)*[‡]

April 20, dusk[2]: opening[‡‡]
April 21–May 26:

[‡]Tito Vincenti / Vincenti Studio
[‡‡]Tye Larkin Hayes

[1] fog, Tito Vincenti, Tito Vincenti, transsexual, The
Robert Mapplethorpe Gallery

[2] carbon dioxide, The Robert Mapplethorpe Gallery,
Tito Vincenti, Tito Vincenti, Tito Vincenti, The
Robert Mapplethorpe Gallery, [obscured]

The evening of April 20, Tye repeated the tableau with Albrecht that should now be pretty familiar. A Thomas von Frisch look-alike was placing blocks of dry ice on the overturned barricade. If you weren't paying attention, you wouldn't notice that he was eventually replaced by the real Thomas von Frisch, who continued bringing out dry ice, and eventually by an older woman who did the same. She was dressed like Tom, as his look-alike had been, and she, too, was a pretty close ringer. Like them, she had short white hair, black pants, a plain white shirt, and no breasts. The fact of her breastlessness was evident when she was dressed but became even more apparent when she came out with a load of ice naked from the waist up. Her sunken chest was mapped with scars.

Tye's scars from his top surgery are relatively discreet, and fading.

Tye had told me a little about meeting this woman, and there were some personal facts that I mentioned in that e-mail. You don't need to know those things. Most people who saw this piece didn't know those things. Tye did tell me afterwards that the woman also found it strange that people didn't look at her, but they were fascinated by the dry ice.

I'm also not showing you the video I made on my cell phone. There are some things you can't see but you just have to trust my description of them. There was a little fog still coming off the ice, and it was melancholic.

On a cheerier note, I have a friend who's a disability activist, and she sometimes posts interesting links on Facebook to articles or videos on the topic. Early on, when I was first getting to know Sami,

I watched a short documentary she'd been involved in that was, in part, about Asperger's. It was very interesting. Anyway, in late April she posted a link to an article in the *Huffington Post* about a young man named Rafe Biggs. He fell off a roof while traveling in India, and became paralyzed from the neck down. The article said that he had learned to experience orgasms through his thumb, which was the one part of his body, besides his head, where he still had sensitivity. About a year after his accident, a girlfriend was massaging his thumb, and then she started sucking on it, and he had the most amazing sexual climax of his life. They were both surprised. Neurologists confirmed that there's something called neural plasticity, which means that the brain can learn to find new neural pathways if the old ones are damaged. Biggs was really happy to figure this out. There was a picture of him smiling broadly. He founded an organization called Sexability to teach other people about alternative possibilities. Biggs isn't at all shy about talking about his sexual techniques. He says that there's actually a difference between his two thumbs: the right one is better for giving pleasure, while the left one is better for receiving it. I found this very heartening.

We all have parts that are sensitive. Some are more surprising than others. The first time I made love with a woman, the great revelation, to me, was that the hand was a receptive sensory organ. I'd never touched something so soft. Well, it's obvious that hands feel, but in sex I think I had tended to think of my hands more as giving things. I have other parts that are very good at receiving. They're not spectacularly original, but they're also not the very most obvious ones. You'll remember what I told Tye. My body is an extension of my body.

My friend who had posted the link to the article also found it very heartening. She wrote underneath it, "GO RAFE!"

I just realized I haven't said anything about the uke covers I made in the spring. Believe it or not, I never gave them up, even at the height of my confusion. When I was riding the train through Düsseldorf, I remembered that song by Regina Spektor, "Düsseldorf," and after I got home, as soon as I pulled myself together, I recorded it. I gave it to a writer I know. Sami liked that one, despite my mangling of the German. Lauren Berlant suggested Martha Wainwright's "Bloody Mother Fucking Asshole," which is much sweeter than the title would lead you to believe. When I was writing a little essay somebody had requested about Pussy Riot's use of the balaclava (which I linked to masks used by the Zapatistas as well as the black blocs and the Occupy protesters), I did a nice little cover of Romulo Fróes's "Máscara." I sent that to my friend Narcissister, who only ever performs masked, though otherwise often quite exposed. I read something about the singer/songwriter Angel Olsen in the *Times,* and I got a little obsessed with her uncanny voice. It was like a cross between Patsy Cline and Meredith Monk. I like it, but it's disconcerting. I don't sound anything like any of them, but I decided to record "Always Half Strange." The words to that song are also disconcerting. It's about persisting in believing something you know is probably only half true. I didn't send that one to anyone.

Sami also hardly skipped a beat in posting his music. Well, there was that week he was mostly in the bathroom throwing up, when he was going through withdrawal, but after that he produced a fairly steady flow of things, a completely incongruous mix of genres and instruments and approaches. One day he posted a torrid, passionate rendition of Piazzolla's "Le Grand Tango for Cello and Piano" with Bronislawa. The interplay between the two of them was like tango itself. You could practically hear the pressure of their foreheads pressed together, of their grip. You could practically smell the sweat. I wrote him that it was beautiful, and he said, "Yes, Bronislawa came last night, we played until very late. She just left this morning, after we had coffee." He didn't have to tell me about their lovemaking. You could hear it in the music, and besides, Sami is pretty discreet about that kind of thing. He said once he thinks that's the gentlemanly way to be. I also try to be gentlemanly about that kind of thing.

It didn't make me jealous, of course, but it did make me wish for a minute that she had been me. Sami had posted another Piazzolla piece—"Verano Porteño" for solo guitar—and I did my own duet with it. It was another of the hand dances I can't show you. It's too bad I can't show you because it may be the most technically perfect dance I ever made. I'm serious. In that one, we were in perfect sync. Also, I'd been thinking about that young man with the sensitive thumbs. I used what you might call "extended technique." I wasn't playing the obvious parts. Even I thought it was kind of impressing. When I sent it to Sami, I said, "I know you just played that beautiful Piazzolla with Bronislawa, maybe you just want to remember that for a while. You don't have to watch this dance if you don't want to—I just wanted to make something with you. I hope you don't mind." He didn't mind. Later I made him another gold dance, the one to words. I did it to one of the first voice messages he ever sent me. That one I can show you. It's very pure.

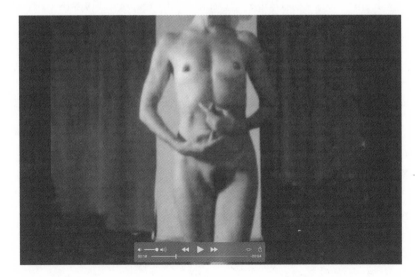

Around the end of May, Karen Finley was doing a project at the New Museum called "Sext Me If You Can." The idea was that during a period of several days, Karen would set up a studio in the lobby of the museum and volunteer patrons would slip into a room in the basement and sext her. She would then create original artworks based on the sexts she received. Her patrons would commission the works, which would remain on display in the museum until the end of the show. At that time, the models/patrons could retrieve their artworks and take them home. The commissioning fee was paid online, in advance. Then each patron was given a ten-minute time slot. The website assured you: "Sittings are completely private, discreet, and anonymous. During your sitting, you will receive access to a private phone number for the purpose of sending Finley a 'sext.'" The commissions were surprisingly affordable. I couldn't resist. I really love Karen's drawings and paintings. They're not what she's most famous for, but they're wonderful—sometimes whimsical, sometimes uncanny, often very beautiful.

I didn't tell Karen that I was doing this. I loaded my phone in advance with a couple of very carefully composed photos that I thought would translate nicely into works on paper, but when I got to the museum for my appointment, I realized that I'd have to trash that plan: they gave me an index card with my identification number printed on it, and they also gave me a sheet of rules and tips for the sexting transaction. If you were typing text, you had to type in your patron number in the subject heading, and if you were sending a photo, then the index card itself had to be visible in the shot. That is, no precomposed photos. They had to be taken in that room in the basement. Those were the rules. The tips were assembled from some silly article in a men's magazine that advised you that if you were going to send a gal a sext, you should not expose your face. There were a couple of other little pearls of wisdom having to do with getting a flattering shot of your special parts.

I was coming straight from the gym, and I was a little discombobulated. The room they took me to was really not sexy. There was a fluorescent light and a dressing room mirror with a Formica countertop. There was one folding chair. I had ten minutes to strip, photograph myself, send the photos, and get dressed again. Plus that card had to be in the shot. Ack. I got undressed quickly enough, and I awkwardly held the card with my left hand against my hip as I turned to the side and arched my back a little. I was able to make it somewhat flattering, but it looked tacky and dumb. There was nothing really sexual about it. I did another from the other side. I texted those to Karen. I was kind of fumbling with the BlackBerry. I was nervous, and I didn't like what I was getting. She texted back something friendly like, "Hi!" I wondered if she knew it was me. I didn't think so, but it was possible she'd recognized my tattoo. I was feeling a little desperate. I didn't want to give her something that banal to work with. Suddenly I realized that if I put the card down on the countertop, it would be visible in the photo, but I didn't have to hold it. This freed up my left hand. I reached down and touched myself. I took a picture of that. That one was really straightforward. No arched back, no coy pose of any kind, just that: me touching myself. I sent that one. Then I actually felt kind of sexual. The card was still on the counter. I turned to the side and leaned against the wall and touched myself again. I took another picture. That one was really beautiful. But really beautiful.

That was exactly the moment that the museum security guard started banging on the door saying, "Time's up!" It sounded like they were putting a key in the door. I scrambled into my gym clothes and got out of there. I was told to go upstairs. I was still tying the drawstring of my shorts as I walked up the staircase. I hadn't had a chance to send that last image. Karen's assistant was at the top of the stairs, and I sadly explained that I'd run out of time and hadn't sent the one good shot. She was very nice. She said, "Oh, you can still send it, it's OK." But when I pulled out my BlackBerry and tried to open the image, for some reason I had a hard time finding the cell number from the texting chain, and I got flustered and confused again, and my shorts were still kind of half on, and my hair was a mess. The assistant leaned in to help me with the BlackBerry, and as she took it and started typing in Karen's number, I suddenly realized that my hands smelled like sex. I thought, "Oh my God, she's going to turn to me and say, 'What the hell were you doing in that room down there?'" She didn't say that. She was very polite.

We got Karen the image. She texted me back, "Ur gorgeoud." Then she corrected herself, "S." Then she said, "I think I got something." I thought maybe she sent nice, encouraging messages like that to all her sexters. Karen's very sweet. But I was still happy she said that. I snuck out hoping she wouldn't see me.

She didn't see me, and she didn't know it was me. And the image she chose wasn't the last one. She made a drawing from the straightforward one, the one that wasn't posed at all. It was simple, and perfect: a small ochre pastel sketch of ribs, belly, and thighs, and my hand reaching down. There was a little bit of gold, and my pubic hair was graphite black. She'd signed it on the back, and written, "Drawing— Finger in labia—Sext Me Series—New Museum—5/2013." I loved it. I put it in a floating frame.

I was in a hurry to frame it quickly when I picked it up because Karen was coming to my house, and I wanted her to see it hung. In my rush to frame it, I traumatized myself by accidentally creasing it slightly at the top. I was hoping she wouldn't notice. I had the same nervousness handling the drawing that I'd had fumbling with my BlackBerry.

Karen was coming over because I was having a little potluck dinner for two of the girls from Pussy Riot. I'd gotten an e-mail from the person who had organized a website here in the United States called freepussyriot.org. He'd been trying to help publicize the case for months, and because I'd been writing and speaking about the group, he wrote me to say these two were coming to New York and maybe I'd like to meet them. They were holding a screening of a documentary film that had been made about them. The two who were coming were not the famous ones, who are still imprisoned. Even Samutsevich, who got out, can't travel. These two were, he said, founding members, but because they were at great risk in Russia, he couldn't reveal their names. In fact, I think even he didn't know their real names. I said I'd love to meet them, and if they'd like, I'd love to have them over for dinner. I could invite some feminist performance artists that they might want to meet. To my surprise, he said that would be great. I called Finley and Carmelita Tropicana and Narcissister and some older punk rockers I know and also a couple of teenage feminists and a couple of smarty-pants young theorists. Olivia too.

We all had to keep the whole thing on the down-low because the girls were trying not to publicize their whereabouts. When they appeared in public, they wore their balaclavas and spoke into those special microphones that distort your voice.

That night was like a dream. We all ended up out on my balcony drinking wine and smoking cigarettes. The Pussy Riot girls looked so young, and they didn't speak much English, but they were smart and funny, and they were trying to teach the young smarty-pants how to say "I am poop" in Russian. Ya kakashka. Olivia doesn't really speak Russian, but she'd memorized a few lines from the pro- logue of Mayakovsky's *A Cloud in Trousers* that she declaimed. The girls laughed and corrected her pronunciation. One of the aging les- bian punk rockers gave them an old cassette tape of her band from back in the day. I thought it was too bad they probably couldn't play it, but the guy from freepussyriot.org said, "No, I think in Moscow maybe cassette tapes are still pretty current technology." I wonder if that's true. Anyway, the girls seemed excited to receive it.

I took Finley into my room to see the drawing, and I told her the story about my foiled plans and my panic and the way my hands smelled and how embarrassed I was and how much I loved the drawing. She said, "Oh, I really liked that one." Then she took out her iPad and showed me some of the other images she'd made. The ones of male genitalia resembled flowers or magical sea creatures. There were some that had text, and the images were quite abstract. I asked her about people who had sent her words, instead of photographs. I thought about it after my sitting, why it was that I only sent images, although I generally consider myself a words person. Strangely, I'd felt shy to send words. She said the people who had sent text told her they felt shy to send images. Apparently some of them went into that little room intending to photograph themselves but ended up writing her heartfelt messages saying they just couldn't do it. They wanted to, but they couldn't. She'd write them back something gentle and understanding, and then they'd say a little more about their feelings about sexuality, how they wanted to express it but couldn't. Some of those drawings were very poignant if you thought about the exchange that was taking place.

Karen is also very interested in the kinds of economic transactions that make art possible or impossible. This is why she was making explicit the patronage relationship and thinking about the erotic component of that. But when Karen began telling me about her interactions with her patrons, it was really all about these touching ways in which she was trying to respond to the painfully intimate things that people were telling or showing her. She'd get tears in her eyes talking about it. It's a bit like what Berlant said— even though these relations were "politically saturated," sometimes it's just about one person showing up for another person.

On July 18, 2013, as I was about midway through writing my first draft of this novel, Tye texted me a photo of a check for one hundred dollars with the words, "I'm screwed." I said, "Laundering money for Whitey Bulger?" He said, "Not happy. Thought I was getting five hundred. Still haven't paid July rent." I said, "Oh, I thought it was the down payment on ur soul." He explained that no, this was partial payment for that performance in the attic with the metronome. He was showing it to me because it meant my math was off when I explained what he was getting paid. I'd already shown him that part of my manuscript. I offered to front him some cash for his rent, but he didn't want it. While we were going back and forth on this, I Googled Whitey Bulger and found out that a key witness in the trial had just been found dead. He said, "Whoa." I said, "'Stippo' Rakes. Really." He said, "Jesus." I said, "Watch ur back." I said, not about that, but about the rent, seriously, I could cover him, but he was having none of it. Tye's used to living dangerously.

At one point, when he was reading through what I'd written about him in my manuscript, he said, "I can't show this book to my mother." That's not who I was talking about when I said there was somebody he'd rather not know about this book, but he had a moment there of wondering if it might make his mom uncomfortable. I said I was a little worried about showing it to mine. He said, "Has she read your other novels?" I said yes, but that in this one I appeared to have gone off the deep end. I wasn't worried about the parts about her. It was the business of flying across the ocean to meet a strange, possibly unstable man with an addiction to opiates. And the bit about those hand dances. Tye said, "Hmm."

Tye really loves his mother.

I also really love my mother.

My mother asked me recently if this book I was writing was the kind of book she would like. I hesitated before I answered that. I think she might be interested in some of the thematic issues I'm thinking about, like virtuosity and giftedness and technique and the economic issues surrounding the creation of art and the process of collaboration. I think she might be a little discomfited by the videos. And maybe some other things. She was also a little discomfited by some things I wrote in my other books, though she was very nice about it. She chalked her discomfort up to generational differences. She told me she thought I was a good writer.

This book may be a tough sell. But here's the good news: she's doing really well. I'm going to see her in a couple of weeks, and Leon's going with me. It's been a while since she's seen him, and I know it means a lot to her that he's coming. As I've said, they're kind of kindred spirits. He's also looking forward to it. He likes to ask her questions about her life, and if we run out of things to talk about, he just launches into reenactments of great moments from *Monty Python's Flying Circus,* which she also enjoys.

Sami just took Kakay for a little trip to the seashore. For a minute there it looked like Juliane might not let them go, because Sami had a brief episode of phantom pains and had to take a little morphine. I'm sure you can understand Juliane's concern. I understood it. But this time Sami's period of pain was short, he took the smallest amount he could, they injected it locally, and as soon as the episode passed, he got clean. It was all under the supervision of his pain specialist, and if he'd had to continue on meds, he certainly wouldn't have taken the trip. The trip was exhausting but successful. They ate a lot of salty fish. Kakay played with other kids at the beach, and Sami read in the sand. He wore his "Barbie" prosthesis—the silicone one—which gets a little hot but is good for swimming. Also, people don't stare as much. He said it still looks a little weird because there's no hair on it, and also it doesn't match the color of his other leg when he gets a tan. Anyway, Sami seemed happy when he wrote me. He said he loved watching Kakay sleep. He's that lovely, awkward age, all gangly. Kakay told Sami he thought it was cool that his father's still so young. I don't know if he meant that literally—Sami is young to have an eleven-year-old—or if he meant he likes it that Sami's often childlike.

They were there for a few days. There was one night when Sami got a little anxious, and he wrote me. I told him I thought it wasn't surprising—he's not used to spending so much time with someone else, and as much as he loves Kakay, sometimes it's hard for anyone not to have time alone. I said Kakay was probably even feeling a little bit that way.

I just received two gifts. One was an a cappella cover of "Alabama Song," recorded by that young comp lit graduate student I met at the Free University on May Day. When I first saw the title, I thought it was some kind of anthem for a football team, but then I realized it's by Kurt Weill and Bertolt Brecht. That made more sense. I have to figure out what to send her back. The other thing was a quickie from Natali Pandit. The subject heading was "i thought . . ." and the message continued "that today might be a 13th century french motet kind of day!" She'd attached a recording of exactly that. It wasn't dirty at all.

I also got a message from a student of Lauren Berlant's. She said she's thinking of writing her senior thesis on my novels. That was exciting. She said, "I'm interested in digitally mediated intimacies, especially as they slide between the virtual and the physical (or completely disrupt these boundaries as we think of them)." She'd missed the workshop I gave in the winter because she was studying in Mexico at the time. I looked at that phrase, *digitally mediated intimacies*. I suddenly realized something pretty obvious. *Digital* means "using the fingers." The hand dances were digitally mediated intimacies.

Those messages all arrived electronically, but something else arrived in the post: that package I'd tried to mail to Sami at his fictional address on Von-Ketteler-Straße back in December. It was returned to me in pristine condition with a little green label saying "Zollamtlich abgefertigt," which I had to look up. It indicated that my package had passed through customs, so apparently the Schuler family had just told the mailman to return the package to its sender. I wrote Sami, "I now have two thigh cozies—the one I mailed, and the one I tried to deliver by hand. So if I want to give them to someone, I either have to find a double amputee or else two people who have very long heads, so they can wear them like hats. Then I imagined that the people who live at Von-Ketteler-Straße 11 might have very long heads, like this," and here I attached a picture of the Coneheads from the old *Saturday Night Live* sketch. I said, "I thought it would be very funny if this was what the Schulers looked like. This is how I now see them in my mind. Except wearing green thigh cozies on their heads." Actually, the Coneheads remind me a little of that other couple I met on Von-Ketteler-Straße, the ones who were out gardening in the light rain, who said there was no one of Sami's description living on their street.

After his trip to California, when he was still feeling a little sensitive, Tye texted me, "Barbara, will you still come see my work after your book is done?" I said, "Yes, always! I'm ur biggest fan, u r stuck w me." He said, "Phew."

When I first met Olivia, she said, "Just tell me you're not falling in love with me to write your next novel. And you won't just forget me when it's over."

I find it very hard to stop loving once I've cathected. I guess some people feel differently. Zora Neale Hurston wrote *Their Eyes Were Watching God* at the end of a love affair. The plot of the story was very different from the story of her love for this person, but she wrote it in order to be able to make sense of the fact that she couldn't be with her lover anymore because they hit each other. Later, in her autobiography, she said that when she wrote the novel, "I tried to embalm all the tenderness of my passion for him." I've already indicated how highly I think of Hurston, but I wouldn't ever use that figure of speech to describe what I'm trying to do when I write about a person in my real life. I wrote one novel just so that I could figure out a way to continue loving someone, not to give up on them. I don't ever write about people so that I can be done with them. When I read the things I've written, I still laugh about the funny things my characters say, and I still cry when they do the things that made me cry when I wrote them. When I read those things, it's like when I look at old photographs of Leon. I see him as he was then, but also as he is now. I still want to be with the real people, as they are now. The one person who's never expressed any anxiety about this is Sami, I think because he feels the same way I do. He's still in love with Juliane, even though she's often angry with him now. He loves Sabine too. And although they don't talk about a lot of intimate things, he also loves Bronislawa. He's told me so.

You might be thinking that the difference with Sami is that there's a possibility that he's not who he says he is, so he has less to risk. But Olivia's entirely fictional, and it doesn't keep her from feeling vulnerable.

Oh, Rebekah's also not worried about whether I'll keep loving her; she understands these things. I've been a minor character in any number of things she's written.

Somebody just sent me a message about my ukulele covers. Apparently he found them by Googling "twiztid," and somehow he ended up clicking on the ridiculous version of "Woe Woe" I made with Leon. I guess this guy's favorite genre is horrorcore. But he listened to a whole bunch of my covers and said "niiiiiice." I wrote back, "thank you!" He answered, "Oh yur Welcome Luv yur Style of music by tha way, even tho i don't noe wat iz said. ahaha. nawt really my type, butt I likez it :D." Sometimes art makes for unexpected bedfellows.

On July 16, 2013—just a couple of weeks ago—it seemed that Pussy Riot had released a new song, "Like a Red Prison." There was an accompanying video on YouTube. This time, the chummy relationship under attack was not that of church and state, but rather that between Putin and the oil industry. The video showed several masked young women dousing a portrait of the head of the Russian state-run petroleum company with black liquid. Days later, however, Pussy Riot released a statement indicating that the song and video had been produced by a group of Pussy Riot imitators. Interestingly, though, they didn't seem to be particularly angry. The statement published on freepussyriot.org said, "As we struggle against the system in the courts and prisons, and thus do not have the opportunity to perform new actions, a group of anonymous activists presented a gift to us—by releasing a music video." There was a hint of anxiety about how others might be using the name of the group in order to promote their own agendas, but since this song had a message they could get on board with, they seemed OK with it. I thought that was nice, that they called it a gift.

I worry sometimes about the two young Russian girls who came to my apartment that night. Before they left, we hugged, and I had this intensely maternal feeling toward them. I looked them in the eyes and said, "I'm so proud of you." The next day they went down to Zuccotti Park to have their pictures taken there.

Tye told me a story once about a trip he made to Detroit during his freshman year of college. He was at Berkeley, and his main focus when he got there was political activism. He hadn't been dancing for a while, though he'd get back into it the next semester. But right when he got to school, he was a little disoriented—he wasn't yet identifying as trans, but he was out as queer, and there had been an ugly incident when he first got to school. He was also experimenting with drugs, methamphetamines specifically, and he got this idea to run for student government on the Defend Affirmative Action Party ticket. He knew he wouldn't win, but the idea was to get visibility for the party. Actually, the election was surprisingly close, and his candidacy attracted the attention of some radical labor organizers who passed his name along to the Workers Aligned for the Revolution (WAR), an underground Trotskyist organization. That's not the real name of the outfit, but you get the idea. Their headquarters were in Detroit, and they sent Tye a plane ticket during the winter break. He was couch surfing at the homes of various members, but each day he'd be taken to the leader's house. This guy's name was Lorand Sandberg. Every day for one week they'd leave Tye sitting on Sandberg's couch in this old ramshackle house. And every day he'd have to wait for about three hours for Sandberg to come downstairs. Tye could hear him up there, moving around. As I mentioned, Tye was pretty tweaked at the time, and he was still a bit unsettled from the homophobic incident. Eventually, Sandberg would come down, and then he'd lean forward in his chair and talk at Tye for eight hours, practically without interruption. Sometimes Tye would talk softly back. Sandberg seemed to know a lot about him. He knew about the bashing incident and also that Tye had had some family drama. Sandberg liked to talk about the pathologies of capitalism using metaphors of the pathology of the nuclear family.

There was a front organization for WAR that was significantly more user-friendly. FTP—Fight the Power. After that indoctrination trip, Tye continued for a time to maintain ties to WAR. They had some very severe rules about what kind of language you could use. They didn't like the phrase *people of color* because it evoked the moldy racist term *colored people*. You couldn't say *queer* because it was taking on the negative language of the Man. Tye still digs some of these people's political aims, but the indoctrination experience was a weird one. I thought it sounded very creepy that Sandberg had so much information about Tye's personal life.

Obviously, part of the attraction was having an alternative father figure, even if Sandberg was lecturing him about the pathology of the patriarchy.

Why am I telling you this story? Because I think Tye thinks it's important. He told me about that trip just in passing, a few months ago. But there were certain things he couldn't remember when he first told me. He just sent me an e-mail saying, "Lorand. His name was Lorand. I'd forgotten that. FTP is the front organization for WAR. You only figure that out if you Google them together." I guess he'd been trying to remember that. It wasn't that long ago, but he was strung out at the time.

Tye also told me that after his recent trip home, he had a kind of crisis about his art. Even though on paper things are going well—he's got some interesting gigs on the horizon, and he's been getting good press—he still wonders sometimes how much difference it makes. He said that recently he'd been having intense fantasies about disappearing—just relocating to the Midwest or the South and changing his name and devoting all his energy to community organizing. Naturally, when he told me this, I insisted that his art was very important. He told me he's starting to feel back on track again. He had a very good meeting with one of the curators from the Whitey Bulger, and the guy was smart and enthusiastic and didn't balk at any of Tye's ideas. As usual, his project will involve some pretty major inconveniences for the hosting institution. They're going to have to apply for some building code dispensations. Tye seemed happy that when he told the curator what he needed, the guy didn't bat an eyelash.

The story of Lorand Sandberg makes me think of some conversations Sami and I have had about alternative father figures. We've both looked for them over the years. I mentioned Farrokh's parents. It was very important to Sami that they accepted him into the family. I also mentioned that Günther's been quite supportive, and that was especially helpful after the accident.

But there have been various teachers and mentors over the years—usually other musicians. They weren't necessarily more proficient than Sami at music—in fact, most of them were less capable than he was and often sort of in awe of his talent—but it helped him when an older male figure would express affection or pride.

I've also had a few of those—older men that I'd hoped would take me on as a kind of artistic or intellectual protégée. Sometimes they were very helpful. A couple of them wanted to sleep with me.

One wouldn't give me the time of day. I actually preferred it when they wanted to sleep with me. One of them I slept with.

Sami's quite a bit younger than me, but as I've mentioned, he often makes me think of my dad. When Rebekah was going through her Wili thing, telling me what a terrible idea it had been for me to fly to Cologne to meet a man with possibly serious mental illness, at one point in the conversation she threw up her hands and shouted, "AND CAN WE JUST TALK FOR A MINUTE ABOUT YOUR FATHER?!" I really didn't think that was necessary.

I checked in with my mother today. She's looking forward to our visit, but she's still having a few problems with her health. When I called, she'd just gotten home from a visit to her new doctor. My sister set her up with a geriatric specialist, as we'd discussed. Even my mother's now acknowledged that it was time to move on from Billington. Her new doctor thinks some of the pain she's having in her back may actually be due to a bit of kidney malfunction, which is probably related to some of her prescription medication. He ran a battery of tests. She found it a little exhausting, but she's glad he's so thorough. I am too.

She's pretty philosophical about the fact that new problems keep popping up. She says, "Well, what is there that's eighty-five years old that doesn't start to malfunction?" Good question.

The end of that part of the story is not going to be about living happily ever after. But all things considered, she's doing well.

Sami is too, though surely he'll continue to have some hard days. After he and Kakay got back from the trip to the shore, they were going to spend the last few days of Kakay's vacation together at Sami's place, but now he told me that he was still feeling slightly overloaded from the trip, and he started to get a little anxious again. He had a heart-to-heart with Kakay, and they decided that maybe it was best if Kakay went back to his mom's place early. Juliane was OK with that. Sami seemed to feel a little defeated, but I thought it was good they could all see that this was best, under the circumstances. I told him it was lovely they'd spent that much time together and that the trip went well, and they both would remember the things they saw and did, and they'd have plenty of chances to spend more time together.

That's also never going to be easy.

Olivia's hand healed pretty quickly. There was no displacement, so it was basically a question of ice and rest, and after a few weeks, she was supposed to do some exercises. She had health insurance from Bard, thank goodness, but there were still a few unexpected charges. She'll be fine, but it's another one of those situations that makes you wonder what less fortunate and prudent people would do if something like this happened to them. We have some friends who have been following very carefully what's going to happen when Obamacare goes into effect. Jean-Christophe, for example, has chronic asthma, and for a while he's only been able pay for very basic services. If anything catastrophic were to happen, he'd be, as his own GP once said to him in a moment of unusual candor, "shit out of luck."

This is also not going to be easy. Sorry I keep repeating that sentence.

I have a confession to make. I haven't been doing my ballet exercises. Tye, I'm sorry. I've been working so hard on this novel. I had a plan to write the whole thing over the summer. I told myself I'd write three pages every day. I've been very disciplined about it. My writing is the one thing I'm pretty disciplined about. I got a little bit ahead of schedule on it, and I'm still hoping to spend the last couple of weeks of August on the dance, after I get back from seeing my mother. I realize that two weeks is not long enough to work on my petits battements. I should really have been working on them for the last year. But I have to make the dance, because I promised I would. Also, you really have to hear Sami playing music—

real music. I'm pretty sure I won't rise to the occasion, but I'll try. Sami, I promise I'll make the gold dance. It's the last thing I'll do.

Sami told me one other thing about Kakay. It had to do with that thing he'd said about how he thought it was cool that Sami was young. I guess a day or two after that, while they were having dinner, Kakay suddenly looked up at Sami and said, "I don't think you're like a child." Sami figured this was probably something that Juliane had said to him. Then Kakay said, "You're also not like a father." Sami asked him what he thought he was like, and Kakay said, "You're like someone who knows too much and pretends not to know anything." Sami said he thought Kakay was very clever. I think that's right.

Uh-oh. The horrorcore guy wants to friend me on Facebook.

Have you been wondering what happened to Abner Berg? I had a sort of strange exchange with him recently. We have a long-running Scrabble game going on Facebook. I'm not a big Facebook person, but I like to keep a few Scrabble games going. I check in once a day and make a couple of moves. You can chat with your opponents if you feel like it. It's a nice level of contact with certain people. If you feel the need to say something personal, you can, but you can also maintain that sort of phatic contact through your moves, without actually saying much—or sometimes anything at all. Well, I happened to mention to Abner on there that I'd written him into my novel. I said I changed his name to Abner Berg. I said I thought he came across as a "smart, funny, concerned friend." In fact, that's pretty much how I think of Abner. He e-mailed me almost right away to say that he liked the name Abner Berg, and he had no problem appearing in my novel, but he said that, frankly, he'd been a little worried about me, and he thought perhaps we should meet to talk about it.

That kind of threw me for a loop.

He said something about "this story of you and 'Sami.'" He always puts Sami's name in quotation marks. It's a little irritating. Abner's message said, "Yeah, I actually am a bit concerned about you. Although the weirdness was in part about you and in part about our friendship and whether at some level (conscious? subconscious?) the performance art theorist and practitioner in you might sometimes have some splitting issues, as my former shrink used to say, and if you use (take that word advisedly) friends in part to play out your art. I don't mind at all figuring, for example, in the last section of a book. But I mind if the known hard facts (OK, I know, but still) of the Barbara-and-'Sami' performance are shaded/obscured in, say, an ongoing conversation with a friend (me, for example). You know what I'm saying?" I said, "Totally confused. Read that 'shaded' sentence several times." He said, "Easier to chat in person," and he proposed a window of time if I was free. I said, "Are you a little bit pissed off because you think I might be lying to you and calling it 'fiction'? I'm not! I was about to explain the relationship between truth, lies, and fiction as I see them but then realized that's what the book is about and maybe I should just give it to you when it's done. I'm so honest! Also, I'm such a good friend! But you may find this similar to the time I asked Sami (right after the catastrophe of my trip to see him) if he was at all dangerous, and then I said, 'Well, that's a silly question to ask somebody who said they lived in a house they don't live in.' Anyway, he answered that no, he wasn't at all dangerous. I'm not at all dangerous. :) I'm mostly around also—busy Wednesday and Friday, but otherwise fairly clear . . ."

Abner said, briefly, that he was curious about my "deep subconscious motivation" to have a "'relationship'" with "'Sami'" as opposed to, "say, someone you love who is corporeal and present." And then he proposed getting together the next night. I said, "OK! I'm tempted to begin to answer your question, although you'd probably say better to discuss in person. But I like to write, which is part of the answer. But also part of the answer is that I love to have real, corporeal, present relationships with people, and I do that often and with pleasure. Olivia, of course, but not just. I really wanted to see Sami in person. I went all the way to Cologne. You keep putting his name in quotation marks, and I have to acknowledge that there's reason for doubt, and I can't be 100 percent sure he exists, and I have to kind of make fun of myself, both when talking to you and in writing the book. But I'm about 98 percent sure he exists, and I think he's very largely the person he purports to be. As much as any of us are. Which is maybe on average 95 percent true. Not because we're 5 percent liars but because we can't see about 5 percent of ourselves. I know you think I'm Paul Frampton in this story. Possibly. My friend Lun-Yu, the psychotherapist who's dealt with social phobic patients, thinks everything rings true, but naturally, everybody has his or her investment in wanting to believe or not believe. I still hope I'll meet Sami. We still talk about it. But if we don't, I'm pretty sure we'll keep corresponding, because we keep making our best art for each other. I'm not sure why we'd stop. In the meanwhile, as I said, I'm all for spending time with people in restaurants, talking in person, and so on, so yes, let's meet tomorrow. Say where. Oh also, the one thing I think you should not be judgmental about is my resistance to promissory sexual relations, that is, bourgeois marriage or any of its offshoots, including gay marriage or something approximating it. It's particularly bad to pathologize this resistance in a woman. My resistance to it is partly constitutional but also political and feminist. Can say more. Also about great correspondences, which far predate the internet (hello, Emily Dickinson). OK. See you soon. I'm still leaving your representation in my book as a smart, funny, concerned friend, although in your recent missives, you've sounded vaguely judgmental and a little grouchy. xoxo"

He said, "Before I even start reading this, I want to say this: your message went straight to my spam filter! I had to rescue it!

Now I'll read it. Let's meet inside the Time Warner Center at Columbus Circle—right at the top of the Whole Foods escalators. Then we can choose one of the bars upstairs for a drink." Mysteriously, he signed this one "J." That was interesting about the spam filter. I wondered if it might have something to do with all those percentages in my message. Maybe they made it look like a marketing ploy. I confirmed the date, and he said, "Weird, my system must be messed up. This latest from you also went to spam. Even though I instructed it to trust you. :)"

He actually wasn't grouchy at all when we met. It only slowly dawned on me that Abner's fear of my psychosis wasn't that I might be delusionally wanting to believe in Sami, but rather that I might have made the whole story up. He thought maybe I was pathologically representing my fictional narrative to him, Abner, as the truth just so I could play it all out in the writing of my novel. But by the end of the evening, Abner had decided to believe in me. He also totally understood the argument regarding promissory sexual relations.

I mentioned my drink with Abner to Sami, and I told him I was surprised to learn that Abner had been worried I might be making a fool of him. Sami said he never really worried about somebody else making a fool of him because he was always doing a perfectly good job of making a fool of himself. In fact, he said, it's not really possible for somebody else to do it for you. He just asked me to promise one thing: to laugh at him when he played the fool. I said I'd do that for him if he'd do the same for me.

Sami isn't *always* playing the fool. It's more like what he said before, about toeing the line between the sublime and the ridiculous. Or that thing that Kakay said.

About a week ago, Olivia and I went back up to Bard—not for anything related to her work there, but to see the very magical singer/

performance artist Taylor Mac. The show was in the Spiegeltent, a canopied pavilion all decked out with crystal chandeliers and mirrors that they set up on the campus in the summer. Taylor was singing tunes from the 1920s that night, and he was also bedecked in sparkly things—stunning. He had a very capable pianist; a discreet and tasteful bassist; a feisty, older woman on drums; and an electric guitarist. Taylor sang a heartrending version of "Bye Bye Blackbird"— slow and cracking with emotion. As he ended the verse, he turned to his electric guitarist and gestured grandly for her to take a solo.

She was a blond woman, a little younger than me, small but strong, also bedecked and bedizened, but with a certain seriousness of purpose as she grasped and addressed her instrument. In that moment, the glaring spotlight and every shard of sparkle and glitter in the tent fell on her, and she played the howling agony of the world, and it was gorgeous, and it was devastating, and no one breathed. The howl of her guitar was the sound of my mother's desire for death and her terror of it, it was the exquisite pain of Sami's missing leg and his father, it was the phone call home that Tye couldn't make, it was Olivia's shattered metacarpal bone and the horrible ache of wanting more than she wanted to want. It was my own clutching fear of disappointing any of them. I leaned into Olivia's shoulder, and I cried like a baby, and I loved the sound of that guitar, and I loved the woman who was playing it, and when she was finished, the crowd went wild.

Olivia stroked my hair. She didn't need to say anything, because she knew: the woman who was playing the guitar was my real lover, the one who asked to be excised from this story, the one for whom I had to imagine Olivia to take her place. After I hurt her, the stipulation she gave me was that the only way she wanted to appear in my fiction was in a brief cameo as a rock star, which is, in fact, what she was.

Well, at least you caught a glimpse of her, in all her incandescence.

I just went back and looked at the ukulele covers I've recorded in the last few weeks.

Sometimes the covers serve almost like a journal. Going over them helps me figure out what I've been preoccupied with, even if I haven't fully articulated these things to myself. The reason people like popular songs is that even though they're often banal—in fact, maybe *because* they're often banal—they speak to some desire or anxiety or pleasure that we recognize as our own. My covers tend to represent the fairly predictable range of emotions that we all have, but I did notice—not surprisingly, I guess—that in the recent batch, there were quite a few songs taking up the question of truth, lies, and doubt. I recorded the Black Keys's "Psychotic Girl" for Abner. That was funny. I recorded Marisa Monte's "Verdade, Uma Illusão," which is very cheerful, although the words tell you that truth is always "an illusion, coming from the heart." "Truth," she says, "your name is a lie." I did another one by Wye Oak called "Doubt." That one's pretty, but very dark. She's telling someone that if they should doubt her love, they should remember one thing: "That I would lie to you if I believed it was right to do." So you're thinking maybe she's the one to doubt—not her intentions, but anything that she may tell you is true—except that suddenly she tells you that *you're* the one she doubts: "What I have learned of you does not assure . . . But I believed it then, believe it still." It's very confusing.

I'm not sure who I recorded these for. Maybe you're thinking I was singing to Sami or to Tye or to Olivia or imagining that one of them was singing to me. But maybe I was singing to Rebekah, or Abner, or Natali, or the horrorcore guy, or maybe I was singing to you.

I don't always think it's bad to misrepresent oneself. In fact, I wouldn't use that word, and I certainly wouldn't use the word *lying*. But in my case, I always call it fiction. Even in my fiction, if I say,

"This really happened," then it's true. It really happened. I like being transparent. Or naked.

I seem to be talking to myself. Before I felt I was talking to you. I'm sorry, it's just a little difficult sometimes to maintain the illusion. Does this sound familiar? In my mind, you were beautiful, damaged, and less freakish than you thought. I wanted to show you that. I wanted to make you something—maybe a little charming, maybe a little funny, or sexy, a small song, or a dance, or this novel.

I was about to apologize for the gold dance to music. I made it, although I obviously failed to rise to the occasion. But then I realized that all this begging pardon is the worst form of bourgeois politesse. How irritating! So here it is—take it or leave it.

I made this for you. It was the last thing I did. It comes from the heart.

Love, Barbara

Coffee House Press began as a small letterpress operation in 1972 and has grown into an internationally renowned nonprofit publisher of literary fiction, essay, poetry, and other work that doesn't fit neatly into genre categories.

Coffee House is both a publisher and an arts organization. Through our *Books in Action* program and publications, we've become interdisciplinary collaborators and incubators for new work and audience experiences. Our vision for the future is one where a publisher is a catalyst and connector.

LITERATURE
is not the same thing as
PUBLISHING

Coffee House Press is an internationally renowned independent book publisher and arts nonprofit based in Minneapolis, MN; through its literary publications and *Books in Action* program, Coffee House acts as a catalyst and connector—between authors and readers, ideas and resources, creativity and community, inspiration and action.

Coffee House Press books are made possible through the generous support of grants and donations from corporations, state and federal grant programs, family foundations, and the many individuals who believe in the transformational power of literature. This activity is made possible by the voters of Minnesota through a Minnesota State Arts Board Operating Support grant, thanks to the legislative appropriation from the arts and cultural heritage fund. Coffee House also receives major operating support from the Amazon Literary Partnership, the Bush Foundation, the Jerome Foundation, The McKnight Foundation, Target Foundation, and the National Endowment for the Arts (NEA). To find out more about how NEA grants impact individuals and communities, visit www.arts.gov.

Coffee House Press receives additional support from the Elmer L. & Eleanor J. Andersen Foundation; the David & Mary Anderson Family Foundation; the Buuck Family Foundation; the Carolyn Foundation; the Dorsey & Whitney Foundation; Dorsey & Whitney LLP; the E. Thomas Binger and Rebecca Rand Fund of the Minneapolis Foundation, the Knight Foundation; the Rehael Fund of the Minneapolis Foundation; the Matching Grant Program Fund of the Minneapolis Foundation; the Schwab Charitable Fund; Schwegman, Lundberg & Woessner, P.A.; the Scott Family Foundation; the US Bank Foundation; VSA Minnesota for the Metropolitan Regional Arts Council; the Archie D. & Bertha H. Walker Foundation; and the Woessner Freeman Family Foundation in honor of Allan Kornblum.

Publisher's Circle members make significant contributions to Coffee House Press's annual giving campaign. Understanding that a strong financial base is necessary for the press to meet the challenges and opportunities that arise each year, this group plays a crucial part in the success of Coffee House's mission.

Recent Publisher's Circle Members include many anonymous donors, Mr. & Mrs. Rand L. Alexander, Suzanne Allen, Patricia A. Beithon, Bill Berkson & Connie Lewallen, the E. Thomas Binger & Rebecca Rand Fund of the Minneapolis Foundation, Robert & Gail Buuck, Claire Casey, Louise Copeland, Jane Dalrymple-Hollo, Ruth Stricker Dayton, Jennifer Kwon Dobbs & Stefan Liess, Mary Ebert & Paul Stembler, Chris Fischbach & Katie Dublinski, Kaywin Feldman & Jim Lutz, Sally French, Jocelyn Hale & Glenn Miller, the Rehael Fund-Roger Hale/Nor Hall of the Minneapolis Foundation, Randy Hartten & Ron Lotz, Jeffrey Hom, Carl & Heidi Horsch, Amy L. Hubbard & Geoffrey J. Kehoe Fund, Kenneth Kahn & Susan Dicker, Stephen & Isabel Keating, Kenneth Koch Literary Estate, Jennifer Komar & Enrique Olivarez, Allan & Cinda Kornblum, Leslie Larson Maheras, Lenfestey Family Foundation, Sarah Lutman & Rob Rudolph, the Carol & Aaron Mack Charitable Fund of the Minneapolis Foundation, George & Olga Mack, Joshua Mack, Gillian McCain, Mary & Malcolm McDermid, Sjur Midness & Briar Andresen, Maureen Millea Smith & Daniel Smith, Peter Nelson & Jennifer Swenson, Marc Porter & James Hennessy, Jeffrey Scherer, Jeffrey Sugerman & Sarah Schultz, Nan G. & Stephen C. Swid, Patricia Tilton, Stu Wilson & Melissa Barker, Warren D. Woessner & Iris C. Freeman, Margaret Wurtele, Joanne Von Blon, and Wayne P. Zink.

For more information about the Publisher's Circle and other ways to support Coffee House Press books, authors, and activities, please visit www.coffeehousepress.org/support or contact us at info@coffeehousepress.org.

The Gift was designed by
Bookmobile Design & Digital Publisher Services.
Text is set in Adobe Garamond Pro.